Praise for

JIMIN HAN

"*The Apology* is an uncanny high-wire act — arch, tender, mercurial. Jimin Han feels like Iris Murdoch's heir, although this novel came from an artistry that is all her own. This is a story unlike any other of Korea and America, with a mother's love made majestic, a deathless avenger, shrewd and wild, and an *ajumma* willing to do anything for her family, even from beyond her grave."

— Alexander Chee, author of *How to Write an Autobiographical Novel*

"What does it mean to be the keeper of the stories? What does it mean to be left behind? *The Apology* shows Jimin Han's talents as a skillful storyteller, interweaving questions of sisterhood and separation, generational secrets and ancestral love, through a singular and unforgettable centenarian voice." — Lisa Ko, author of *The Leavers*

"An intriguing, genre-bending novel that proves that the bonds — and grudges — of siblinghood exist beyond the grave. Insightful about secret-keeping and hopeful about the redemptive power of love, Jimin Han is a literary medium for imperfect families."

— Courtney Maum, author of *The Year of the Horses*

"*The Apology* is a vividly rendered novel about the long life spans of secrets, featuring an unforgettable 105-year-old narrator who is as stubborn and proud as she is spirited. With depth, emotion, and total clarity of vision, Jimin Han has crafted a wonderfully moving story about love and loss, betrayal and forgiveness, and the lengths that one woman will go to in this world and the next to undo the mistakes of the past." — Jung Yun, author of *O Beautiful* and *Shelter*

"Jeonga, a centenarian with two centenarian sisters, has done her best to hide a family secret, even sacrificing relationships with her son and her beloved to do so. Now, at the end of her life, that secret threatens to curse the family for generations. Speaking from beyond the grave, Jeonga narrates the mystery of why we make the choices we make even when they hurt the ones we love. Like magic, this book is at once a page-turning mystery, a supernatural odyssey, a family saga, and a Korean melodrama. Count me forever among Han's audience." — Matthew Salesses, author of *The Sense of Wonder* and *Craft in the Real World*

"Jimin Han's *The Apology* is a captivating multigenerational story of love and secrets, forgiveness and redemption, and how our decisions and actions can reverberate through time, touching the lives of others in ways we cannot anticipate. Han's clear-eyed insights and rich imaginative powers are on full and impressive display in this intricately woven portrait of a fierce, determined, and wickedly funny matriarch at the end of her life (and beyond). An original and memorable novel. I did not want it to end!"

— Mary-Kim Arnold, author of *Litany for the Long Moment* and *The Fish and the Dove*

"Bold, original, and utterly captivating, *The Apology* is a sweeping intergenerational saga, delivered by one of the sharpest, most memorable voices I've ever read. A stunning new novel by a writer whose work I've long admired." — Kirstin Chen, author of *Counterfeit*

"In *The Apology*, Jimin Han deftly threads a comedic line through a multigenerational family chock-full of grievances and perceived slights. The impudent yet vulnerable narrator, Jeonga, shows us something she'd never reveal to her sisters: her pain and her joy. She'll fight to the death — and beyond — to do what she thinks is right, and she'll win the hearts of readers while doing so."

— Ed Lin, author of *Ghost Month*

"A riveting, hilarious, and moving tale of a woman on a journey through two countries and two planes of existence. An authentic and wonderfully executed tale of secrets and their consequences."

— Minsoo Kang, author of *Of Tales and Enigmas* and
translator of the Penguin Classics edition of
The Story of Hong Gildong

"What a superb story this is, unweaving the tangle of family history — and the wrongheaded honor that has walled out love — as this remarkable novel moves from the unguessable to the expansively imagined. It's a maze of leaps — across boundaries beyond the known — as one woman grapples with the impossible question of how wrongs can be righted. A memorable and wonderfully original book."

— Joan Silber, author of *Secrets of
Happiness* and *Improvement*

"Jimin Han has woven a marvelous madcap novel of love and loyalty, the living and the dead, and a family that's haunted — by the past, by war, by distance and silence carried across generations. Hilarious and heartbreaking, *The Apology* tells the tale of Jeonga, a proud, isolated, deeply judgmental, and wholly unforgettable centenarian matriarch whose dedication to keeping up appearances leads to her ultimate undoing — and her one chance at redemption. An epic, intricate, and wildly entertaining journey of reckoning and reconnection across oceans and astral planes, *The Apology* is a powerful fable of family secrets and the lengths we go to keep them — and how the truth, in the end, will set us free."

— Melissa Faliveno, author of *Tomboyland*

"*The Apology* is a remarkable achievement, weaving together psychological suspense, Korean myth, and an intense scrutiny of family relationships as these are influenced by war and history. Calling to mind the scathing emotional precision of Elena Ferrante and the Korean gender and social critique of Han Kang, Jimin Han is a force to be reckoned with in this novel — and so is Mrs. Jeonga Cha, a resourceful and brave matriarch in this life and the next."

— Chaya Bhuvaneswar, author of
White Dancing Elephants

"In *The Apology*, Jimin Han has proven herself to be an ace storyteller, observing the hilarious micro-interactions of her characters while also taking us on an epic journey over many generations and many realms. We view the world through the eyes of Jeonga, her 105-year-old narrator, and while we may laugh at her self-absorption and blind spots, Han also manages to make us feel the slights and stings she endures and long for her redemption and peace."

— Deborah Zoe Laufer, playwright, author of
End Days, Informed Consent, and *Be Here Now*

"With a deft brush, Han paints the quirks and preoccupations of old age as the secrets of her heroine jettison her across the world and smack into another one, literally. What follows is an inspiring, often funny, and always engaging tale of the complications of familial love."

— Gloria Hatrick, author of *Masks*

"Jimin Han's riveting, multigenerational family epic is a wonder — a journey that takes us across continents and worlds and plunges us into the deepest reaches of the human heart. In Jeonga, Han gives us the profoundly moving portrait of a family matriarch who must sacrifice all in her determination to save her descendants; in doing so, she also ultimately redeems herself." — Kate Brandt, author of
Hope for the Worst

"In *The Apology*, Jimin Han gives us a complex centenarian character motivated by love and family in Jeonga, the youngest of four wealthy Korean women. Han's exquisite descriptions and unfolding of secrets kept me engrossed, even when Jeonga was at her most undesirable. Seriously, I did not want this book to end! It's refreshing to have such a new take on tradition, reputation, and the smallness of our world." — DeMisty D. Bellinger, author of *New to Liberty* and *Peculiar Heritage*

"Jimin Han's *The Apology* delights and surprises at every turn — in every chapter, on every page. The narrator is a cranky centenarian. There are family secrets plus wonderful comedic passages in a novel that doesn't shy away from history or death. It's a comic novel with a serious touch, a serious novel with a comic touch. It's that rare combo, serious and comic all at once, deeply felt, deeply alive, brilliantly rendered, and willing to explore the complicated affiliations that form along bloodlines, generational divides, class, and love. Also? A hell of a good read, generous with its ghosts both literal and figurative, told with wit and relish." — Juan Martinez, author of *Best Worst American* and *Extended Stay*

"The sins of the parents visited on the children — it's an iconic theme but one that feels razor-sharp in Jimin Han's new novel, *The Apology*.

Jeonga, a wealthy and prideful South Korean centenarian, gets a rude awakening when a decision of passion she made decades ago seems destined to cause catastrophe for her progeny. Her need to correct her mistake takes her around the world and even into the afterlife, where she confronts truths she never wanted to face as she pursues a better outcome. Unique and totally absorbing, *The Apology* is a story that delves into matters of family, love, tradition, and harsh self-awareness as it exposes the secrets we keep from others — and those we keep from ourselves."   — Barbara Josselsohn, author of *The Lilac House* and *The Cranberry Inn*

"Han's remarkable story, at times hilarious, always gripping, took me on a journey with her unrelenting 105-year-old protagonist who refuses to let anything, even death, stop her from saving her family from the impending disaster she put into motion decades earlier. I couldn't stop reading until I reached the last word, and then I read it again."
— Patricia Dunn, author of *Last Stop on the 6* and *Rebels by Accident*

"It begins with a bus accident, but really it began so long ago. *The Apology* is a work of tenderness and empathy, a portrait of family and memory, of different generations colliding across multiple dimensions both literal and in the afterlife. Jimin Han has conjured more than ghosts here, and you should listen to her story."
— Michael J. Seidlinger, author of *Anybody Home?* and *Scream*

Also by Jimin Han

A Small Revolution

THE
APOLOGY

JIMIN HAN

Little, Brown and Company
New York Boston London

Copyright © 2023 by Jimin Han

Hachette Book Group supports the right to free expression and the value of copyright. The purpose of copyright is to encourage writers and artists to produce the creative works that enrich our culture.

The scanning, uploading, and distribution of this book without permission is a theft of the author's intellectual property. If you would like permission to use material from the book (other than for review purposes), please contact permissions@hbgusa.com. Thank you for your support of the author's rights.

Little, Brown and Company
Hachette Book Group
1290 Avenue of the Americas, New York, NY 10104
littlebrown.com

First Edition: August 2023

Little, Brown and Company is a division of Hachette Book Group, Inc. The Little, Brown name and logo are trademarks of Hachette Book Group, Inc.

The publisher is not responsible for websites (or their content) that are not owned by the publisher.

The Hachette Speakers Bureau provides a wide range of authors for speaking events. To find out more, go to hachettespeakersbureau.com or call (866) 376-6591.

ISBN 9780316367080
LCCN 2022935977

10 9 8 7 6 5 4 3 2 1

MRQ-T

Printed in Canada

For
F, S, and J

THE
APOLOGY

CHAPTER 1

Fleeing in a panic is not recommended. A week ago, on my last day alive, I was at my grandson's house in Chicago, America. I was frantic. I got myself to my feet and ran. The heavy cypress door of the stocky house couldn't keep me in. Outside, I hurried as fast as I could along the sidewalk, head down. Chill seeping into my skin, through my taupe linen suit jacket over my white blouse, cotton undershirt, and wide-legged linen slacks. This was what it was to be old: no protections despite layers of clothing. It was summer, for goodness' sake. To my left, houses and houses and trees, vicious large trees, and across the street to my right more trees, as if I were inside a large endless cavern of trees that blocked the sun. In the very periphery of my vision, they crowded me. Judged me. What gave them the right? I raised a fist at them and then hurried on to increase the distance between me and the house I'd left, increase the distance between me and my family in that house. Judge me? Yes, they were judging me. I suppressed a sob that rose in my throat. *Ignore them, Jeonga,* I told myself. *Breathe and get oxygen to these old-woman legs of yours. Breathe and hurry.*

Finally, the trees disappeared and then there were traffic lights and tall buildings and American people and too bright of a sun. I was at the mercy of an onslaught of screeching car tires and belching truck exhausts. The stench of rotten wet vegetables, gasoline, and grease assaulted my nose. I swerved right and then left. Where could I find a place to rest a moment away from everyone? I meant *everyone*. I was sick to death of the world. I needed to think. Think, think.

People swarmed around me, so close I thought at first it had started to rain but it was sweat from a stranger that had landed on me. I flinched. Too close. Everyone was too close. Hot air; actually, hot breath: "What the hell, lady," someone shouted in my face. Right in my face. How dare he. I wrenched my arms out of my jacket and dumped it in a trash container on the side of a building. I assumed it was a trash container; who cared. A stranger's perspiration, no, thank you.

I'd resented the trees and wished for warmth, but now I was in a worse place than before. Was it always going to be like this? Something worse around the corner?

"Foolish Jeonga," my sister had called me many times. Really, everyone had. They were right. They'd all been right. What could I do now?

Long, long time ago I had a sister, and now this fact was returning to snatch the future away. Who would have thought my great-granddaughter and my sister's great-grandson would have found each other on this huge foreign continent and fallen in love, not knowing they were related?

I picked up my pace. Across the wide American street was a bench flecked in gold. It beckoned. I could sit there. An answer would arrive if I could only sit. I'd come up with plans to cover up my secrets before. All I had to do was make it past these crowds of people who had no respect for personal space, this stream of relentless machines on wheels, on this cruel, cruel day.

I hated people. They had always been terrible. In the neighborhood I grew up in, people spread rumors about my family. My parents stuck to their version no matter the consequences. *Never give in to them,* they told me. *Cut your losses. Even if the gossip is true.* My father was especially adamant about this. Our family had a reputation to uphold, a household to protect. Save what you can. Save who you can, especially for the family's reputation. Posterity. Upholding traditions would ensure that future generations would survive. What didn't help the health of the family was removed, like a branch of a tree for pruning. It had been done before. That was the way it had always been done. But now I had doubts.

What if I had chopped the branch that would bring down the family tree? Why had I followed my family, our traditions, so blindly? Was there anything left to do now? Decision after decision had led to this moment. Foolish Jeonga. I wrapped my arms around myself as I walked. I raised my chin to encourage myself to stay strong. *Don't let them know they hurt you, Jeonga.* I didn't want anyone to see me like this. My cheeks were cold when the wind hit my face. I let go of the present as I searched. I hurried along in this life as I walked but memory pulled me to the past. Where was the mistake? What could I have done differently? I'd protected our family's reputation. I had hidden my son's indiscretion from society. I had banished the woman he had impregnated. All I had done, I had done to save us. That was my duty, wasn't it? But now, any day now, the secret would be exposed. In fact, it had to be exposed or the family would be cursed for generations. What to do, what to do? I was being squeezed from both sides. To tell or not to tell. I didn't want to tell; so help me, I didn't.

Step by step through that busy intersection, my body traveled while my mind crossed into the past. I remembered my son's face as he bent his head down all those years ago. I'd feared he'd never raise his chin again, the despondency weighing him down. All I could do was stare at the beautiful thickness of the hair on his head, the hair that the midwife said was responsible for the heartburn I'd experienced when I'd been pregnant with him. I didn't care. I'd held him tight to me, infant with a full head of hair, and I wished I could do the same now. I extended my arms but he shrank from me. We were in the courtyard in front of our house in Seoul. He was collapsed in the dirt. "Why, Eomma? Why?" he asked.

"My boy, my foolish boy, I've fixed your mistake," I'd grumbled at him, but I was swallowing my own guilt for allowing him to spend as much time as he had with a young woman in our employ. It was my fault I'd overlooked how grown he was by then. A young man old enough to be a father.

How I wished the entire episode had never taken place. I gasped and held on to that memory for a moment too long and that is why what happened next was the end of me. I relinquished my grip on the here and now.

People were shouting, "Bus, bus," and I was glad to be able to make out that one English word. *Bus.* I imagined they were late to catch it. I pitied them. Maybe the man who had shouted in my face was one of those who had missed the bus. *Serves you right,* I thought with satisfaction. Some of my misery eased. Bus drivers never stopped to let people on after they closed the door. Korea, America, all the same. I heard the wheeze of the hydraulic system as the bus rose from its kneeling position. Off it went. "Watch out." People gasped and the rest was garbled speech, the beginnings and endings of English words run together. I couldn't understand. But it didn't concern me; I was almost across the street, nearly upon the glittering bench that was my destination. You think old ladies can't run? We certainly can.

My first thought as I was struck was that someone had slapped me across the face, and I was astonished anyone would want to do that to me. And I found it curious that I was on the pavement because of it — a simple slap by someone, and I was horizontal on the street? But then I couldn't breathe and it seemed that a huge metal blanket had collapsed on me. It was swift after that. The dawning realization that the slap was much more than something a person could have done to me. A flash of excruciating pain and then — blissful reprieve, which carried the price of blindness, dense and complete.

A bus was my undoing. Simple fact. I died in Chicago, America. If I had only paid attention to what was around me. That could be inscribed on my headstone: IF SHE HAD ONLY WATCHED WHAT WAS COMING. Ha!

I can find some humor in it now, but in the moment the metal made contact with me, I wasn't laughing, I was astonished. A bus crushed my flesh and bones. Agony and then nothing. No feeling at all. With relief came reluctance to give up the pain — isn't that curious? Hand in hand, the relief and the pain. As if pain was familiar because a blank forgetting arrived that frightened me more than anything I'd ever experienced before. I was scattering outward. Who was I? What did I want? What had I cared about? I wrapped my arms around myself, but they swept through without resistance. I could see nothing when I looked down — was I looking down? I reached for my face and felt nothing.

Like in a dream, I felt all around me the vastness of a solar system in outer space but with no pinpoints of stars. The first sense to return was touch. Prickles of damp against my skin. Skin in the afterlife? My outer layer tingled. A mist enveloped me. Slowly the feeling beneath me solidified, a hard surface; moment by moment my body claimed me again.

Smell seeped into my being; that was next. The dampest whiff of an orchard of persimmons. I inhaled and the soft texture of a ripe persimmon slid in my mouth — a faint taste memory. Next was sight. I opened my eyes to an orange mist — the shade of a persimmon. In front of me, the outline of a town square.

Then, under my hands, the edges of myself formed, fingers and toes. I was sitting in a crouched position, my chin on my knees — I was hunched over, shielding my head with my arms. When I lowered my hands, I saw that my legs were covered by the skirt of a white hemp hanbok. I touched the cloth, a rough and simple cross-hatching of thread from the crudest loom. Why was I dressed in this old-fashioned funeral garb? My feet were in white sneakers, the only material item that had carried over from my life — that and my white socks. My travel socks and shoes. I flexed my toes. New clothes but old shoes. Why?

I was doomed; this knowledge descended on my shoulders. Remorse in waves washed over me. I was sorry, wasn't I? But for what? Orange dust scattered beneath my feet. I alternately flailed my arms at the air around me and covered my head with them in fear.

And then a whisper. "We were sisters."

I raised my head. A memory was crystallizing in my mind. My touchstone. My sister Seona. I had a sister named Seona. She was two years older than me. Old enough to tower over me and yet be my play-mate. "Jeonga, Jeonga, your turn," my sister's voice called to me.

Long, long time ago we were sisters.

I remembered even though I was dead and in the afterlife. I knew this as surely as I knew I had once been alive. There were songs about where I was right then. The five-hundred-years one, my favorite, though I didn't know then what I know now. Consider that: How can a person live for five hundred years? I was most interested in love. How it bound us together, how it ripped us apart. There were four children in our family. The two older ones and then Seona and me. Seona and I were a team. I looked up to her. She was brave.

Jeonga was my name. The relief to know this. When I was a child, Seona and I used to play in a dusty town square waiting for our mother, who was at the market. The town square, where I remembered being happiest, even if boys would come and snatch our tea set made of hollowed and dried gourds. A cup taken once, a teapot another time. We'd huddled over what remained, our backs to the thieves.

Old women used to gather in threes and fours in the corner farthest from us, under the shade of a straw shelter. Crouched down like us, they sang the five-hundred-years song: *Why does he ask for five hundred years and then leave me behind? We can't go on. Nobody would ever love him as much as I loved him. Nobody would ever love me as much as I loved him.*

I remembered we were two little girls in a big, empty, dusty square in summer. The boys would come and steal our play set and run. The other girls, our older sisters, would walk by, talking about us, leaving us behind. We would become old women with empty hands singing songs like this. Was this the lesson?

"No worry, no worry," Seona used to say after the marauding boys left us. "See?" She held up a cracked gourd. "We still have this one." Her small hands scooped up dirt, let it funnel into the cup. She raised her chin and sang the song, and I tried to follow along.

"Remember the song," a voice sounded now in the orange mist. Was that Seona's voice?

I looked about. Before me was such an expanse of emptiness. I remembered the song of the old women: *My love has gone, who asked me to live together for five hundred years, compassion nowhere. I cannot go on. Geureochi, amuryeom geureochi. Five hundred years.* I was a child with my sister in the town square in Korea long, long ago.

The song essentially said, "You remember the love. That remains, the feeling of love; everything else you forget." I remembered my sister's love.

I had a sister.

Maybe I could stand up. I pushed off the ground with my hands. At least the ground was solid. I flexed one knee, then the other. I stretched my arms above my head. Not easy. I felt as old and creaky as I'd been in life on my last day. One hundred five years old. If I was dead, why didn't I have the litheness of a gwisin? Ghosts were free from their bodies, weren't they?

I took a deep breath. *Focus, Jeonga,* I told myself. *You heard Seona's voice. There must be a reason.* Korean folklore said everyone was assigned a guardian to traverse the afterlife. Seona as my guardian — the thought gave me hope. I had lived more years without her than with her, but I remembered her every day. I swallowed and called to her, "Seona, big sister, help me." I waited for a response, but none came. The mist drifted around me and still nothing else in the great expanse. No voice replied, but I wasn't discouraged. My memory was returning. I recalled the faces of my family. I remembered I'd had a problem in Chicago, America. I had to do something; I couldn't just wait in this empty town square. I was not one to give up, not ever. I chose a direction and walked forward.

I was looking for a second chance even in death. It shouldn't have been a surprise, but we get comfortable in our modern age with what we hold on to. We become attached to who we think we are. I had to go on, had to try, in hopes that something, anything, would give me a clue as to how to save the living. Love was my way back.

CHAPTER 2

Ten days ago, I was in my sitting room in my apartment in Seoul. When you're one hundred five years old you know your life is near its end, but that didn't make me use my time wisely. I complained about having nothing to do. I thought my secrets were safe, my losses behind me, permanently in the past. How content I was in my arrogance. The room faced south with windows through which I could see the garden one story below. If I didn't look too carefully, I could imagine I was in my childhood home. If I concentrated on the purple and pink hibiscus that bloomed in late summer, I could forget how much the city had changed. Selective memory — isn't that what it's called? I was an expert at it.

I sat in my favorite chair. A Finn Juhl Pelican in gray cashmere. Say what you want, but the chair was not a hug from a person in its soft curving form as it's marketed to be, simply a chair I liked for its proximity to the floor. How I miss it now. I was short, even for an old Korean woman. On the wall to my right was a painting, an abstract of the Golden Gate Bridge in the United States: a streak of uncanny orangish red over a blue expanse.

Both the chair and the painting were gifts from many years ago. I added other Finn Juhl pieces of furniture over time. All original. Sleek and simple. Some would say the modern imitations were even better with their low prices, but I say who needs so much? Buy a few. Less to clean. More space in a room to breathe. This is what I thought back then. I thought I was wise.

I wore my short hair in a bob, easy to care for, hid the thinning that happened in your advanced years. That day I must have been wearing a pair of my simple, loose wide lounge slacks and a lilac tunic. The tunic was tied at the side of my chest in a new interpretation of a jeogori by a Korean designer. Skirts were preferable but wide-legged pants were comfortable and modern, and I wanted to match my furniture in case anyone was watching. From wherever. I suspected even then, but how little I knew.

Those days, I felt like I was always waiting. How I hated waiting. That's where I was that day. It was closing on noon, and I was reading a book. Not an exceptional book, domestic drama that it was. Not much thought required, which was a blessing. Some people — my sister Seona, for one, and a man I used to love, for another — would have scoffed at it. But I admit I wanted to escape my reality more often than not. That particular day I was close to that back-cover closing. I was dismayed that the story would be over and I still had the entire day before me; not even lunch, and I'd be finished.

What else could I do? The menu for the week had already been planned; the grocer had come and gone; the doctor had examined me yesterday; I'd been to the acupuncturist the day before that. A walk would take an hour at the most, and it was summer, so the afternoons would be a sauna. I liked a day to clear my head between reading books. I couldn't bear to start another story after being deeply immersed in one. It seemed to lessen the experience, or, more to the point, it felt like a betrayal somehow. I was reputed to count loyalty among the highest attributes one could have. I was not unlike my parents in that way, especially my father, whose respect I had always longed to have.

So there I was, reading this fine novel. I relished each word, knowing I was near the end and hoping some pages were stuck together so there would be one more and another and another. There I was, the last three, four, maybe five pages until I would have to close the book, and then the author gave me a gift. The gift of an epilogue.

I'd seen them before, but I'd never allowed myself to expect them. They were rare. And here it was, a few short pages that encapsulated years that the author wouldn't cover in his novel but that would give me a sense of what would come, and I could savor every sentence. Each bit about the main character's life, the children he would never see grow up, the generations who would move to remote corners of the world, and I could picture it: The spoiled one, the youngest in the family, would find work in Amsterdam; the tender one, my favorite, would strike out for Peru and become a mayor (imagine that — a Korean-immigrant politician. I knew it happened, but it surprised me how far we could venture into the world); and the middle child would become a doctor, saving children's lives in America. Just before the main character died, he said, "You can't control love. You can't conceal it from each other. The world is too small to hide in."

In all my years, I'd seen it happen several times. People losing control, throwing away their futures for what they thought was love. He was right — you can't control it — but I didn't agree you couldn't do anything about it.

I reread that line about love several times, then finally closed the book and held my hands folded on the back cover in my lap.

An epilogue was what I wanted in my own life, it occurred to me then. Greedy to live longer as a centenarian? It was not unusual in my family or even among Koreans. My grandmother had lived to one hundred eleven. I wanted more, and the more that I wanted didn't have to have me in those pages. I wanted a summary. I wanted an overview. I wanted to see what happened.

Reading books helped me push away a habit I'd had as a little girl. I used to have visions when I was awake of people walking through our stone walls into our yard, sometimes beckoning for me to follow, sometimes not aware I could see them.

My mother used to say, "Ignore them; they're in pain and will pull you into their sorrow if they can. Put your attention on something else, like reading books."

She was right. Reading books directed my mind to focus on stories in a disciplined, contained, safe way. That's how I learned to cope in life. The scenes I saw of gwisin used to be debilitating. The anguish in their faces, how they wailed; they were as vivid as if I were watching a movie — I didn't know this at the time, but later when I went to the cinema, suddenly it was as if the world saw what I'd been seeing for years. My own private film — though I hadn't been able to choose what I saw. And it seemed I had not been the only one who saw things many others could not.

As a senior citizen, I kept my life simple and quiet. Part of my secret to longevity was to do so. Unlike others who had large staffs, I had one trusted aide, named Chohui, who cooked, cleaned, shopped, replaced batteries, drove the car, had remarkable insights to ease my day. I tried not to express to her how much I enjoyed her company beyond the day-to-day tasks. In retrospect, I should have shown her how much I appreciated her.

"Ready for lunch, samonim?" Chohui said that day I was finishing the novel. *Samonim* was the word a respectful person used for someone as old as I was. It irked me, though I had no reason to object. She walked into the sitting room with my cell phone held out in front of her.

"Food again? Is this all we have to talk about?" I snapped at her. "Why did you bring me that phone? Did someone call?"

"You're always hungry," she said. "It was charging on the kitchen table where you put it. Remember, I'm going to the park this afternoon, so you should have it by your side."

"Well, I have no use for it. Go ahead with your friends; I can manage lunch," I replied.

"Samonim, I know you like to have it in case someone calls," she said.

"All the errands are done, who would call?" I shot back. She was right — I often checked to see if I'd missed calls, though there never were any.

My irritating criticisms seemed to roll right off her, but I know they must have hurt. Thinking about my actions now makes me cringe. Chohui didn't know what was in store for us that day. Neither did I.

She proved to be tougher than she appeared.

In practical terms, I appreciated that she was exactly my height of 153 centimeters, which had been a benefit over the years, as I did not ever have to peer up or down at her. On occasion she offered me her arm when we walked up steps or she'd go ahead to see if I'd have trouble with the steepness of the terrain based on her stature relative to it. Compared to me at her age — twenty-four — or at any age, she was lovely. While I had a narrow face, she had a broad forehead; she also had pleasant eyes, which she squinted when she was nervous. We'd been to several ophthalmologists, all of whom claimed she had perfect vision. She wasn't squinting now, simply waiting for me to agree to lunch. As usual, she had talked me out of my bad mood.

Chohui had been working for me for the past twelve years and was an adequate housekeeper. I knew I was fortunate but not how much so. The first time I saw her, I noticed right away that she was unusual. She was standing outside a pharmacy, a child half the size of the adults around her, her head tilted upward, staring off into space. My watch told me it was an odd time to see a child in this part of town. In her plain navy and white school uniform, she was out of place on this busy street with shops. Adults walked past her as if she weren't there. Admittedly, my first emotion was fear. Maybe she was a gwisin, and I had let down my guard.

I had not seen one in years, but still, I was relieved when I saw an old man stop short to avoid colliding with her. She was real after all. I approached, my heart relaxing from its clenched state. As I neared, something about her reminded me of myself at that age.

I walked right up to her, and I said, "What's wrong?"

"Everything," she said. "I'm terrible. You shouldn't talk to me."

"That can't possibly be true, you're only a child — go on, tell me," I said.

"I hate school," she said, her mouth wobbling with upset. Having struggled with academics as well, I understood this particular affliction. My father had considered me obstinate when I had trouble understanding the simplest theorems.

I did then what I wished others would do when I felt tearful: I pretended I didn't see how overcome she was. I walked into the pharmacy, paid for my medications. When I came back out, she was still standing there but this time looking anxiously in my direction.

Her face blanched and she squinted at me as if something awful were on my nose, so I turned my back to her and prepared to cross the street. Before I had a chance to step off the curb, however, I heard a commotion behind me. The cashier who had helped me with my purchase earlier was berating the child. I couldn't believe my ears. The woman was shouting at the girl, telling her to obtain a job.

I stepped officiously between the woman and the child. "A job?" I said. "If she's bad at school, you should pay for a tutor."

"Who can afford that?" the woman said. She squinted as well. A family resemblance. The rest of her was pinched, her face like the pleated seam of a dumpling.

"Is she your child?" I replied.

"She's no business of yours," she said in a harsh tone. The cashier who used to work at the pharmacy prior to this woman would never have spoken to me thusly, but everything had changed in recent years. I was sorry the old cashier had died. I chose to ignore her replacement.

"You're in luck, then. I need some help. Will you be my helper?" I asked the child, and she seemed to give it some thought, squinting at her scuffed white sneakers as if the answer were there.

"She's twelve years old, so she can work four hours a day, at the minimum wage, paid to me," the woman said. "If she cooks, it'll be twice the minimum wage."

I spoke only to the child. "You'll go to school and I'll pay for a tutor and you'll come to my house two days a week to help the cook prepare meals. I'll have my driver pick you up and take you home afterward. Two hours per day should do it," I said. "Could you manage that?" I handed her my personal stationery; the woman snatched it away from the child.

"That's close to here," the woman exclaimed, studying my address.

"A tutor can work wonders, don't worry," I told the girl. "But I don't want to hear any complaints about you from my cook. Understood?"

Her eyes widened. "Why are you helping me?"

She was suspicious, a trait I admired and shared myself. "You remind me of someone, understand?" I said. She nodded and thanked me in such a soft voice I nearly missed it.

After that, I went home. It turned out that the child's name was Gwak Chohui, and the woman at the pharmacy was a distant cousin of hers — another Gwak with a first name I don't recall now. Koreans put surnames ahead of first names, a custom that I approve of but that Americans do not practice. One of many challenges I had to face in my life. Chohui was born in a small rural town south of Seoul, the youngest of a large family. Her parents had fallen on hard times, so they sent her to live with a relative. I paid for her to be taught English as well as her other subjects by an expensive tutor after school. In time, Chohui graduated from high school, and she agreed to be my live-in aide rather than commuting from her cousin's house. I'd also arranged for her to get driving lessons, so when she moved in, both the cook and the chauffeur could retire. They'd always talked about me behind my back anyway. *Good riddance*, I thought, though on occasion I missed them. Especially the cook, who routinely made my favorite kimchi with my suggested modifications. No matter, these days there was a plentiful selection of kimchi at grocery stores.

That day, Chohui put the phone on the table beside me, its gleaming white surface a contrast to the black cellular device.

I ignored it and raised high the book in my lap for her to see. "What should I read next?"

"*Our Eternal Price* is in bookstores tomorrow," she replied.

"Curious title," I said.

"Yes, but samonim, everyone's talking about it."

Chohui knew the latest trends. She knew which new books were coming out, being as she was active on social media and listened to podcasts. I relied on her for recommendations. She was an exceptional young woman; everyone seemed to think so.

"All right, then, I guess it's time for lunch," I replied, getting to my feet, resigned to a long afternoon of boredom.

At that moment, an astonishing thing happened. The phone rang.

My oldest sister, Mina, was on the line. She reminded me that today was in fact the anniversary of our father's death. I felt ashamed to have forgotten and had no reply for a moment.

I tried to recover, grateful that she had not simply appeared at my door. I preferred speaking to her on the phone rather than in person because she had always, even as a child in my memory, had halitosis. The worst sort. And lately, she blew her nose constantly, as if she perpetually had a cold. She was one hundred ten years old, so a little sniffle alarmed all of us, but we couldn't tell her our concerns without being criticized for knowing nothing about anything.

I didn't tell her I'd forgotten or that Chohui had already prepared lunch. Instead, I was silent and let her ramble on, then reminded her of practicalities when she insisted we meet at his grave site.

"By the time we go out to the cemetery and back again, it will be too late to eat lunch." This was precisely the excuse she'd given me last year when I'd requested we meet on the exact anniversary of our father's death. I'd given in and we'd met a week after.

On this day, Mina ignored me. She had a voice that was in direct contrast to her height. She was the tallest of my sisters and had the lowest voice. Had the longest face too. They say your earlobes continue to grow as you age, so you can imagine how long hers were.

"We'll go to the Gentle Grove. They'll still be open," she said. "I'll see you at the cemetery." And then she hung up as if she had nothing else to discuss with me. That was clear from her tone. While I changed into suitable cemetery clothing — a white collarless Chanel suit jacket, a white tie-neck blouse, and a white skirt — Chohui texted her friend about her delayed arrival at the park and left to bring the car up from the high-rise's subterranean garage.

The journey was arduous. Cars weren't equipped to travel on dirt roads with boulders in their paths. Steep inclines and sharp turns made me fear for my life. How I suffered, despite Chohui's best driving. The whole trip one way took over an hour.

When we arrived at last, I took a deep breath as I glanced about. The cemetery was far from residential areas, on the side of a hill, and the wind seemed to blow constantly. It pleased me to know that we'd paid a handsome sum for our parents to be buried beside each other. These days it was common to be cremated, but back when my parents died, we arranged for suitable proper burials and only twice had we had to move them to make way for new condominiums. They rested in a dignified part of the cemetery, in the ground, not in urns in cubbies in those large buildings close to the parking lot we drove toward now.

It wasn't hard to spot Mina, tall as she was, walking in slow motion toward a low shrub several meters away. I said farewell to Chohui and exited the car. Only a smattering of people were out and about. I felt a surprising burst of affection for my oldest sister at that moment. I saw how bent her neck was, as if her feet couldn't keep up with her nose, and how, although she had long had the most beautiful figure, even for an elderly woman, in these past couple of years, she had been altered by age at last. She paused in her classic Burberry beige plaid belted dress and turned her head at an angle toward me as if feeling my gaze. In that gesture I saw my sister Seona. So many years had passed and yet that one movement took me back in time. How had I never seen the similarity before? We're all related, after all. It was more poignant somehow that day. I can't describe it. With a pang, I wondered how Seona was faring in North Korea. What part of her had been altered by time if she was still alive? I waved at Mina, who waited for me to catch up.

On the walkway a few shrubs ahead, we encountered our sister Aera. She was sitting on a low stone bench, her head bent, poking her blue-gloved fingers at the screen of her cell phone. Aera always wore gloves, even in her sleep. She swaddled her hands in cotton gloves of assorted colors that she'd had made specifically for her. They had a special material on the fingertips so she could use her phone.

I didn't know how she stood it in the heat of summer, but she did spend her time in air-conditioning and was rarely outdoors. Today, this humid weather seemed particularly intolerable, and I imagined her mood was sour as a result.

Aera also had the thickest hair still. At one hundred eight years old, she dyed it dark mahogany with red highlights — her daughter-in-law's

20

idea — but it was still as thick as a horse's tail and just as coarse, cut to a lob just above her shoulders. One could dye and highlight one's hair, but that thickness was pure Aera. One could not buy that in a store, although some tried with oils and vitamins. Seeing her gloved fingers clicking on her phone, I let out a chuckle. Silly when we all knew cell phone service here was weak. But Aera was not one to believe it. She was the second oldest, after Mina, the one obsessed with the latest news about viruses and illnesses and scientific studies. If there was a list of recalled products, Aera was the one who would send you the link about it. In recent years, she had become paranoid about germs and getting sick. The change had been sudden and happened after her third grandchild was born. The gloves protected her, she insisted, and she gave us gloves as gifts but I didn't take mine out of the package. I confess I sometimes wanted to rip those gloves off her just to see what she was hiding underneath.

We'd adjusted, as family members do, to how we appeared as a group. We calibrated our color palettes in what we wore so we wouldn't clash — sisters' territorial intuition and quest for harmony. Aera wore jewel tones (a sapphire pantsuit today), Mina wore neutral tones, commanding in her height (the Burberry belted affair), and I wore pastels, except today, when I wore white. I always upheld traditions, whatever they might be. In this instance, it was wearing white to my father's grave site to show respect. Black funeral garb was a modern phenomenon. I pictured Seona, wherever she was, in bright primary colors. As it worked out, our birth order clearly corresponded to our heights: Mina, the oldest, was the tallest, then Aera, then our sister Seona, and then me — the youngest and shortest.

Mina talked about the large buildings as we passed them the way she did every time. I didn't bother to tell her she was repeating herself. That would have provoked an argument. She said she'd purchased an entire wall of glass cubbies for her family's urns, that they faced the best view of the mountains in the distance, that she'd rest in peace in such a spot.

Aera agreed and admitted she and her children had bought several rows in one of those buildings too. I thought it was rude, considering that our parents were buried in this exact cemetery, for us to be talking about which was better. Plus, why did they want to exhibit themselves and their children for others to see? Did they want admirers even after death? Did they want to show off their riches for other mourning families? I thought this as they chattered. My arrogant sisters, I thought. I didn't admit I had made no arrangements whatsoever. I was like our mother in that regard. She'd said we were not to speak of things related to our demise or it would invite death to greet us. I'm curious now when I recall this. Death came anyway.

We finally found ourselves standing before our parents' austere burial plots. After our bows, we had our private silent conversations with each of them, leaving extra time for our father, since it was the anniversary of his death, after all. I promised him I'd protect the family as I had all these years, that I'd do what he'd expected us to do even if I was the only one doing it. I wouldn't let him down the way others had. He had shown more affection to me, the youngest of his children, than he had to my sisters. He had let me sit on his lap when I was a very young child, allowed me to eat from his rice bowl at dinnertime. A treasured memory; I knew it set me apart, marked me as more special than anyone else.

Afterward, we took Aera's car. I'd already sent Chohui off to meet her friend as she'd originally planned. Though my sisters agreed that Chohui was the most skillful driver, Aera insisted on the special air-filtration system she had in her German car, which she preferred. Her chauffeur was competent.

We traveled without incident from the cemetery to the Gentle Grove, which wasn't a favorite of mine but, as Mina had said, was open. The hostess of the restaurant seated us at a table for four, so there was a chair for our sister Seona — emphasizing her absence. Seona, the third sister in birth order, was two years younger than Aera and two years older than me.

Aera put her blue Birkin handbag on the empty chair deliberately. She was willing to step right into the space our sister left. She was greedy, that one.

If it were up to me, I would have made sure there was food at Seona's place in case she was already in the afterlife. We didn't know. Seona had eloped to what is now North Korea when she was a young woman. Eighty-nine years had passed since we'd seen her last.

Silly how time plays tricks on us. I'd swear it was yesterday that she ran off. I missed her as keenly as if it were so. I was not hungry at all. I didn't even imagine hunger. But I ordered something to eat because the living know it's a necessity to keep up the rituals of life.

The waiter brought us tea and we were busy on our phones, checking e-mails and texts, as we waited for our food to arrive. The three of us lived in the same city, and you'd think we'd meet more often than biannually, our children grown and all three husbands dead now. But we were — no, *they* were — too busy, so all we managed was to meet once for Father, once for Mother, summer and winter. Those were the times. Summer when Appa died, winter when Eomma died. I wished that my sisters invited me on more outings. One never imagined how loneliness persisted. On that day, however, the visit was already longer than I could bear.

The usual bragging began with Aera telling us that her CEO grandson and his family were in Bali until next month. Mina commented that her son and his wife had just returned from there.

There were things neither of my sisters could understand about me. Mina drew all the wrong conclusions. She said I kept too much to myself. We talked about this at lunch that day. Mina turned her terrible bad breath in my direction.

"Jeonga, you were too busy with that son of yours. You spoiled him with too much attention. You shouldn't have been overly emotional. Aera and I each had three children to manage, but you — you could hardly take care of one." We were old women but we still talked about the years when we were in the prime of our lives; this was the time that was most real to us, before we turned into these creatures who looked and felt so unlike ourselves.

"Well, it's easy when children are as astute and ahead of their peers as yours were," Aera said to Mina.

"You're too doting an aunt. Yours were clever too," Mina replied, patting Aera's gloved hand. How that blue glove clashed with her sapphire suit, I thought.

"Logically, it doesn't make sense. One child as much trouble as three?" Aera said, joining Mina in her criticism of me.

"Good point," Mina returned, her bad breath churning every word into guttural acid.

This was a special jab at me. How could they speak so flippantly about my son when he had died too young? And there they were, smugly discussing between themselves my feelings. They were really telling me that they believed that I had caused his death.

I had to grit my teeth. "Arithmetic was never your strong suit, sister," I said.

"True." Mina laughed. "Jeonga, you were never good in math either. I'm the oldest, I remember our childhoods best. Seona was the quickest, wasn't she?" And we all looked at the empty chair, and I took that moment to rise, pick up Aera's handbag, and hang it on the back of Aera's seat. No more sweet complying baby sister. *Fight me — go ahead*, I hoped my eyes told them both.

Mina stood up and went to the powder room and Aera said, "Oh, for God's sake, Jeonga, don't be angry. We don't mean anything by it. I understand. I lost a husband at a young age too, but there was still the house to manage and the responsibility to keep up appearances for the sake of our children. Don't prove Mina's point about being intense. We're too old for all that sentimentality now."

"You think you know me?" I said. It was true, Aera and I were both widowed as young mothers, but I didn't believe that Aera and I had anything in common even so. Her children were all still alive.

"Well, you don't have to snap at me." Aera drew back. "Quite honestly, it's up to sisters to look out for one another, isn't it, and I can trace many of your troubles to that son of yours. Hear me out. For once, listen to your older sister."

CHAPTER 3

She was wrong, of course. I looked at her mouth moving and thought how old she was. Her narrowed eyes peering at me even with glasses on, myopic from looking at her phone all the time, searching for bad news. All those wrinkles, extra skin hanging off her face. She couldn't be my sister. It would mean we were all nearing the end. I couldn't look at her, but where else to look?

Aera was saying, "It seemed rather more for your own sake than for your son's that you hovered over him. I'm your sister, and it's my responsibility to be honest. Do you remember that time I came to see you and you shut the door in my face?"

I remembered that day she came to my house. I did close the door on her. Couldn't she see I was upset? And not about my son. That's what's so awful, that my own sister would believe I was overwhelmed by taking care of my child. Can you begin to understand how preposterous that was? Never mind that Aera didn't know me well enough to even suspect the kinds of things that would overwhelm me — but how could she blame my son?

Gwangmu was the easiest baby, the most eager to please — he rarely threw a tantrum. From the moment he was born, with that beautifully shaped head, perfectly formed, that whorl of hair I'd trace lightly with my finger, he was a sweet, sweet boy. He told me he loved me without any prompting — he was gentle and attuned to people's moods. He never caused me to worry or indeed gave me any problems as a little boy. I wanted him to grow tall, so I'd stretch out his legs and press on his knees as I sang numbers for him to learn, and he'd repeat them after me: "Hana, deul, set, net..." And of course, as I encouraged him to count, I was silently hoping he'd live forever.

"Again, Eomma," he'd chant. "Knee numbers again." Easy to please, that baby boy. Easy for me to believe it would always be so.

I did not obsess about him as Aera accused. There was plenty for me to pay attention to. A household, a business, and a family to run. Widowed at age twenty-seven, I had only myself to rely on. In fact, even before my husband died, we'd lived in my childhood home and I'd continued my father's business because my husband had not been able to manage his family's fortune. I was grateful for my father's foresight in buying properties that brought in rents that could sustain us even during the worst of the Japanese occupation and the Korean War that followed. I looked after my mother and kept the finances in order. I did so by imagining how my father would handle matters. I did so by picturing how pleased and surprised he'd be that I, of all his daughters, had been capable enough to take care of his business and our family. Mina and Aera had gone off to manage their husbands' families, their in-laws, their children.

Speaking of Aera, let's be honest, as she said she was: She didn't lose her husband until she was thirty-five. She had three sons and she was always comparing their childhoods to how we had been raised. How accomplished in academics they were, especially the third one, who was like Seona in math and science. He'd worked for a research laboratory before moving to Samsung and was now retired. Dull, I thought, but strategic, and I couldn't say a bad thing about him. Except Seona would have done more than simply make money if she had not eloped. She wouldn't have been content with a company job. She was never ordinary.

So that day that Aera came to my house, I didn't want to see her. She was right about that. She was the last person I wanted to see at eight in the morning. I was frantic when I heard the knock. I was hoping it was someone else. I assumed it was, but that was wishful thinking.

"I have no idea what you're talking about. You must be confusing me with someone else," I said to Aera now in the Gentle Grove. "My son was no trouble at all. Absolutely none."

"Sounds like you're losing your memory," Aera replied. "Vitamin B twelve, ask your doctor for a monthly shot right away."

"You're losing *your* memory," I retorted.

That last bit was said with Mina standing over us, back from the powder room, and she interrupted — her breath stinging my nose — "Can you two stop bickering? We don't have all the time in the world, don't you think?"

"'Don't you think,' 'don't you think.' You're always saying these things as if you're asking a question when you're not. You don't want an answer because you think you already have the answer. And I'm sick of it," Aera announced.

"Well, I'm sick of you telling me how much you've sacrificed. We've all sacrificed. Our sister Seona is the only one who lived the way she wanted and look what happened to her," Mina returned.

We were silent as the waiter set the food before us, and we ate without another word. As the waiter cleared our table minutes later, Mina added, "Seona was the happiest of us all."

Aera sniffed. "She was the bravest. She did what she wanted."

"Well, since we're talking about Seona — a letter came from her granddaughter," Mina said.

"Who would that be?" Aera lurched forward, upsetting my teacup. I had to reach over and right it again. It was empty, but she didn't know this. She didn't even apologize or attempt to correct her careless gesture.

"Her name is Joyce, remember?" Mina said and pulled a long letter envelope out of her handbag.

"From America?" Aera exclaimed. Being a know-it-all, as usual. Show-off.

"You're the best at English," Mina said, thrusting it at me. "What's it say?"

Aera grabbed it before I had a chance to accept. "I'm good at English too. It's from Ohio," she said as she scanned the envelope. My stomach flipped about. Seona had eloped when she was a teenager, never to be seen by me or my sisters again. However, during the Korean War, years after she'd left us, her husband had appeared at my house. I learned that he and Seona had two children, a daughter named Taeyang and a son named Daeshim. The son accompanied him. In time, Daeshim moved to America, married, and had a daughter. She was named Joyce, and she had written the letter, according to Mina. I'd never gotten over how Seona herself and her daughter had not come south during the Korean War. I'd resented her husband and son for arriving safely without them. It all felt confusing and entirely unfair for the women to have been left behind.

My hand hovered in the middle of the table. What did Joyce want? It took Mina clucking her tongue for Aera to surrender the envelope to me.

I read the contents immediately. The writing was black and thickly scrawled, as if with the broad side of a felt-tip marker. It had bled through the thin paper in several places. I made out some phrases: *Trouble you . . . My son needs . . .* And then I looked up. "She has a son named Jordan," I said.

"Easy to remember; sounds similar to Joyce. I have trouble remembering American names, so that's a relief. What else?" Mina said.

There were too many words for me to translate all at once. And the script deteriorated as it progressed down the page, slashing right. Why hadn't she printed it out from her computer or e-mailed us?

"How can she be too poor to have a computer?" Mina said, leaning toward the letter in my hand.

"Not all Americans are rich," Aera said in exasperation. Sometimes she surprised me by being well informed.

"I need time to translate each word," I told them and tucked the letter in my purse.

Mina nodded. "I hate to bother my children or grandchildren with this, but you know they're all expert in English."

"I wonder if it's an emergency, but if it were, she'd use KakaoTalk or call us," Aera said.

"How would she know our KakaoTalk names?" I said.

They looked at me as if I had Alzheimer's. Thankfully, the waiter came by with an electronic pad for our credit card and Aera paid because it was her turn, and my sisters called their chauffeurs and then we left.

It was only a few minutes before four o'clock. What would I do with the time? The hours stretched ahead of me. I put off alerting Chohui for a while longer. I walked around the block. More people driving cars than walking in this part of Seoul. Sidewalks needed sweeping. A few stray pieces of paper were carried by a breeze here and there. The city had become enormous in my lifetime. Gray concrete and glass, everything in tidy compartments. Our individual goals and desires didn't matter. These buildings would remain long after we were gone. I had done my part for the greater good.

Here's the thing: I was merely asked to translate the letter — keep that thought in mind. The letter was addressed to Mina. If she had handled the whole thing, I would have continued to live my days in peace in South Korea for who knew how many more years.

Instead, I was thrust into a role unexpectedly.

Chohui picked me up several blocks from the Gentle Grove. Once we arrived home, I set to work on the letter. First, I took the *Oxford Eng-*

lish Dictionary from the shelf behind my desk. There was comfort in
the heavy weight of the large volume. Second, I used my laptop to
access the website translator, which would bring me up-to-date on any
vernacular usage. My sister Seona, the intellectual of the four of us,
would have been impressed. It was a talent of mine for which I wish
I'd had a better outlet. I could have been an academic. That would
have astonished Seona and impressed my father. I remembered how
he would challenge my sister with difficult philosophical questions,
and when I'd offer an answer, he'd dismiss me with a wave of his
hand. "Quiet; your sister is thinking," he'd say without even turning
his head to address me. "Build a house with those books on the floor
for your dolls if you want, but don't disturb us, you're too young to
know," he'd add.

"But — but — give me a chance, I think I know the answer," I'd
chirp. He'd act as if he hadn't heard me. I'd be left waiting for his
respect, which never came.

Well, back to my excellent translation skills. Suffice it to say, it took me
four hours to decode the entire page with deep concentration. It began
easily enough:

Dear Great-Aunt Mina,

I'm sorry to trouble you. I'm Daeshim Yun's daughter.

Well, why was she being so formal? Of course we knew who Joyce
was. Maybe it was the way Americans wrote letters. I read on.

I found your address in a box of my father's things. It had a list
of several names with addresses. Yours was first. I hope it is still
current.

I'm sorry I haven't written this letter in Korean. I think that would help get the meaning and feeling across. Do you remember meeting me in Chicago? I hate to remind you of that terrible day that you went to the cemetery for your son, but I was there. We met you at the airport. I remember how beautiful you looked, even in your sadness, in your white suit. And how you gave me, a ten-year-old girl, Korean makeup. I still have the compact. I'd never seen such a well-dressed Korean woman like you. You had elegance and sophistication. You were almost unreal, otherworldly. Korea became a fanciful dreamlike place for me after I saw you. I know now, of course, that not all of Korea is like this. But you made quite an impression on me.

Anyway, I'm writing to ask you for help. I don't know where else to turn. I wish I could visit you in person but it's impossible for me right now. I have a son named Jordan who is twenty-nine years old. He's become very ill. It's been going on for months now. The doctors are completely baffled. He has been in and out of the hospital. We've run out of money for his care. Jordan needs experimental treatment, which is very costly. Please help us. We need to raise $70,000. I have no one else to ask.

We've exhausted all our savings. Everyone here has been helpful, especially Jordan's fiancée. She's a lovely young woman named Ellery Arnaud whom he met in college. We hope you'll be able to come to their wedding someday soon after Jordan recovers.

The name gave me pause. Surely a common name, Arnaud. And how startling that Seona's great-grandson was ill. But Ellery Arnaud? A marriage?

I calmed my nerves. Maybe I'd misread it; maybe it was Amand. *Concentrate,* I ordered myself. *Concentrate on the letter.*

But we need more money. My father once told me that my grandmother Seona was disinherited. I wish I knew about her. As you know, my father died several years ago and did not share any more about my grandmother than that. Even so, is there anything you could give us now?

I'm hoping you will help us. I would be so grateful. I know it sounds as if that's all we want from you — money, that is — but that's not the truth, I assure you. I would never even ask except for Jordan's condition.

A most unpleasant sour twittering sounded outside my window to underline my unease. A bird with a crown of orange feathers sat on the ledge and seemed to be peering in even as it emitted rude squeaks. I got up and tapped on the window. "Away with you," I shouted. It thrust back its head on its neck as if wincing in disappointment. I tapped the glass pane again and hissed, "You rascal, be gone." At that, it flew off.

I returned to my desk and the letter. Any details about Ellery Arnaud? I continued to read.

I hope you won't be upset by this letter. That is not my intention. I hope you will find a way to help us. As one mother to another, I beg you. He's my only child. I would do anything for him. I know you understand.

Your grandniece, with love,
Joyce Ko

Ko must be her husband's last name. She was using the American fashion of taking on the married name. Also, she had adopted the American way of placing the surname after the given name.

In Korea, we kept our names from birth. I would always be Hak

Jeonga, but in America, married women took their husbands' last names, in which case I'd be Mrs. Jeonga Cha. Or would I be called Mrs. Jeonga Hak Cha? Terribly confusing to me.

Anyway, back to the letter. Joyce had made an error. She had confused me with Mina. I saw immediately how that could have happened. Mina's son, Bogum; my son, Gwangmu; and Seona's son, Daeshim, had all met briefly at my house — cousins who were all the same age. Now Bogum was the only one still alive. It was most likely Bogum's letters to Daeshim that Joyce had found among Daeshim's things. I remembered that day in Chicago. I remembered wondering how Gwangmu could have died swimming in the lake in winter. Bogum was the one who came to my apartment in Seoul and told me the news. He said Gwangmu had been doing research for his lab.

"A tragedy," Bogum had explained.

I told him Gwangmu's body must be returned to Korea and me at once.

"But he has a wife and children," Bogum said with surprise.

"I'm his mother," I said. "I'll pay for everything."

"His wife has arranged a funeral in Chicago, Youngest Auntie," Bogum said. "She's not sending Gwangmu to you in Korea."

I arranged for him to wire money to Gwangmu's wife, hoping it would persuade her to let me have a funeral for him in Korea, where he belonged. When there was no word after weeks went by, I tried to pretend Bogum had never delivered that terrible news. Six months later, Bogum called me. "The grave marker is in place," he said in a gentle voice. "Don't you want to see where your money has gone?"

I wanted more than to see the headstone, but I was unable to do anything because my son had had a wife. With bitterness, I agreed to see where he was buried, but that was all.

"So you won't see your grandchildren?" Bogum said in dismay.

"I'm not meeting his widow or his children," I said. "Not when she wouldn't send his body to Korea."

Turned out that Bogum couldn't accompany me because his child was sick with something. But Bogum called Seona's son, Daeshim, who was then living in Ohio, and asked him to escort me to the cemetery.

I walked right past Daeshim at O'Hare. He caught my arm to stop me. I was astonished at how he had matured. He had been in America for many years, and his face had filled out on the sides. He was dressed in a well-ironed suit, though his tie appeared too tight around his wide neck. I was taken aback by his eyes. He had the same hooded eyes as Seona. I hadn't seen the resemblance to his mother when he was a boy.

"Youngest Auntie," he said and bowed deeply. "Grateful to see you again," he said. America agreed with him.

He introduced me to the little girl by his side, his daughter, Joyce, who slipped into the back seat when we reached his car. He had a right to refuse to help me at a low point in my life after how I had treated him when he was a boy; I knew this. I braced myself for retribution. I was vulnerable and could do nothing to shield myself. My son had died — imagine. Instead, he drove me to the cemetery and waited for me in the car.

At Gwangmu's grave, I was pleased to see that my money had been well spent. I'd had a recurring nightmare that when no one was looking, the American cemetery company would pocket the money I'd sent instead of keeping Gwangmu's site clear of weeds. I'd pictured it overrun. Worse still, I imagined Gwangmu's ghost in torment because his coffin had been moved or crushed because another coffin had been dumped on top of his. The businesspeople could have resold his plot out of greed, taking my money and the money of someone else. Maybe two others. Who knew how deep they'd go, piling coffins on top of coffins.

I had worn a white suit; Joyce was right. Similar to the one I wore to the cemetery that day with my sisters, but the one back then had been my Chanel bouclé, as it was chilly in Chicago, the weather report warned. At the airport in Korea before I departed, I had bought Daeshim's daughter a present. I didn't know how old she was. Imagine, giving a child makeup. I knew only that I'd wanted to give her something. I couldn't go empty-handed; there were customs, after all.

I remembered Joyce as a little girl in Illinois, America, in the back seat of the car as we drove to and from the cemetery. She was a jumpy child, unable to sit still. Impatient, like her grandmother Seona. Bangs in her eyes. *Why doesn't her mother keep her hair tidier?* I remember thinking. Makeup was certainly not an appropriate gift for her. But she flipped the compact open and looked at herself in the mirror. And that's when I thought I had done her a service: showing her how she appeared to the world.

Now this many years later, I was flattered she'd kept the old compact. I could give her the current stylish items the young people were using now. That was my first thought. I pictured it and her gratitude — a present I could send in the mail; that was simple enough.

Her request made me think of the book I'd just finished reading. I could be a character in Joyce's story. The point could be that I arrived and saved Jordan. Maybe I could be in the epilogue of her life. And then I caught myself.

Maybe Joyce didn't care about me. Maybe I wasn't a character at all. Why should I bother? What if I was completely wrong? What if I was being used? I felt a depression coming on, and I stayed seated in my chair and didn't want to help her. I didn't.

Why had it taken her this long to contact me? Why did people come to me only when they needed money? It had been the case all my adult life. I'd been the keeper of my family's fortune. I reread the part of Joyce's letter where she expressed curiosity about her paternal grandmother, whom she had never known. But of course, in the end, all she wanted was her inheritance. Again, only money. How could she have known the truth?

And then there was the more uncomfortable possibility of that name, Ellery Arnaud. So much came with that name.

A chill entered the room. The sky outside darkened at once. A cloud, no doubt; large, by the way it persisted. But then another bird landed on the windowsill. This time a bright cardinal. He looked right at me. An accusation in his look? Did I have a right to be in anybody's epilogue?

It would be up to Joyce to decide the role I'd have in the book of her life. What did I need to say in my letter in reply?

I was deep in thought when Chohui interrupted me. Unable to decide what to do, I was still staring at a blank piece of stationery on the desk. She announced that it was time for dinner. We had simple red leaf lettuce wraps with potato soup — I'd taught Chohui how to make this, as it was a staple during lean economic times and comforted me, reminding me of my childhood. How I relished it. Much better than restaurant food with all the salt they put into everything.

A good night's sleep was what was warranted. My mind was truly fatigued.

The next day, I woke early, had a light breakfast, and returned straightaway to my desk to write Joyce a letter. I'd decided what to say. I smoothed a blank piece of stationery and began this reply:

My dear grandniece Joyce,

How lovely to hear from you. I have thought of you often. I am in receipt of your letter and your request. It was not your oldest great-aunt who visited you in Illinois; it was I. I am the youngest of the four sisters. Your grandmother Seona was the third in the order of siblings. I wish your son the very best recovery. You should be grateful that he has a fiancée. Is her last name Amand or Arnaud? I could not make out your handwriting. While I cannot answer all your inquiries here, I can wire you 10,000 American dollars. Any more than that, I am not at liberty to send without my lawyer's approval. Your son deserves excellent care and your grandmother would want that for him, I can assure you. Again, I wish your son the utmost speedy and complete recovery.

> With great affection and wishes to you
> for a happy and fulfilling life,
> Hak Jeonga
> (Mrs. Jeonga Hak Cha)

Then I put the letter in an envelope. At first, my intention was to go to the central post office myself to send it on its way. Probably by express mail; that was the least I could do. The thought of fresh air appealed to me. A reason to leave the house. But the post office was located in a part of Gangnam that I didn't like to frequent. The buses, so many buses, especially near the terminal, drew my eyes. I couldn't look away. They called to me in a manner I couldn't describe. Maybe the right word is *feel*. My mother used to say we feel close to significant moments in our lives — they leap toward us, a vibration. All the knowledge we need is within our reach, she used to say. I wished I'd paid more attention to her words — she'd tried to help us navigate our lives, but I was too busy thinking she knew nothing about life, sequestered as she was in our narrow neighborhood. Seona had disdain for her, and it had been contagious, my sister's scorn.

On that day, as I was tucking the letter into my handbag, an additional worry nagged at me. With the extensive time it took for letters to arrive overseas, Joyce might believe at this very moment that we had forgotten her. There must be no delay in sending the money. It must arrive even before my letter, perhaps. I changed my plans.

CHAPTER 4

Whenever my father had a crucial decision to make, he'd consult his books and seek advice from experts. My attorney was such a resource I called upon often. I'd also need him to handle the money transfer to an American bank. Chohui drove us to see him. We walked through the glass doors and went up the elevator in our crisp suits. I'd bought Chohui several suits, so she looked equal to any of the city women, but she always swapped the skirts for pants and never buttoned the jackets. I didn't mind; I was pleased she took my fashion advice in these official matters.

"It's so quiet," Chohui said as we walked on the thick carpet of the hallway and gazed up and down at the floor-to-ceiling glass windows around us.

"Much better than the loud clacking of our shoes in the lobby, don't you think?" I said and felt foolish. I sounded like Mina now with that ridiculous phrase, *don't you think.*

My lawyer was standing at the receptionist's desk. I liked that he was eager to see me. Chohui stared from him to me as if she found something odd about his expression of joy at my presence. I wanted to believe it was because he truly had missed me, but I suspected he was thinking of the hours he was billing at his very high rate. Maybe meeting me in the reception area counted as part of his billable hours. He bowed his head curtly and let us go ahead of him down the hall.

Once we entered the conference room, I made note of the time so I could compare his invoice to my accounting of my time with him. I waved Chohui toward the sideboard. Might as well get something extra if we were being charged. Her fingers hovered over the pastries on the plate. I whispered to her to take one of each if she couldn't decide. Honestly, anyone watching would believe I didn't allow her to eat at my house. The truth was she was a selective eater.

Attorney Kim simply stood by his chair until she was seated. I already sat in my favorite chair, which was at the head of the table. Attorney Kim had offered me that chair the very first meeting we had in that room and it had been mine ever since. The chairs were quite comfortable, in tufted leather, and I was glad some of my money to this lawyer was being put to good use. The only problem was my feet didn't reach the floor, but I pretended to ignore this fact because I wanted to be seated as high as he was so as to be chin level when he turned to me in that conspiratorial way that was his particular professional talent and why I'd chosen him of all the lawyers I'd interviewed after my longtime attorney retired two decades ago.

Chohui sat across from the attorney with an éclair on a napkin. I wanted to remind her to obtain a plate, but I remembered the ticking billable hour.

"Mr. Attorney Kim," I began. "The occasion has arisen in which I'm considering giving my grandniece in Ohio, United States, a generous amount of support." Then I gave him a concise summary of Joyce's letter. Only what he needed to know.

A wide smile spread across his face, as if I'd made a genius statement, and he said, "In that case, I am pleased to put in every effort to amend your will so that she receives the allotment you feel appropriate to meet her needs commensurate with your own very generous kindness."

The poor man must have been stressed because his chin had a few adolescent pimples, and I made sure not to pay them any mind. A regular visit to the dermatologist could prevent that, but perhaps he wasn't as reckless with his earnings as so many of his generation were, doting as they did on their appearance. He had two children of college age — I'd inquired, in previous meetings, about his family to show him how concerned I was for his continued emotional stability. Divorces were becoming more common throughout the country.

I tapped his hand, which was on the table, palm down, between us. A brisk pat. A show of approval and an urging. I didn't let it linger. "I'm pleased to hear this, Mr. Attorney Kim. Might I say that it is not my will I wish to change but a specific distribution I wish to wire to her. I've prepared a deeply thoughtful letter in response that expresses my heartfelt wishes for her to apply these funds in the manner that would be most helpful to her and her dear immediate family."

Chohui brought the éclair to her lips and paused, and then, when Attorney Kim began to speak, she took a bite. I wondered if she thought he disapproved of her eating it. I sent her a look and nodded, a signal I hoped she received, but she was staring hard at the éclair, which she'd returned to the napkin in front of her. Then she busied herself with her phone, which I thought was rude, but young people these days were constantly on their devices.

Attorney Kim spread his fingers in my direction. "I see. Well, Lady Hak," he said. (I quite liked it when he called me this, though it was not a term used much anymore.) "I'm at your disposal, of course. Lady Hak, what is your grandniece's name, her bank's name, and her account number, and how much of your wonderful funds would you like to send from your bank here in our lovely Seoul to your grandniece? It is your grandniece, is that what I heard?" he asked and paused in his very breath.

42

"You're correct," I said, and he seemed to be effectively released from his paralysis and began to nod.

He waited. I waited.

His brow wrinkled. Finally, he said, "Lady Hak, I need to know the name of her bank and her account information."

He looked nervous, so I placed my hand over his hand closer to me — it was surprisingly cold and clammy — to slow him down. Patience; I feared he had none. Chohui coughed and I looked over to see that her eyes bulged as if ready to pop out of their sockets — I think that's the phrase children use these days — with the éclair fully in her mouth. I removed my hand at once. "How could we find this, Mr. Attorney Kim — isn't there some way with the technology of the banks, as you say, to make sure this money would reach my grand-niece in proper fashion, as opposed to, good fortune forbid, some other United States person's bank account?"

He clapped his hand to his narrow forehead as if I'd surprised him with my extraordinary caution. I had not survived all these years without some amount of wisdom, keep in mind. Our old-world ways had held me in good stead.

"Lady Hak, you are once again as wise as I would expect from a personage of such talent and fortitude —" he began.

"Fortitude?" I asked.

"Tremendous depths of beautiful intellect; your reputation is out-standing in that regard — dare I suggest, Lady Hak, perhaps you could review your grandniece's letter once again and see if she included her bank information?" He looked at me with such sincerity that I was struck by how insincere he was. He dared to question me? I didn't have the bank information. I knew what the letter had included and what it hadn't.

I felt my neck flush and I glanced at Chohui, my cheeks pinked with mortification — surely she could see as well as I did that he

43

thought I was a ridiculous old frump. I pushed my chair away from the table and slid off the seat in my cream dress oxfords and stared down at him. "Mr. Kim," I said, leaving out the honorific *Attorney*. "I take issue with your tone, sir."

He blushed crimson, far redder than I, and I heard Chohui let out a loud single laugh. "That was not my intention. My apologies, Lady Hak. I'm out of practice taking meetings with you and I'm caught unprepared by your esteemed request. Shall I dash to the bank manager and call you as soon as possible with a satisfying answer? Perhaps he could offer an alternative form of action? Do you have an address for the grandniece?"

I nodded. This was more like it. I handed the envelope to Chohui, who copied in her elegant handwriting the Ohio address onto a piece of stationery that Attorney Kim provided in a genuine leather-bound folder. Then Chohui returned the envelope to my safekeeping.

With Joyce's address securely on a piece of paper in his folder, Attorney Kim requested permission to take his leave of us and scrambled for the door. I heard him call to someone, and then he was off down the hallway. The bank was across the street and on the corner. It had many offices throughout the city now. Too many, in my opinion. I pictured a monstrous tentacled beast of a company making a profit from every person on every corner, as if banks were as important as hospitals or grocery stores, which they're not — they're simply banks. Must we encounter them at every turn?

"He could have just called," Chohui said from the sideboard with her hand on a lemon Danish.

"Hardly. How was the éclair?" I asked. "Is there anything to drink here?"

She looked around, which made me inspect the room in turn. On the end of the sideboard were two carafes, which I assumed contained coffee and hot water; beside them were four teacups in elegant stoneware. Did no one offer plain water anymore? Most people my age preferred hot drinks, but I enjoyed room-temperature water — filtered, of course.

"What to do?" I said to the air.

"We'll get some water at home," Chohui returned.

This is when I began to think about what was left of the day and the day after that and after that. No matter how many assurances this bank manager gave my silly lawyer, how would I know for certain that the money reached Joyce? I imagined not knowing for weeks, months, years to come. How would I know what happened? It was not just curiosity; I had true worry about her and her son. I could hear her voice through that letter. I pictured her sitting down to write it and then waiting for the postal person to bring her an answer, and what if it didn't reach her, both of us on opposite sides of the world waiting indefinitely? Also, that tug at my conscience: the name Ellery Arnaud.

The thought of waiting for Attorney Kim to find Joyce's bank information was suddenly intolerable, even that small amount of time. I directed Chohui to drive me to see Bogum, Mina's son; he kept an office in a building a few blocks away. What had he told Daeshim in letters that Joyce would have read? Did Bogum know about Ellery Arnaud?

Parking was atrocious, so Chohui dropped me off, and I walked in alone. I remembered Mina saying he had returned from Bali — why would anyone want to vacation there at the advanced age of eighty-three? He was officially retired, but he still went to an office every day to feel useful; that's what I suspected. So many folks were unwilling to relinquish control.

He was available, and we engaged in amiable banter. After all, he wasn't a scholar or a researcher or anything; he sat at a desk all day reading the news on his computer. He was Mina's only son, the one we had talked about at lunch, the one who was the same age as my son, Gwangmu, and Seona's son, Daeshim. He was gracious and not at all bothered or behind schedule after having been to Bali. He didn't look as if he'd been in the sun at all. He was paler than I was with my best cushion powder and seemed confused when I asked him about the weather on his vacation. Still, how delightful to see someone who shared my bloodline. I extolled the virtues of travel, especially to the United States. We chatted about it, since he too had visited America often.

"I hear you used to write letters to Daeshim, Joyce's father, in Ohio."

"Not as much as I would have liked." He sighed.

"You were good to be in touch," I said. "By the way, do you know Jordan very well?"

He raised his eyebrows. "I don't, but I've not been in touch with Joyce as much as other people in the family. In fact, it's only recently that Ned, your grandson, contacted me. Sharp man, curious man. Enjoy our talks immensely. You should visit him, Youngest Auntie. How many more chances do you think you'll have?"

The sting of that remark took me aback. A criticism in there somehow. Should? I should? I should visit my grandson?

"Who's lucky enough to have time for selfish trips like that? I'm too old to be traveling about, even if I could possibly manage it. And I might not be able to at my age. Exploring the idea, Bogum, that's all," I said. I was not going to tell him I was mulling over plans to go to America to obtain Joyce's bank information and see for myself that she received the money.

"You look healthier than people half your age." He laughed.

His compliment immediately returned me to a good temper. Of course I was in fine health. I told him I took all the precautions for such and gave him advice on how he should include exercise in his daily routine. "Don't sit in an office," I said. "And did you even go outside of your hotel room when you went to Bali?" He seemed confused again by my reference to Indonesia. Was I pronouncing it incorrectly?

He changed the subject at that point. I should have been more on guard. "How did you hear about Jordan, Youngest Auntie?" he asked.

I was in such a good mood, I came clean. "Your mother received a letter from Joyce, didn't she tell you?"

He shook his head and became very quiet.

"But do you know," I said, leaning in, "Joyce was actually trying to reach me. Probably got your mother's address from one of your letters to her father. Her son has a fiancée! See the role your letters played here?" I chuckled.

He gave me a weak smile. "Easy mistake to make. We do have a big family," he said.

I nodded. "Indeed. And we must help the younger generation. Even you, you're not as young as you used to be," I said with tenderness. "Jordan's fiancée is named Ellery Arnaud — would you say it's a common name?"

He smiled at that and shook his head. "I don't know anything about American names. So, you think you'll be going? Is that what the letter was? A wedding invitation?"

"Absolutely not," I said. "It's just an engagement. It could be a long engagement, for all we know."

"Weddings are nice, aren't they, Youngest Auntie?" he said.

I refused to answer and left at once. A wedding? He had no idea how dangerous that was.

CHAPTER 5

As I walked outside, I smelled roasted chestnuts. I associated them with the war, what Americans call the Korean War. I was a widow; my sisters were busy with their families, and my parents were long gone — I remember the uncertainty in the air. The fear. What was I supposed to do? How would our country move forward?

I focused on my son and lost track of what I thought about anything. It happens when a child is growing. Things I thought I'd never forget — *poof*, vanished. My sisters couldn't even come across town to visit me because the fighting was so bad. We all kept our gates closed. I wouldn't have opened the door, except one day — that day stands out — a note was slipped under it that the maid found. The note was written in the most beautiful form you can imagine. I remember how time stopped and crystallized into a moment I'd never forget.

It was dusk. I was about to eat dinner alone when the maid brought the note to me. I thought at first, as I did with every note, that it was from Seona, something from her asking how we were faring, completely unaware of how much our family had declined.

I quickly unfolded it and there it was — the most refined handwriting I'd ever seen. More uniform than that of any of our teachers. The note inquired about my needs. I misread it at first. My needs? Who would be concerned about what I needed at a time when I was running about making sure we had enough provisions for everyone in the house? And when my sisters sent their own messengers to me, asking for more items from Father's hidden storeroom to exchange for food for their families? The note was clearly written by an educated person and I knew, sensed immediately, that here was the beginning of something momentous. I could ignore it or I could respond, knowing that my life would change forever. Just from this short note, inquiring politely if I needed a tutor for my son.

That's all it was. And how frivolous.

At a time when no one knew which way the war would turn, it was hard for me to entertain the idea that my son's education was necessary. But in the back of my mind, in my heart, was this worry that it had been two years since his school closed. I was beginning to wonder how he'd ever go to university. Gwangmu was about to turn fifteen years old. His father had died ten years earlier. He was an inquisitive boy who had been methodically reading the books in the library his grandfather had accumulated. But the books weren't sufficient to give him an education in those subjects, and I knew I wasn't a good enough teacher to help him further, especially in mathematics and the sciences. He was becoming a man without anyone to guide him; he was no longer a child. I wished for him to become a scholar.

What was education when we were facing life and death? But some parental concerns never changed. Every day was a lost day of the rest of his life.

Maybe it was the civility of the request at a time when civility was the last thing on everyone's mind. But it was what I longed for — what I tried to keep a semblance of, for my son's sake. I needed to believe there would be a time again when life returned to the daily rituals of meaning, beyond whether we survived another day, week, or month. There had to be more to my life than this waiting. So there he was.

He was like any man. Average. I'd try to remember this first impression later to remind myself there were others, plenty, just like him. Not special, I told myself. But it was no use. He was nothing like he appeared to be. Far from average. I was wrong, even about his age. Prematurely white strands were scattered throughout his close-cropped hair, making him look older than he was. I'd learn later that he was twenty-six, ten years younger than me. If I'd known his actual age at the start, I would never have allowed myself the beginnings of those feelings that grew with time. It was unseemly. I knew later how unseemly they were. A humiliating, pathetic age gap for the gossips to seize upon.

By his side was a girl — sixteen years old, but also young-looking. Malnourished. Not developed in the chest. All the children looked younger while the adults looked older, with our frown lines of hardship and worry. I thought she was his daughter, but he said she was his sister. Not even half — wholly his sister. I knew it was possible. With mothers having children so young, they could be ten years apart. He called her Hayun.

So there he was. Conventionally handsome, except you could see that he didn't know it. And there was this girl beside him. Hollowed cheeks. Her head was down but her eyes scanned the room, taking in the valuable chest of drawers, the scrolls on the walls. In contrast, he kept his eyes in a respectful gaze on me.

There was an immediate connection. I felt it. Internally, all my organs snapped to attention — I felt as though I could smell more acutely, see more acutely. I felt — when our hands touched by accident — more alive.

I could have been suspicious. Never mind what happened later; I wouldn't believe it was all false, that he hatched a plan on the street and then made his way to my gate and sought to take advantage of me so he could have a career in America. No one knew I was lonely. I was not a brooding type. I had my hands full as a mother and a widow who had to manage household affairs on a dwindling fortune. I didn't complain to the people who depended on me or let them see how frightened I was. I acted as if nothing had changed, or at least very little. I was not an obvious target.

I thought he was genuinely surprised by how welcoming I was of the skills he could provide. His name was Jin Siwon. He was a teacher in need of a student to teach. Was I in need of his services?

I invited him and his sister, Hayun, to sit and eat supper, and he blushed and obliged out of courtesy. He was nearly paralyzed with embarrassment at how greedy his sister was. He seemed to want to say something to her but stumbled on his words — the only time I saw him in such a state. He would have stopped her if I weren't sitting there. I think that I saw him as he truly was in those first few moments. He had held up pretty well and didn't stuff honey balls into his mouth the way she did, her form hunched over, collapsed on the floor practically. He clearly had manners.

I had the maid take Hayun away after an interminable amount of time with an offer of sweet rice cake in the kitchen with my son. She was a year older than Gwangmu, and I imagined they'd have very little in common so I didn't impose any rules on where or how they could see each other. I was also consumed with the details of daily life, about keeping us all safe and out of the line of fire. But that's not the entire truth, of course. I knew how much was in my hands. I knew what he was asking. Not only to educate my son but to live in my house with me, within the safety of my walls. Not only him but his sister. Surely she was included, indivisible from him.

If I'd learned anything from my father, it was to negotiate with silence. *Pause,* my father would say. *Don't worry that they think the game is over. Your adversary will hang on every word if you slow down the conversation.* I turned the teacup in my hand, took a sip, placed it on the table, looked at it for another long moment. I noticed he was

51

waiting. I admired the fact that he had made his inquiry straightaway, even though he'd seemed reluctant to do so. I thought it meant he had character, not that it was his approach to everything, which it was, I'd learn later. Finally, I picked up the teapot and offered more tea.

"No, thank you," he replied as if he were punishing me for the delay.

"Where were you educated?" Of course I had to ask. I returned the teapot to its place.

"Does this mean you are in need and asking about my qualifications?"

"Why do my motivations matter here?"

"I'm only saying that if you'd like, I could show you my references."

"How comforting." And then I let the silence in again.

"It's nothing I'm embarrassed about," he began, sitting taller and giving me the satisfaction of seeming nervous.

I would have hired him on the spot even if he'd been self-taught. But he didn't know that then. "Where did you say you studied?" I asked.

"The professors left the university — there wasn't —"

My heart raced ahead. University? He had to mean Seoul Dae. It would be easy to justify a job for him now. No one would question my judgment, even during wartime. But how old was he? "Such mayhem between the Japanese occupation and this war," I offered.

"Exactly," he said with a sigh.

"So was it called Keijō Imperial University when you were there or Seoul Dae?"

He looked away.

"Of course, well, then, when can you start?" I finished. No need to humiliate him. If he didn't want to tell me how old he was, I did not have to push him. I'd heard many graduates were embarrassed by the upheaval their studies suffered during this time. If they had even graduated. No matter; I'd gotten what I'd wanted. He was an accomplished scholar. A solid truth. But it was an easy truth, and there would be more difficult ones to come.

I enjoyed being near him. Even that first night. If I could have paid him just to sit beside me, I would have — if I could have justified it to my sisters and the rest of the world. The cook came in once or twice and I could tell she was suspicious of his motives. But I was glad, for once, because then I didn't have to be. She'd tell me if she learned anything.

It felt like a secret, to be together having dinner, me and a stranger whom I wanted to be near, whom I didn't want to be a stranger anymore. Besides my husband, I'd known few people and I'd never been allowed to choose someone for myself. I felt like I understood for the first time too that night why men go to a gisaeng. Why they claim nothing even happens sexually, that they just want to sit and look and inhabit the same space as beauty. A grace that could be called beauty.

I knew it sounded foolish. *Beauty?* Seona would have scoffed the way she did when I worked hard on my crocheting. She was all for speed and size. I thought it ironic that she'd said that about the man she eloped with — that he was handsome, she said. Like the men in the books. The opposite of the boys from the families around us. A man, she'd said about her fiancé. She'd picked a stranger, and looking at my own, I realized how she'd felt.

I remembered the day we celebrated Father's fiftieth birthday, we all had new hanboks. Individually, each one looked pretty enough, but not special; in fact, Mother said they were too garish, but Grandmother said my sisters and I looked like autumn trees on a hillside, and we did, all together, the four of us girls, the year before our oldest sister married. We looked beautiful together as a group.

That's how I felt beside Siwon: prettier than I was by myself. My husband had never made me feel like that. He had been sloppy. Not in a roguish manner, but in an absentminded way — like a messy child. That was his character. And it made him weak. Some women like that sort of partner in life. I wished I did.

But Siwon commanded your attention. I'll tell you, he had only two shirts, but they were clean and pressed and looked expensive even when they weren't. Even in those terrible times, he was crisp and neat, and I had faith in his knowledge. I wanted my son to be like him, to exude that kind of confidence and speak with authority and grace. My boy was showing signs of being too much like his father. Not his fault. How can you blame a boy? But from this man he could learn another way of being in the world. You might even call it military, how he carried himself, except there was no forced arrogance, nothing artificial. Sometimes with those soldiers I knew without their uniforms and guns, they were cowards. And in the Japanese occupation we'd grown up in, who wouldn't be drawn to that kind of strength to stand up to brutality? But honestly, all that was secondary. I was attracted to him from the moment I saw him enter the room.

I didn't like to consider my behavior too closely in those early days. I was stunned, drawn in, enchanted; does that sound too irresponsible? I was enchanted by his eyes that sought the floor by my feet, his eloquent but simple speech, the way he said he didn't require anything from me and then proceeded to ask if I had read this book or that. Instead of making me stumble over my words, his presence brought out my sharpest negotiating instincts, a sense of humor no one ever appreciated. I felt better than I ever had before, a whole person, wise, witty, attuned to my own desires, vulnerable. I thought of Seona often. She knew what it was to love and be loved like this. She'd given up her sisters, her parents, for a love like this. We knew that there were no easy truths in what comes with love. How small that word: *love*. How small for how much it demanded for the illusion of what it gave.

I relished that time. I let myself enjoy my days for once. Conversations. Walks. The belief it would always be this way because we wanted it so. Back then, I'd basked in the company of this man. Later, I gazed at him in the afterlife and remembered everything.

He sat with me in the sun on the porch of the house and dazzled me with his knowledge. It was impressive to me to hear Siwon talk about his books. And it was in books that he'd learned about America. I hadn't even known that my father had such books in his study. Siwon discovered them and read voraciously.

We spent our days in that gated land of the house and by the pond with our books, my son copying the passages Siwon gave him, Hayun playing with the ducks. For her age, she was terribly childish. But this didn't matter in the least. I tried sometimes to teach her how to knit and crochet, and she learned to fetch the things needed by the cook and maid. But she didn't pay attention for long. Always an excuse to run off somewhere. Little did I know she was running off to be with Gwangmu. How did I miss all the signs?

Siwon might have known. He said something that astonished me.

He said to me back then, after he announced his sister's condition, looking at the floor: "Who could blame them? They had only each other to entertain themselves."

I was stunned. Who could blame them? "They were children. Children don't become pregnant."

Except they weren't children, were they? Gwangmu was fifteen and Hayun was sixteen. Inquisitive, lonely young people. I was the one who didn't consider their attraction to each other. I was the one who blamed them. It was a terrible mess. If I was guilty of anything, it was of not paying attention. It seemed Siwon and I talked endlessly about nothing, walking with our heads bent together about geography and politics, while Gwangmu and Hayun had been alone with each other too often and for too long.

Those nine months of Hayun's pregnancy were horrifying, like looking at a giant wave in Busan during a summer storm coming in at you while you stand waist-deep in the ocean. You're too slow to run back to shore and not far enough out to dive beneath it. It will break over your head, no question. Even at this distance, you recognize this inevitability. And you are stuck in place by the receding sand, despite what you know will happen.

We couldn't keep the foolish children apart during this time. My son was as solicitous as an old grandmother. Siwon couldn't get him to read a single page out of any book.

After we learned of Hayun's pregnancy, I didn't panic. I believed, even in the stark reality of our predicament, that if Siwon was with me, we would find a solution. My son a father at fifteen would be a disgrace if anyone knew about it, with a war on, with supplies dwindling, and I was still in an enchantment of love. Part of me didn't want anything to change and was in denial about impending doom. Part of me, the one that would begin to take over eventually, was terrified about what my sisters would say, what the neighbors would say, how they would see that I had been caught myself in love, and untoward love at that. Siwon was ten years younger than I, a widow. My sisters would have accused him of fortune-hunting. How could he love me for anything else? I was fearful of old patterns, believing the traditional grooves to hold even as society changed around me. Maybe I could have stood up to them all, but, you see, I had my doubts too. I'd seen how people could be tricked into love. I couldn't face the possibility I too had fallen victim.

After Siwon told me, we walked around and around the yard, talking about everything and nothing. I watched for signs. What did he expect from me? Was I supposed to make his sister part of our esteemed family? Would he love me less if I refused?

He was a gentleman, to be sure, and he loved his sister dearly; you could see that in how he helped her from the table, gave her extra food off his own plate to eat, looked at her with tenderness, as if she were in fact his child and not a sister who could fend for herself, someone of his own generation. Maybe it was because he'd always played the role of her caregiver. But a father would have been stern and ashamed of her condition. And he was not. Which I didn't approve of, but I deferred to him. I let him know I deferred to him. I told him we'd come up with a plan together. We walked the yard each night, especially when everyone else was asleep. We were in love, after all. With the moon high in the sky, we considered our choices.

I was the mother of the boy and there was not the same honor to defend in our case. I imagined what my father would have done in my place. And the answer came to me: I made it clear we would provide a certain amount of legal tender, that despite the illegitimacy, the baby would always have a home in this house, as diminished as it was by then, lacking a man to run the business my father had run. We still had value, though, in this house, this land. We had a name and a reputation of which we were proud, and this baby would have, if not the name, at least the courtesy of financial support. I suggested we hide Hayun until the baby was born and then pass the child off as a relative of the maid. I'd overheard my parents talk about a similar situation once. In that case, a Japanese soldier had gotten the daughter of a prominent Korean family pregnant, so they'd sent her to live with extended family in the northernmost part of Korea until the baby was born, then given the infant away to another family to be raised. The soldier had been returned to Japan by his commanding officer.

Hayun could move to Mina's house and be the cook's helper. That position had recently become vacant. I assured him that Hayun would be able to visit often — as the teacher's sister, she'd be welcome anytime, and it was close enough to walk in under two hours. There would be ways to allow her to spend as much time with the baby as she liked. I thought a farther distance was more suitable, but I knew Siwon would want to see his sister. Gwangmu's face when he looked at Hayun made me think this might be a healthy compromise.

Siwon weighed the practicality of this idea against his knowledge of his sister's emotional state. He didn't think, ultimately, that she would accept that option, and it was not safe for a young woman to be traveling alone. It hurt my feelings, to be sure, that he refused to persuade her of the sense I made. Or even to present my solution to her. He said she had taken to weeping — which I had witnessed — and needed to be soothed for the baby to be healthy.

The days passed with his sister pregnant. I don't have much to say here except that Siwon left the gates of the house more and more frequently and returned with academic journals and newspapers. He took my son with him too, as a favor to me, because I didn't like the way Gwangmu had grown wider around the middle and softened around his face. He should have been interested in the world outside our walls, not acting like a servant to this timid girl. But I kept my opinions to myself. Siwon praised him for his attentiveness.

Before he left my room in the early hours of the morning, Siwon would often share that he wished he could continue his university studies. It was I who suggested he apply to graduate programs in America. I was the one who reached out to the priest at the Catholic church to see if he would sponsor Siwon in his studies at a university abroad.

San Francisco was where he was invited to study. I decided that Hayun and the baby would accompany Siwon to America. It felt like fate had opened a door, a release from the pressures and the questions, a freedom for my Gwangmu, who had an entire life ahead of him, choices, if he could escape from the weight of a baby and family and a woman he hardly knew.

The baby was born and named Jiu. I convinced Gwangmu that he could join Hayun and Jiu in a year or so if he still wanted to. I promised we'd visit often and then move there possibly. Korea was a mess, wasn't that obvious? We presented San Francisco as a temporary separation.

Before the three of them left, in the days immediately following Jiu's birth, I noticed a difference in Gwangmu right away. A quiet boy, he suddenly couldn't stop talking. He was bewitched by this baby's existence in the world. He said, "I can't believe I made a human being. A miracle — science, but still miraculous."

It was unnerving. It was unlike him. Love can do that to people. Turn them inside out. Grow parts of the heart that had not been in existence before. They say that about the brain, but I think it happens to the heart too. Or the soul or whatever it is that we call the heart. I know this is not the way to think of actual human anatomy, but it felt that way then. It felt like the heart had grown wings and that the ankles sprouted them too and I knew what he meant but I couldn't acknowledge we had both fallen into this beautiful trap of loving people we couldn't be with.

In the summer, Hayun and Jiu traveled to San Francisco with Siwon, who had entered a graduate program in physics that began in the fall. I let my love go to America with his sister and the baby and kept my son with me at home. I admit I had no idea how the distance between Korea and America would feel to me until he was gone. Some days, I thought I would not be able to live an hour longer without him.

The day my sister Aera knocked on our door, the morning she had spoken about, was the day after my love had left with Hayun and Jiu. I stayed up pacing the entire night and when I heard the knock, I thought he had changed his mind and returned. Seeing my sister standing there with her hopeful face made me shatter inside.

In the year that followed, Gwangmu was despondent and raged at me, but I kept my head. I took the verbal pummeling and remained firm. My constant refrain: "You'll go someday to see your daughter if you want to, but first you must go to college and get your degree, and I'll pay for all of it. Be patient." I survived only because letters and books from America arrived regularly. Siwon recalled our conversations, described his days in detail. I wrote back even more often than he wrote me. Two, three letters for every one of his, which he acknowledged with gratitude. They were the only reason I was able to get up each morning.

Five years later, Siwon took a tenure-track position in Colorado, but Jiu was in school by then and Hayun seemed to be managing well with a job as a nursing-home aide, so the two of them stayed in San Francisco. As the uncle, Siwon remained in Jiu's life, inviting her to Colorado and orchestrating her undergraduate enrollment when she was college age.

We did not visit as I'd promised. I never considered leaving Korea in all those years we corresponded. Air transportation was expensive in those days. Gwangmu asked me once, years later, when he felt I'd tricked him into letting his baby and Hayun go to America without him, "Why did you lie to me? Why did you say I'd be able to see my baby often?"

"You failed your exams," I burst out. Not a proud moment of motherhood, but it was the truth. "You had to take them again. Look at the progress you made because you concentrated. You would not be proud of yourself if you hadn't gotten into college. The shame would have destroyed you."

"Destroyed *you*," he scoffed, but he didn't push it.

I didn't tell him about the family business. Seoul was in upheaval. I had to collect rent; I sold and bartered. I ran the remnants of my father's business the best I could. The buildings he'd owned through the chaebol, those judgmental old men, I bartered with them. I fought for our lives.

Eight years passed from the day Siwon, Hayun, and Jiu left. Gwangmu excelled in biology. When he was accepted to a graduate program in Chicago, I arranged for him to stop in San Francisco to visit Hayun and Jiu. He never said what happened when he arrived there. Neither did Hayun. He enjoyed his studies in Illinois and fell in love with someone else, an American woman. So there it was. Strands of a life I thought I'd saved. I thought Gwangmu would be grateful. Unlike my father, who had battled Seona fast and firm, I had delayed and coaxed, and Gwangmu had stayed home. But ultimately the result was the same. He left me like Seona had.

I eventually visited America three times. First in 1960 to see how Hayun and nine-year-old Jiu were doing (Jiu was not a pleasant child). I also saw Siwon in Colorado then but I didn't go as far as Chicago, where Gwangmu was, as he was attending graduate school and said he was too busy. My second visit was in 1974, six months after Gwangmu's death. That was also the last time I visited Siwon in Colorado. Finally, my third visit was twenty years ago, to see my great-granddaughter in San Francisco. Completely the opposite of her mother, Jiu. A child who had taken delight in everyone and everything around her — my great-granddaughter Ellery Arnaud.

CHAPTER 6

Three days after I saw Attorney Kim and Bogum, I wrote up a list of our preparations and told Chohui to give the food in the refrigerator away to our neighbors. When she appeared with my cell phone in her hand, saying it was Mina calling, I assumed my sister was asking for an update on the letter. I was pleased to hear from her.

"Yes, hello," I said. "I was about to call you — we're on the same wavelength."

"Why must you constantly embarrass me?" Mina's voice came hissing through the phone.

"Are you talking to me?" I said.

"Why do I come home after a long morning comforting my friend whose dear neighbor has died to a call from my son saying you went behind my back and visited him in his office?"

"I was in the neighborhood for another reason —"

"You never said you were going to see him. Did you think I wouldn't find out?" She was the hysterical type. I gripped the arm of my chair with my free hand. Bogum was a little gossip. Why did he have to tell her right away?

I waved Chohui out of the room. She was fiddling with the leaves on the rubber plant and annoying me no end.

"By the way, do you need honeydew melons?" I said to Mina.

"Melons? Don't change the subject."

"Honestly, Mina, I didn't plan to see him. Joyce mentioned in the letter —" I said in as clear a voice as possible, but she interrupted me.

"That's always your excuse. I don't believe you. You couldn't translate the letter, is that it? I'd told you I wouldn't bother him with such a trivial matter, but you couldn't translate it, could you? That's what this is about. I thought you were better in English than all of us. Well, give it back to me, then, give me that letter immediately. I'll ask Bogum myself to do the work. He was upset I didn't tell him about the letter."

Well, this was a surprise. I tamped down my own upset. "I didn't ask him anything about it," I said.

"Don't you dare say anything against Bogum. He has a soft heart — he said he was concerned that you were going to America."

"But he wanted me to go," I said.

"Exactly, you admit it, you went to see him about going to America but you — you're too old to make such a trip by yourself. I'll go too," she spat.

Mina continued shouting through the phone about this and that. *Think, Jeonga,* I told myself. *You do have to go to America. Of course you have to go. But how can you plan your trip to America if snoopy Mina is acting as a chaperone?* There was something I needed to do alone.

I stood up and made my way across the room with the phone in my hand to the window, and I wanted to punch right through it with this veiny dry fist of mine. But I took a few deep breaths and was able to calm myself down.

"Oh, dear, Chohui needs me, the grocer's here to be paid, I must go, but don't worry, I've changed my mind, I won't go to America," I said, running over her words. She was going on and on still about how old I was and frail and weak and reckless. I pushed the button that ended the call. I could lie. Two could play at this game.

The phone rang again.

"I told you I'm too busy to talk with you," I answered.

"Mina says you're going to America and she's going too to keep an eye on you, so how could you leave me behind?" It was Aera with her scratchy voice.

"Are you catching a cold?" I asked.

"Don't change the subject, she said you'd try that. Do I sound sick? Could I have gotten sick from seeing you and Mina?"

"She's mad I saw Bogum."

Aera's voice lowered. "Bogum? He has nothing to do with this. It's Mina's dream about Seona — I find it upsetting too."

"A dream?" I repeated. Mina had not mentioned a dream. But Aera could be relied on to blurt out the truth without realizing she was giving away a confidence. "Tell me about the dream."

"If you're having trouble with the English words in the letter —"

"I know all the English. What dream?" I squelched the urge to shout at the phone.

"I think she's reading too much into it, but she doesn't listen —"

And then I remembered I could hang up on her just as I had done to Mina. Small answers we forget. "Have to call you back," I said, and I immediately dialed Mina.

"Tell me about your dream," I said as soon as she picked up.

Mina let out a breathy sigh. Then she proceeded to say, "I'm still mad at you about going to see Bogum but I've been on edge because Seona came to me in a dream. It's true."

It stunned me that our sister had appeared in her dream and not mine. Seona and I were far closer. Why would Seona send a message to her and not me? Small bombs burst in my cheeks, but I didn't let on. "I'm listening," I said in my most inviting voice.

Mina didn't miss a beat. She rambled on, and I had trouble following what she was saying. "I really sensed something in that letter even though it was in English. I stared, trying to get meaning from it. I put it in a drawer, and don't you know, when I went back to my room, it was on top of the bureau. Thinking I had not actually put it in the drawer, I put it away slowly, deliberately this time, under my eyeglass case in the drawer, and I closed it and saw that it was closed and went to see the gardener.

"Later that night before I went to bed, I opened the drawer for my pills and the letter was missing. Searched all around to see if it had slid toward the back of the drawer. I checked the other drawers in case I'd put it in another one, but I couldn't find it anywhere. Well, I couldn't sleep, and I was flustered and I thought I was imagining things in my old age, don't you think?

"I took a sleeping pill and then the next morning when I was dressing, I found the letter in the pocket of my sweater. It was a sweater I hadn't worn since the early days of spring when it was cold, so I called you and Aera. I knew I had to get that letter out of the house."

A dull chill fluttered through my heart. I walked over to my desk and opened the top drawer. The envelope with Joyce's letter from America was exactly where I'd placed it yesterday. I took it out and laid it on my desk. The cursive slashes of Mina's name seemed to form into the eyes of a human face. I blinked and the eyes disappeared. "Mina, the dream?" I prodded her, urgency quickening my voice.

"What?"

"The dream? What did Seona say?"

"But don't you see how that letter was making me pay attention to it?" Mina's voice boomed.

"Dear, dear," I said. "You didn't lose that letter and that's what matters. Now, what about the dream?"

"No, I didn't, I couldn't lose it, it wouldn't let me lose it. It didn't let me forget. Imagine that...do you still have it?"

"Right here." I picked up the envelope and tapped it on my desk.

Aera and Mina were trying to scare me, I decided. And my mind was playing right into their hands with these hallucinations. "You're forgetful, that's all. I can be that way too," I said, trying to placate her.

"Stop patronizing me. I'm not old — you're old," Mina snapped.

"You're older than me, so if you call me old, then what does that make you? Oh, never mind, tell me about the dream."

"Oh, what was I saying…oh yes, oh yes, the dream I had when I couldn't find the letter. It was that terrible time when Seona had smallpox."

"I wasn't born yet."

"We were all young and sick. It was a memory from that time except Seona did something that she didn't do in real life. Aera agrees Seona couldn't have done this. Why did she change it in the dream, do you think?"

"Change what?"

"It was as if Seona knew that little boy next door was going to die, but of course none of us knew at the time. He was as old as me, so it wasn't expected."

"You're not making any sense," I said with a sharp edge to my tone, but honestly, if she kept rambling, I was going to pull my hair out of my scalp. She was such a talker. Seona used to say so. Always gabbing, gabbing. Seona told me Mina was clueless. She was harsh about it. She had no patience or respect for her. Even though she was the oldest, Mina didn't speak like she knew more than us. The prattle, the incessant noise of her gossip. Her interest in marriage and having children and a household, on and on. It's why Seona took me under her wing. I was the quiet one who always listened to her.

"I'm getting to it," Mina said, her voice rising in pitch. And then she paused. I could imagine her pinching her cheeks to remind herself of what she wanted to say — that and to make her skin more firm, which was a lost cause at our age.

"Get to it," I said.

"How, when you keep interrupting me?"

"I'm listening." I returned the letter to the drawer so I wouldn't crumple it, which I was likely to do in response to the way Mina was annoying me.

"What's that supposed to mean?"

This was suddenly devolving into chaos and I wanted to hang up on her just as I had earlier. I didn't care that Seona had appeared in her dream. I was tired of her voice.

"Are you still there?" Mina sounded frantic.

My oldest sister had always been the most excitable one of all of us, the easiest to frighten, and what was she frightened about anyway? But I felt sorry for her just then. "I'm here. Go on," I said in a soothing voice.

"I thought I'd lost my hearing. Mrs. Park lost her hearing. Did you know that?"

"Say your name."

"What?"

"When you think you've lost your hearing, say your name aloud and you'll know. I do that sometimes when I wake up in the night and it's dark and I don't know if I'm still in my bed."

"Where else would you be, Jeonga?"

"Please, Mina." I looked up at the ceiling, a calm white, then returned to the phone call. "What did Seona do in your dream that she couldn't have done in real life?"

So then she told me. She said Seona had smallpox and was sleeping with Aera and Mina in their room, which Aera confirmed hadn't happened, especially when Seona had smallpox because she was in quarantine then. But in the dream Seona was there and she woke up both of her sisters and said they had to help the neighbor who was going to die. So in the dream all of them went together outside, which Mina said was strange because the snow was fluffy like cotton balls and not

67

cold even though she was barefoot. And there outside the gate, there was a young woman with long hair in modern clothes, jeans and a sweater like young people wear now — not the neighbor boy — and she was crying in loud sobs that Mina said she was afraid would wake the whole house.

Seona told her to come in and offered her a coat and boots. Mina warned Seona that they were all going to get in trouble and had better go back to bed. Seona patted the woman's arm and tugged at her to come inside, but suddenly she captured both of Seona's arms and pulled her toward the street, and Mina grabbed Seona's waist, and Aera held on to Mina, and the two sides battled over Seona like a tug-of-war. Seona was shouting. But that stranger, she shouted too. She said, "Why did you keep so many secrets?" And that's when Mina woke up and was certain that the woman was Joyce Ko, in America.

"What a strange dream. Secret? Whose secrets?" I feigned ignorance. I wanted to lie. I'm telling you, in that moment I wanted to keep the contents of that letter to myself. Some of it was to protect Seona's family. Most of it was to protect me and Gwangmu. The dream captured the essence of the letter. By writing the letter, Joyce Ko was reminding us we were tied together, even if she thought it was simply about money. She was making us pay attention to branches of our family in America that I'd tried to keep separate. I did my very best to stall, but Mina was persistent. She could sense I knew more than I was divulging, and I felt trapped.

"Well, why didn't you tell me about the dream when we met for lunch?" I asked.

"I had the same dream, the exact same dream, again last night and the night before."

I didn't know what to say to that.

"So what did the letter say, did you translate it?" Mina asked.

I tried to stall but the fact that the dream had repeated each night frightened me. In the end, I capitulated. She asked question after question. I was brutally honest, but only about the words Joyce had written. I translated every line for my sister, told her exactly what it said. Even Ellery Arnaud's name — there, I said I was sorry. Mina balked a little at the money but then, in an about-face, said, "She's right about the inheritance."

"But we should split it, twenty-three thousand from each of you and twenty-four from me," I sputtered.

"Seona's portion of the inheritance when you sold our childhood home, what did you do with it?"

"Invested it," I said.

"We should give Joyce some of that too," Mina said. "Aera and I will front half of the total and you can pay us back when you cash out the investment. You have enough for that, don't you?" It was a rhetorical question.

I was glad to focus on the money rather than on the series of secrets that the sequence of sisters being pulled through the gate made me shudder over. The one promise I was able to extract from Mina was to be silent about Seona's great-grandson's illness. She promised. She assured me that the illness would not be discussed outside of us three remaining sisters as long as she accompanied me to America.

That day a foreboding seeped through me as I listened to Mina promise up and down how silent she would be, and I found myself with an upset stomach, not least because of the money. I knew I couldn't underestimate Mina. She wasn't as oblivious as I had once believed. I needed to dissuade her from coming with me.

CHAPTER 7

My sisters won out. I couldn't stop them from planning to go to America with me.

I walked to the shelf where I had a trio of books prominently displayed. The series was one of my prized possessions. I'd never let a single volume leave the house, not even this room, because they were from Siwon: *I'm giving you these books because I want you to know what I know about this country, this tremendous country, and because I hope you'll see it someday in person.*

Running my palm over the covers now, I felt my heart soften at these books. They were leather-bound, smooth, rich tree-bark brown with a dark green rectangle around the gilt title: *Encyclopedia of North American Geography.* Hefty, a solid weight in both hands, I returned to my chair with one of them and opened it to the first page.

For Dayton, Ohio, United States, I'd have to know the climate this time of year to know what to pack. I studied the maps to orient myself. I'd learned how to approach this, had applied it before I'd gone to Colorado. I learned it from Siwon. "There's a method," he'd said once.

It was the opposite of what Seona had done. She'd disappeared into the night. Preparing had never been her style, and maybe that part of Korea back then hadn't seemed far away. She'd scoffed at me. "Slow,

slow Jeonga," she'd said. "Scaredy Jeonga," and then she'd hugged me to show me I shouldn't mind her teasing.

I read that Dayton was a small city in the middle of America. We'd have to stop for a layover, I saw. Good. I wouldn't have to lie. I needed to make a stop. I called Mina at once.

"We'll need to transfer planes," I said.

"Bogum will book the flights. He'll find the cheapest," Mina said. I didn't like the sound of that. I'd flown business class and would do so forevermore, I'd promised myself after one particularly horrible experience several years ago.

"You know my knees bother me —" I returned, scrambling for an excuse.

"If I'm fine, you'll be fine," she said. "Let's not bother him with particulars."

"If you're too busy to go, remember, I can go by myself."

"Seona came to me in the dream. Not you," Mina said. "She obviously wants me to go. Since I decided, the dreams have stopped. My son will make all the reservations."

"We must have a layover in San Francisco," I replied. "You'll enjoy the famous Fisherman's Wharf," I threw in, hoping to sway her. My sisters' idea of traveling was composed of plans I abhorred. They preferred to travel based on what their friends told them, making a beeline for tourist traps.

There was a click, signaling the end of the call.

I was left holding the phone. Had she agreed? I had other goals besides being able to boast about famous sights I'd seen. I hated having her involved. For a few seconds, I was stumped. And I felt my body protest. All this sitting was not good for me. My feet were tingling. I stood and began to pace. I sighed as I walked, beating my fists onto the tops of my thighs under my lilac drawstring linen slacks.

Chohui came into the room, no doubt from the creaking of the floorboards, and I unleashed my frustrations on her.

"I go weeks and weeks without hearing from my sisters and now they won't leave me alone," I said.

"They boss you around, samonim. Tell your sisters what you want," she said in a show of solidarity that irked me. Sympathy was not helpful at that moment.

"You obviously don't know what you're talking about," I told her. "I have to split off somehow from them." As if to punish me, pins and needles shot up and down my calves. I had always had terrible circulation, and it continued to sneak up on me at will and hijack whatever resolve I had.

"Make them go where you want to go. Call them back, samonim," Chohui said.

"You think it's so easy?" I sputtered, massaging my calves. "My oldest sister is involving her son, and I have no say in the matter."

"Your sisters listen to you more than you think," Chohui said.

"You don't know them," I spat, the pain increasing in my legs.

"Samonim, you always tell me to stand strong," Chohui said.

She was right, but I didn't tell her so. Instead, knowing she was witnessing my ridiculous invisible enemy, I ordered myself to handle it. The flare of pain in my legs made me want to shout, but I didn't. I stomped my feet. *Stomp, stomp,* gritting my teeth.

When that didn't work, I told myself, *Damn it, walk. Walk anyway. Keep going. Circulate, damn blood. Release me,* I ordered. And then it did. Come and gone. Chohui had too, it appeared, when I looked around the room again.

I decided I'd call Mina right back and tell her I did not need her pushing me around. It was my fate, my life. I would decide how I traveled and with whom. I would make separate airline reservations for myself.

No doubt she'd accuse me of hiding something from her, so I arrived at some excuses she might accept. I was determined to fool her. Let her make her plans; I'd tell her I had to go on my own for medical reasons. No, then she'd worry. I dismissed that excuse. I'd tell her I had to go next week, so she and Aera should leave before me; Chohui needed me here — what could I say about why?

"Mina," I said when she answered the phone. "I'll meet you in America. Something has come up. I'll join you later."

"I was just about to call you because Bogum says we should take someone with us. My aide or yours? Someone who could get our bags at the airport, that sort of thing. I think your aide would be adequate. Mine is needed to run things here. For the great-grandkids, you know. My children rely on me and my staff. Even if I'm not here, they can come and stay as they do every week; we must not break their routine."

"Did you hear what I said? I can't go with you."

"You're always so difficult. Well, not this time. This time we're going to save our sister's great-grandchild. And you're going because you speak the best English of us all. I'll expect you at the airport in three days. It's a nine-thirty a.m. flight. I'll meet you at the gate. And if you don't come with us, your sister's great-grandchild's life will be thrown away by you and you alone. Have that on your conscience."

I wished I could say she was wrong, that our going would do nothing to help Seona's great-grandson. But I knew that was ignoring reality. My chest felt as though ice had formed within it.

"Would you listen for once?" I shouted.

There was silence.

"Mina?" I said, my heart racing; had she hung up on me? "Are you there?" I added.

"We don't have time for this," she said.

My heart slowed again. "Well, then, tell Bogum we must have our layover in San Francisco for at least two nights so we can adjust to the time change. Aera won't be able to handle the jet lag." I sniffed. I could figure out a way to lose them in San Francisco so I could do what I needed to do. If they came with me to Ohio, that was fine. It was San Francisco where I needed to be on my own.

"I heard you. We'll stop in San Francisco," she said.

"You sure?" I said.

"Two days in San Francisco. I've never been there."

Chohui came into the room just as I was hanging up. "Samonim, did your sisters upset you again?" she asked.

"Of course they didn't. I've decided we can all go together."

She nodded, squinting to my left and then my right as if there were people she didn't recognize standing on either side of me. I kept talking because I didn't know what to make of her inspection. "Ask Mrs. Ahn if I can call on her this afternoon. I'd like her aide to come by here to water the plants and look after our place for the next month."

"Samonim, I don't need any help. I can do it myself," she said and stood a little taller.

"You can't if you're with me, Chohui. Just do as I say. Lunch would be nice. That turnip kimchi should be ripe now. I'd like that instead of the cabbage one today."

Chohui stood staring at me.

"Go on," I said.

"Oh, yes, samonim," she said, excitement in her voice.

"It won't be a vacation for you. Don't get the wrong idea. My sisters are not easy. I'm sorry in advance."

"I don't mind, I don't. I'd love to go. How much free time will I have? Do I have to stay with you the whole time?"

"My lunch, Chohui."

"It'll be like in the movies," she said, her eyes blinking rapidly.

74

"Go on, Chohui," I said, waving her out of the room.

She turned and left, talking to herself. I stood at the window. There was a swath of black clouds whispering to the white ones beneath. The rain would come within the hour. I thought of my sister Seona. How many times had I been comforted by the fact that we would see the same sky? Was she looking out her window at this exact same moment too? Before the Korean War, it was only a day's drive, but now the DMZ blocked travel in either direction. Ridiculous, Koreans fighting with other Koreans, with this armed border, with a fence — how I wanted to tear it down with my bare hands.

I wanted to ask Seona, *How did our lives turn out so differently? Why did you leave forever?* I'd never been one of those who sought adventure. I was content, my world inside the gates of our house. She — on the other hand — she was always looking to leave. Neolttwigi was her favorite game. It was our version of a seesaw, made by standing on a board. If we jumped high enough, we could see over the wall, see out of our yard. Did she ever get to go beyond North Korea to the greater world? Did she know that I had gone to America? And even, twice, to Europe? I allowed that I could be wrong. If Seona had risen in the ranks in North Korea, she would have traveled too, but it seemed unlikely. Wouldn't she have contacted us or her grandchildren, someone in the family, if she had?

My temples twinged with pain. A headache coming on. No need for this stress. I reminded myself that Mina had agreed: San Francisco before Ohio. I would not think about San Francisco any more today. I laid my head on my cool desk surface. I wouldn't think about children or grandchildren or great-grandchildren in America.

"Samonim, are you all right?" Someone was kneeling and shaking my shoulder. "Samonim, I've been calling you over and over. Haven't you heard me?" Chohui's voice materialized from the murky mass of my son's smiling broad face; his sharp cheekbones showed he'd suffered from hunger. Clearly, he wasn't taking care of himself and needed me. "Gwangmu, I'm sorry," I said. His face dissolved into Chohui's concerned expression.

She was bent, her face at an angle. I was apparently seated in my usual chair at my desk.

"Samonim, here, take this," she said and patted my face dry with a soft handkerchief. When she stepped back, I could see the handkerchief was mine. I kept it and a few others in my desk drawer — a desk drawer that was open now. No one seemed to carry handkerchiefs like this anymore. This particular one, Seona embroidered when we were children. Missing stitches, frayed at the edge, but I'd kept it. I'd replaced the backing of it with other cotton material, but the needlepoint had been preserved. A rabbit and a smaller rabbit beside it outlined in light blue thread. She'd thought she was being witty. Seemed wasteful to throw it away. I took the handkerchief from her brusquely.

"Took you long enough. I'm famished. You're starving me, Chohui," I said in a stern voice.

"Oh, samonim, I'd never let you go hungry," she said and looked down at her feet. Chohui took everything so hard. I feared that after I died, people would be cruel to her, so I had to teach her somehow to shield herself.

"You were only trying to be helpful, don't apologize," I said.

"But you were slumped over. I thought the worst had happened," she said.

I sighed. "Go on, I'll join you in a moment." She kept looking over her shoulder at me as I followed. At the door to my bedroom, I waved her on. I wanted to put some powder on my face. In the bureau mirror, I saw someone who never ceased to shock me. My face was a cross-hatching of tiny wrinkles, not unlike an apple's skin as it was perishing. I was surprised each time to see it. I shook off a foreboding feeling, inspected my teeth.

As long as my teeth were good, I'd be fine. I'd heard stories of people my age going to their death because they couldn't eat.

My eyes were smaller than ever, swollen skin all around them but still showing wrinkles, so I filled them in with some cushion powder, then returned to the small dining room. I made a mental note to have Chohui remove the mirror from above my bureau. I could use the mirror in my compact to apply my makeup and moisturizer and anything else I needed. And this way, I didn't have to see the whole face at once, just parts of it at a time.

CHAPTER 8

We arrived without mishap in San Francisco, though I was peeved that Chohui had refused to sleep during that long fourteen-hour flight. Not only that, but she kept looking around, her eyes taking in everything, and kept fidgeting with the airplane tray table that flipped up and down as if she couldn't believe it was possible. And then all the channels on the tiny screen mesmerized her. The person seated ahead of her kept turning around to glare at us. I glared right back. What did you expect but rudeness from people in economy class?

Through passport control and out into the larger hall of the airport, we completed the necessary documentation protocol in two hours. Everyone around me withered from the wait. I was tense with all I knew I had to do, which gave me a strange kind of energy. I considered ways to have time on my own.

My sisters were complaining as they waited on a bench in San Francisco International Airport for Chohui to collect our luggage from baggage claim. Already they'd discussed their next meal. Always talking about eating. Bogum had given Mina a list of restaurants with high ratings.

"So many, but how far?" Aera said, pointing to Mina's list. That piece of paper was already looking worse for wear after having been handled a multitude of times. I'd read that the gustatory modality is the last of the five senses to diminish with age, and my sisters proved it. Cuisine was all that mattered to them; I cared less because eating meant I'd have other medical ailments to concern myself with. Digestion didn't happen as efficiently as it once did, for example, and so I didn't like to tax my system.

"Where's that famous harbor with all the fancy stores you said everyone talks about?" Mina asked me.

Already bothering me about sightseeing. I admit I'd thrown that tidbit out there so she would stop complaining about our layover in San Francisco.

"Well, we're not going there tonight. Focus on the hotel," I said.

"If your girl would hurry, we could surely be there in thirty minutes. San Francisco is rather quaint, wouldn't you say?" Mina sniffed.

Poor Chohui. Already she'd been browbeaten more times than necessary; the plane had had flight attendants to be at my sisters' beck and call, but instead they used Chohui as if she had no feelings. And now she was nowhere to be found.

I said I'd see what was keeping her and made my way around the corner, where my sisters couldn't hear me. I'd just pulled out my cell phone and was about to make a call when I smelled Mina's halitosis. She stood right over me and barked, "There you are!"

She'd followed me; it was clear. I was so startled I put my phone in my pocket, a guilty response I couldn't help. But then I regained my voice. "I was calling Chohui."

"She's at the baggage carousel," Mina said. "You passed right by her."

"Oh, for heaven's sake. Why don't you help her, since you know everything?" I said.

Mina rolled her eyes to the ceiling. "If you're blind now as well as old, then admit it, why don't you?" She pulled me by my sleeve around the corner and pointed at Chohui, who was wrangling Aera's big red suitcase off the conveyor belt.

"My son arranged for a taxi, and I don't want the driver to over-charge him. We must keep our wits about us. Money doesn't flow like water," Mina scolded. She looked rather stern, and I was glad she'd bought my lie. "Get some eyeglasses like the rest of us, and not just for reading."

"You're right," I said and made a show of nodding with resignation.

"I don't think we should spread out like this," Mina continued. "It's a waste of our energy. Follow the plan. Stay close. If you can't find someone, come back, and we'll all go together."

My bossy oldest sister. How difficult this would be to get used to again. Though we planned to be in America for a month, it felt as though I'd be stuck in her presence every moment of every day for the rest of my life. How would I have any privacy? I felt panicked for a few minutes but then I remembered that I would share a hotel room with Chohui while my sisters roomed together, and there would be plenty of time for phone calls.

Feeling my painfully swollen feet in my shoes after so much sitting on the plane, I saw my own mortality. I reminded myself that, though it was not likely, the rest of my life could be just one more month. And for my sisters as well.

Chohui was standing in front of Aera when Mina and I reached them. She looked exhausted. Her bangs fell into her eyes, and she blew them off her face rather than sweeping them away, which required more effort; her shoulders slumped. Four large suitcases sur-rounded her. "They have wheels," Mina announced as if we had failed to notice and waved us on down the large hall. Aera followed, her black Prada tote slung over her shoulder, headed straight for the ground-transportation signs, leaving me and Chohui with all the suitcases.

I gestured to the metal caterpillar of luggage carts in the corner. Chohui seemed perplexed. "We'll do the same," I said and pointed to a man pushing an assortment of suitcases on a metal wagon as he strolled past us. Chohui nodded and went to retrieve a cart. It was not obvious how to detach it from the others. I didn't know how either, so I waited as patiently as I could as Chohui researched the mechanism on her cell phone. Finally, she was able to release one and pile all our luggage onto it.

For this too, I tried to be patient. She had never been outside of Korea before. I remembered how it had been for me, so I walked alongside her, remarking on how glad I was to stretch my legs. I told her she'd have a chance to have her own free time. This arrangement worked for me too, since I wanted to be alone with my own plans. We'd catch up to my sisters in no time. Honestly, I preferred Chohui's quiet company to my sisters' as they prattled on, but I would never tell her this. My father had told me that actions spoke louder than words. To be a hypocrite was the worst offense, in his view.

People slouched in the United States. I observed all sorts of bad posture around us as we walked through the airport. I'd expected it from teenagers, but adults of all ages too? I remembered my own son, how I used to berate him for not standing up straight. Gwangmu seemed to forget the company he was in.

When my sisters and I were children, if an adult came into the room, no matter servant or stranger or family, we stood up straight and were polite. It showed our station in life. It showed our education, the kind our parents bestowed. The hangdog look was for the beggars on the streets, those who had a reason to droop.

In time, I would later see that the slouch was a form of showing ease in the modern world, and when the actors in dramas took that stance, I could understand at last what my own son meant, but it was too late to apologize to him by then as he was well into his grown-man years. Chohui, however, slumped when she was dejected.

My sisters were standing outside when we reached them. A Korean man — who seemed hardly old enough to be called a man — in a brass-buttoned suit jacket was speaking to them in an animated fashion, holding an iPad in front of them and motioning to it. *Must be the driver Bogum hired*, I thought. He snapped to attention and I feared he'd salute us when Mina told him who we were.

The driver didn't seem to understand that Chohui was our aide. He insisted on carrying her suitcase too and opened the van's doors for all of us. I saw Chohui blush as he waved her in as if she were a dignitary. Mina shoved me with her elbow so I would make note of this. Aera was oddly quiet. I wondered if she was sick from the food on the plane. Chohui and I had eaten noodles, but she'd chosen chicken.

"Do you know where we should go?" Mina asked the man once we were all buckled in. The driver replied, "The Fair Hotel," and I saw her relax. As we shot away from the curb, Aera folded over and clutched her stomach, and I wished she weren't sitting next to me. Chohui looked back from the front seat, where she sat beside the driver, and I resolved to straighten up and not lurch so obviously away from my sister. If it was anything, it wasn't contagious, surely, and if she vomited on me, we'd have to cope.

What kind of example was I setting for Chohui? Or this American chauffeur? Sure, he was Korean, but he acted like an American. His holding the door for Chohui, for one; the way he kept glancing at her, for another; and the way he let other cars pass him before merging into traffic. Korean drivers knew how to fight for their place among other cars because everyone believed you can't always concede if you intend to get anywhere by a reasonable time. What did lanes mean anyway?

"After the hotel, which restaurant did we decide on?" Mina said over her shoulder.

"I'll need to lie down for a bit," Aera answered.

"Sure, but I want to give Mr. Yang a time frame for when he should return to the hotel to take us to dinner." She peered closer at Aera, adjusting her posture in her bench seat. "What's the matter with you, anyway? You were the one who said you were hungry."

"I'd like to get some rest too," I said, as if either had asked me.

"Me too," Chohui said. Mina threw her a disapproving look. I saw Mr. Yang's neck stiffen. I could practically see his ears at attention. Young love? The signs were obvious. I had to shake my head clear of that. What was the matter with me? Chohui had only met Mr. Yang minutes ago, and perhaps he was sympathetic. It was certainly not love. I was terribly suspicious of romance after what I'd seen in my many years of living.

Aera's forehead was smattered with dots of perspiration even though it was a comfortable twenty-one degrees Celsius when we arrived in front of the hotel. "Everyone thinks everything in America is better than in Korea, but this is not so. Do they even know what air-conditioning is?" she said, fanning herself with her hand and looking peeved.

I didn't tell my sisters I'd been to this hotel before. Mina chided Aera, going on and on about how it was the location of some American television show and how fortunate we were that Bogum was able to reserve us rooms. A testament to her son's influence in the international sphere, her point.

Their voices whined on as we walked through the lobby. We eventually checked in and then I wandered away; I didn't realize I was leading the group until Mina bumped into me from behind.

"You found the elevators," she said in surprise.

The bellman walked up from his position in the rear of our entourage to press the call button. With a bow, which I suspected was facetious, he nodded and then returned to the luggage cart beside Chohui. He appraised her a bit longer than was required. It seemed Chohui was the focus of our little traveling group wherever we went. I noticed that Chohui was getting used to it and stood confidently now. What I hadn't known about my power at that age. I had been oblivious to the value of breath. That's what I thought it was about. You have more oxygen, proportionately, and it made you buoyant and light, and energy surged outward. Seemed limitless, but of course there was a limit. From there on after, you deflated and had to forge ahead.

Even in gray lounge pants and a sweatshirt, Chohui's figure was apparent, and her skin shone like a nectarine. She walked differently, as if on air, even in plain white sneakers. Her hair in its ponytail had a sheen. She had no idea how she glowed. All of us had been as healthy once, my sisters and me. And we had no idea back then. Wasn't that the way, though? If we'd known, what a force we would have been. Was it a good thing we didn't have mirrors about? Or would we even have been able to see, blinded by our own untrusty vision of ourselves made by all we didn't know? Bound by our uncertainties? Why did we have to be so certain before we could venture forward? Never mind — we go on. The hotel. I was speaking about the hotel.

What had struck me before and struck me now as the elevator stopped on the fifth floor and we walked out and down the hallway to our rooms was the plushness. Americans like to pad everything around them with cloth and furniture, fill every space. The proportions were different from Korea. Here they'd built a giant hotel and then they had proceeded to decorate it with gilt and marble. The hallway was dotted with paintings and mirrors every few meters.

Mina and Aera wanted to see both rooms before they decided which lodging they wanted to take as their own. Even though they'd be here just two days, they had to inspect each space as if they were going to occupy it for months.

The rooms were three doors apart and identical save for the location of the headboards. They were on the left in the first room and on the right in the second. In each one, on the dresser by the pair of coffee mugs, was a green ceramic bowl with a single ripe persimmon. The green was very Korean, of celadon fame. It should have made me feel comforted; instead, I was uneasy. For some reason I couldn't fathom, Mina seemed disturbed too. She walked back and forth three times before choosing the second room. The bellman stood at attention because there was nothing for him to do. Once Mina decided, she instructed him on which bags were to be left in which room. Four suitcases on the brass bellman's cart didn't take long to distribute.

"I'm going to lie down," I said to my sisters.

"Not too long," Mina said from her doorway. "We'll be going to eat soon."

"Maybe a shower will make me feel better," Aera said.

"That will delay our dinner," Mina said, but I closed my door. That was for the two of them to work out. Just to have several solid walls between my sisters and myself was a victory. I told Chohui to lie down too. She did so but made so much noise tossing and turning in her queen-size bed beside mine that I sent her down to the lobby for some toothpaste. Korean brand was preferable, but Chohui would enjoy seeing the offerings in the hotel store. And then I walked to the window and pulled back the filmy curtain behind the first set of drapes. Layer after layer to pull aside before I touched the glass pane through which the evening light poured. Streaks of sun shone in long rays through the clouds. For the first time in twenty hours, I was completely alone.

Now that I was about to make the call I'd known I had to make ever since I'd read Joyce's letter, I hesitated. "Jump, jump," Seona used to call when it was my turn on the seesaw. And when I didn't go right then, she'd call Aera to switch. I pretended like I didn't care but it stung, how impatient she was. By the time I could react, I was too late. Aera had run over and taken my place.

CHAPTER 9

The cell phone showed that it was 6:07. I'd been sitting here doing nothing for ten minutes. I heard Seona's voice in my mind again. *Hurry, Jeonga,* she called. Carefully, I took a phone number from my wallet.

"Hello?" came a cheerful voice through the phone.

"Ellery?" I asked. It didn't sound like my own voice, this English I put on.

"Someone Korean, Halmoni," a muffled voice said. My heart leaped. It must have been Ellery who'd answered the phone. She was calling for her grandmother when I actually wanted to speak to her. I quickly added, "Just a moment," but I only heard more muffled voices, now away from the phone.

Embarrassing that I'd been identified as Korean. I'd tried my very best English. Siwon used to say no one knew he was Korean when he spoke on the phone; that's how smooth his English was.

"Hello? Hello?" a different voice said in Korean into the phone. "This is Mrs. Jin."

It was a voice I knew. So she called herself *Mrs.*, but she wasn't married; she should be *Miss* Jin. She was Siwon's sister, now eighty-something years old. I didn't want to dwell on her or her age. If she'd married my son, she'd be Mrs. Cha; we'd have the same husband's family name. It pained me to think that Jiu had grown up without the name of her father's family, but I'd had to suffer it. When she married Ellery's father, Jiu had kept the last name Jin for professional reasons. I would have preferred her to change it to Jiu Arnaud so the mistake might have been hidden better. In any case, Ellery was given her father's last name and I had been relieved at the news.

"Hayun, it's me," I said. I sounded tentative, weak; I was surprisingly moved to hear her voice. My love's sister.

There was a gasp on the other end.

"Samonim," she said.

"Let's be American — Mrs. Cha is fine. In letters, you may call me samonim, but when we speak to each other, you must call me Mrs. Cha."

Hesitation trembled through Hayun's voice. "The shock, I'm sorry. Of course, Mrs. Cha."

I relaxed. This was the Hayun I knew. "You remember I promised to visit in person again at some point," I said.

"Oh, samonim, of course," she said. "How are you? Everything all right in Korea?"

I decided not to fight her about what she called me anymore. "I just arrived in San Francisco. Could you send a car for me later tonight? I'd like to see you."

"You're here?" Her voice rose in a tone of panic.

"I think I could be ready at nine thirty. I'd like to see you and Ellery." With Aera looking ill on the drive from the airport, I suspected we'd be eating dinner in the hotel tonight. Chohui would fall asleep as soon as we returned to the room. She never had trouble sleeping. She preferred early mornings and early bedtimes, a rare trait in a young person but one that I applauded.

"That's late. Let me think," Hayun said, her voice measured and calm now.

How rude. *Think? When I've come from halfway around the world?* She clearly didn't want to see me. The truth emerged in a crisis. Siwon had told me that, but I knew it already. How dare she refuse me? Here was the truth: She'd always hated me. A very real possibility. Clearly, she held a grudge against me for everything I'd done to her all those years ago. What had I been thinking? I grimaced but fought on. I had to see if this was the Ellery mentioned in Joyce's letter.

"Ellery still lives with you, does she?" I said.

"You must stay with us, of course. Are you at the airport? Which one? I'll come right now."

An obligatory invitation, but I had never stayed with her and never would.

"Oh, I already paid for a hotel and can't get my money back now — much more comfortable for me in my old age, but I would like to see you, even for just a few minutes. Pay attention, Hayun. Is Ellery with you?"

"She's the one you spoke to just now. You won't recognize her, samonim, she's so grown —" And then a pause before she continued, "I'm sorry, what am I saying? Of course you'd recognize her anywhere — I'll come right away, shall I?"

"Well, if you insist, I'm where I stayed before," I said, comforted. She sounded regretful.

"Oh, yes, you like the Fair Hotel. I'm on my way."

"Not now, at nine thirty."

"Nine, perfect," she said.

"Nine thirty, Hayun. It must be nine thirty. Don't come sooner."

"Absolutely. Nine thirty. I'm so glad."

"Well, drive right up, no need to park. Don't inconvenience yourself. I'll be waiting outside the entrance as usual."

"I'll park and come up to your room; there's traffic that time of night."

I heard Chohui's key card unlock the door.

"Wait for me at the curb," I said and pushed End Call.

My sisters and I went down to dinner with Chohui, who was busy on her phone the entire time and kept jumping up to take pictures of the restaurant.

No one said it but I felt the horror they sensed over the large plate of food set before each person. Instinctively we pushed all four dishes to the middle and used our small appetizer plates as our personal plates to divide up our own portions. So what if the waiters thought we were odd? I did think, as I saw Aera clutch at her stomach, that she was actually quite ill.

Mina had no patience for Aera's weak stomach and berated her for being tentative. "You should eat to get stronger," my oldest sister said.

Aera complied. I didn't agree with Mina's logic, but who was I to argue? I put my fork down. No more sharing of germs with her. We all knew Mina had no compassion for sickness and was the worst person to be around when she herself was sick. Her complaints were unmatched. Growing up, we knew just from that alone that she'd marry the richest man who offered, but she surprised us by marrying the minister's son and then investing her dowry so well that they amassed a small fortune. In all financial matters, it appeared that Mina had beat me and Aera. And in health too. The oldest, she should have been the feeblest, but she was the hardiest due to sheer will. I had been wrong about so many things.

At 9:05, we pushed back our chairs and headed for the elevators. Aera scampered there and pressed the button to call the lift repeatedly — poor thing probably needed the bathroom. Mina dawdled, letting Aera go up ahead of her, and expressed an interest in taking pictures of herself in the hotel to send to her children and grandchildren. Chohui did her bidding while I yawned in an exaggerated fashion, to which Mina said, "Funny, you look quite alert." And Chohui agreed.

I tried to rearrange my face. Why did my body betray me? "But I'm quite tired," I insisted and called for the next elevator. If Aera could leave, why couldn't I? With a peeved expression on her face, Mina released Chohui from photographer duties and followed us into the next elevator.

Finally, we were upstairs, and Chohui went right to sleep. I waited until her breathing deepened before putting on my coat and slipping out to the hall. With the collar up, I hoped I could hurry down to the lobby, through the doors, and out to Hayun's car without being identified. America was vast; one could be anonymous. The elevator kept stopping at floors with no one getting on. My heart beat faster when I remembered to breathe.

Once outside, I recognized Hayun right away. A muscular white bellman was talking to her as she stood beside a small black compact car. Hayun was a short woman with pasty yellowish skin, and her wrinkles made her appear older than me. It had been at least two decades since I'd seen her in person.

She reached to embrace me, but I waved her off and got into the front seat, though I would have preferred the back. She had the door open already; what could I do? The American way of things. I nodded at her and at the hotel doorman who closed the door for me. A little too strong of a push right there. Really not necessary to use such force.

Then Hayun skittered around to the driver's side. *Fast for her age*, I thought; she reminded me of the young woman I had known years ago, quick to do chores about the house despite her pregnant belly, and for a moment I felt young myself. Perhaps I'd been wrong to dislike Hayun as much as I had. She was as earnest as any kitten we'd had as children. Note to self: *Send her the expensive ginseng renewing skin cream and the even more expensive ginseng renewing skin serum.* Hayun needed both. I sent Chohui an e-mail to be sure to order an extra set of creams and serums and then put my phone safely away in my handbag. I didn't want a text to wake her. It was probably impossible to get quality makeup for Korean people here in America.

"You're here! I'm so excited you're here, samonim — I mean, Mrs. Cha," she gushed, pressing hard on the gas. The small Japanese car shot off like a white-throated needletail. I had to put my hand on the dashboard to keep from hitting the windshield, even with the seat belt latched. Is this how she drove normally? How had she survived as long as this?

I gasped and then scolded her. "Are you trying to kill me?" I said.

She mumbled an apology without a glance my way, and I noted with relief that she lightened up on the accelerator.

Now I could sit back and take a good look at her. Beyond the poor skin quality, I mean. Hayun was dressed in clothes I'd characterize as sports-ready. It had happened in Korea too. Women looked as if they were prepared to play golf at any moment. I found it almost rude. They couldn't all be on their way to tee off every single day, could they? Proper attire had gone out the window. I was in a Chanel sweater set — not the Hermès trousers and tunic I'd worn for travel — gray-blue with a pearl pin at the shoulder, and even this felt too dressed down for my taste. It was a color that was appropriate for a woman over sixty. In contrast, Hayun was dressed in neon green, a color I'd never have chosen. Not even in my youth. Did she think she was a social media celebrity? I sighed and then caught myself; maybe I shouldn't dismiss this shade out of hand. Often these same stars influenced fashion, even the oldest fashion houses in the world. Maybe I could wear this color green.

Hayun interrupted my thoughts with a clearing of her throat. *Focus*, I told myself. Wandering into fantasy was happening more often in recent years than I liked to admit.

"I used to have a sister," I began.

"Yes, you told us many times about her."

I was surprised. "Many times?"

"Oh, yes, many times, ever since I first arrived at your house with my brother," Hayun continued, a smile on her face now.

My heart skipped a beat. I didn't recall talking that much about Seona. Had I always been preoccupied with her? Had I never had my own life?

"But surely not about how she left and —" I said.

"I'm sorry, but yes, you did, I remember your son hated it when you brought her up. Your sister running off made him wish he were brave enough to do the same."

She might as well have plunged a knife into my chest with those words. Gwangmu wished he could escape years ago? It was painful enough that he eventually did just that. Abandoned me for America. But back then? Even back then, did he want to leave me for good? I stared at her. Why was she smiling? How could delivering such information to me be joyful for her?

"Here I am babbling on and you must be exhausted and need a refreshment. Forgive me, samonim. I would have prepared your favorite foods if I knew you were coming. Your last letter didn't say you were planning such a trip," Hayun said as she drove, misunderstanding the expression on my face.

I sniffed. Even in her attempt at courtesy, there was an accusation in her tone, as if I should have told her my plans. A car swerved in front of us at that moment and Hayun slammed on the brake, jerking me forward and then back again. That gave me an opportunity to remember I didn't have much time.

Focus, I reminded myself again. I had to keep the conversation on what I'd come to discuss. "So, you know Seona's son moved to Ohio and had a daughter, and she later gave birth to a son."

Hayun peered up at the roof of the car a few times as if Ohio were above our heads. I wished she'd pay better attention to the road, but instead of telling her so, I pressed on. "Did Ellery go to college in Ohio?"

"Oberlin," she replied.

Oberlin? Was that a no, then? I had an inkling that college was in Colorado. Siwon must have mentioned it in passing. It sounded familiar. Therefore, Ellery could not have met Seona's great-grandson Jordan, in college in Ohio, as Joyce said in her letter. No, not possible. He must be engaged to another Ellery Arnaud.

"That's in Ohio," she added.

My hopes took a nosedive.

"What a coincidence. I didn't know your sister's family ended up there," Hayun continued. "Ohio is a very nice place. Ellery liked it very much."

She didn't sound perturbed at all. If she didn't suspect any connection, why should I? My spirits climbed.

"Is there any news about Ellery I should know?" I said. If Ellery was engaged, Hayun would certainly have included this vital information in her previous letters, and if she had forgotten, she would surely tell me now.

She paused, and I saw her blush. I held my breath. "She'll want to tell you herself. She lost her job, but restaurant work is unsteady — you can imagine."

Well, that was terrible news, but it was not a wedding. "I'm sure she'll find something soon. That culinary school she went to was quite reputable."

"It's fine. Jiu and her husband are doing well and sent her enough to cover her for several months. They understand it's her passion," Hayun said.

I didn't like to talk about Jiu, and Hayun sounded as if she were criticizing me for not sending more money in the past when Jiu wanted to study journalism. I'd paid her tuition — wasn't that enough?

She'd sent me a thank-you card. That was all. I'd expected a phone call, but Hayun explained that Jiu was shy and didn't know I was her grandmother. I had made that decision, Hayun reminded me. The nerve of her at the time. I changed the subject again. "I've never seen this part of San Francisco," I said, peering at the outline of a row of Victorian houses in the dark.

"Oh, but you have, this is the historic district," Hayun said. I would have taken offense except her tone was light, and she continued, "My memory is not what it used to be either. Good grief, isn't that unfair? My brother died at seventy-five and here I am, eighty-four. Who knew I'd live so much longer than him? Can't believe how old I am — I've forgotten things I swore I'd never forget. But especially recent events. I check the bolt on the door ten times because I can't remember if I locked it."

"I don't forget things," I said in a firm voice. This was why I'd never felt comfortable with Hayun. She was not someone to confide in. All she did was attack and accuse, telling me what I used to say and what I'd forgotten. How dare she. I had to establish myself as an authority with her. "Try reading or taking walks to clear your mind. Or write more letters. Does Ellery write letters?"

"Young people these days, you know, they use e-mail," Hayun replied.

She turned up a steep hill. Every hill was steep, I noticed. Was she blaming me for not e-mailing with my great-grandchild?

"Well, modern times, but Jiu never wrote to me either," I said. "And she grew up with stamps and letters. But at least Ellery talked to me when I called."

Jiu had been a rude child. She looked exactly like Hayun but had none of Hayun's good qualities. My granddaughter had been moody and uncooperative. Odd that she grew up to be a journalist, interested in other people's stories. If she'd shown any interest in me, I'd brag about her now that she worked for important news outlets, traveling the world. But she had made it clear she had no time. Never called even when her work brought her to South Korea. Though it was true she had no idea I was her grandmother.

I secretly saved all the clippings Hayun mailed to me of Jiu's work. I had filled several albums with her pieces from the *New York Times*. She'd married late in life to another journalist. The photographs that Hayun sent me portrayed a small but elegant wedding ceremony in Paris, where Jiu's husband's family resided. France had not been a convenient place for me to travel to, certainly. I'd suggested Seoul or Hawaii, but I had been ignored. A year later, Ellery was born. I worried when Jiu and her husband continued to travel the world, covering the news. Thank goodness that when she became old enough to go to school, Ellery stayed with Hayun in San Francisco. Stability was important. I approved of this decision.

"Here we are," Hayun said. She pulled into a short driveway on a hill. Every house seemed to be built sideways on a hill. "Ellery will be so happy to see you again."

I found myself giving Hayun a wide smile. Of course Ellery would be happy to see me, and I her. No need to say too much to Hayun; she was bound to gossip and laugh at me about my suspicions. I was glad I had said as little as I did. This would be a quick visit and then I'd travel to Ohio with my sisters, give Joyce the money for her son, and return straightaway to Seoul, where I belonged. It would all be all right. My worry about Joyce's letter had brought me to visit my dear great-granddaughter who happened to have the same name as my great-grandnephew's fiancée. That was all. Easily dismissed. Maybe in this vast land of America, there were three or four other young women named Ellery Arnaud. The thought eased my heart. I even patted Hayun's hand on my arm as she helped me out of the car.

It was quiet, as if it were much later than 9:45. And the streets were very clean; I was glad to make note of this. I sniffed the air, fragrant of persimmons. In August? Early for them; how odd. But this was California, where everything grew. Siwon had said so and now I had confirmed it.

We walked up steep concrete steps and then a trio of wooden porch steps to a blue Victorian with white trim. The robin's-egg-blue paint looked freshly applied.

"This used to be yellow?" I asked.

"You mean their town house in New York; mine has always been blue," she replied.

A vision flashed before my eyes: a photograph on my bedside table of Ellery as a toddler with her parents in front of a yellow town house in Manhattan that Hayun had sent me years ago.

Still, I wasn't going to admit to Hayun that she was right. She sounded smug in correcting me. I was old but not senile. Hayun held open one side of the glossy wooden double doors for me. Under the porch light I could see the intricate details of the stained-glass window in the wood, mauve and white with a sharp emerald-green center. Some would call this charming; I called it busy.

Once inside, Hayun changed out of her shoes into white terry-cloth slippers and then took a new pair out of its plastic wrapping and set it before me on the bare wooden floor, which was polished to a shine. I took off my Gucci flats and slid my feet into the slippers, all the while looking around. Elaborate white crown moldings dripped down like some organic remnant above maroon paint on the walls in this foyer. I shuddered. Stylish taste in design was not something everyone was born with.

Down the long narrow hallway we walked. In the living room, the vanilla leather sofa appeared too large for the small space with its high ceiling. I could tell the sofa's quality was excellent, even from a distance. But really? In a room this size? And who had imagined a rustic wooden coffee table should be put in front of such a large sofa? How could one think or make decisions in a place like this? Simplicity and correct proportions were the standards to live by. My father had reminded us again and again of the importance of one's surroundings to elevate one's mind. I had chosen the furniture in my house in keeping with his principles.

Ushering me to the sofa, inviting me to make myself comfortable, Hayun seemed to be seeing the room for the first time. She looked left and right of me as if there were a mess all about. Then she proceeded to pick up invisible items from the floor.

"Stop that," I snapped, harsh even to my ears.

Instead of complying, she became more frantic, mumbling about dust and dirt in her house. I didn't see any such thing. Even if its taste was questionable, its cleanliness was not. Everything sparkled, just like the floor, actually sparkled — the mirror on the wall, the brass clock on a painted mantel, and beside it a lacquer vase with an inlaid mother-of-pearl flower pattern that was a miniature of one I had. A nice touch, to have a fireplace — very American-movies aura. I could pivot to positive thoughts if I put my mind to it. Most important, I was here to see Ellery. A treat and a relief that my worries were unfounded. I sank into the slippery couch.

"Let me get you some tea," Hayun offered, shaking off her jacket and holding her hand out for my coat. I told her I'd keep it nearby. What if there was a draft? With these high ceilings, that was certainly a possibility. She left the room and I waited for Ellery to appear.

CHAPTER 10

I had closed my eyes to rest them a bit when I heard a clang of ceramic on ceramic. There she stood, my Ellery. Well, she was not mine but I'd seen her as a little girl, and she had been such a delight. Precocious even. Knew how to greet a person and how to ask questions, perfect manners. I knew she was now twenty-nine years old, old enough to be a mother herself. Not the little girl I remembered. I could still see the child in this young woman in front of me. Her keen eyes and generous smile even now on her lips. She had wide-set Korean eyes; anyone could see that. I'd never met her father, but he had been fourth or fifth cousins with Michelle Obama and appeared, in photographs that Hayun sent me, to resemble the former First Lady in facial features and stature. Ellery's dark brown hair needed no permanent-curl treatment from a salon. It had always been that way, since she was a baby. A head of curly hair on that infant. Hayun had sent me a video when she was seven days old. She wore her hair short today, which made her look sophisticated far beyond her years. I touched my own short bob, noting the similarity.

In her hands was a tray with a plate of apples and a teapot with cups, and I got up to help her put it down on the unattractive cabin-style coffee table. The slickness of the sofa required tremendous effort on my part to stand.

"Don't trouble yourself," Hayun exclaimed, coming up behind Ellery. I ignored her and guided the tray to the surface. Ellery thanked me. A gentle, hesitant voice. But her hands shook. From nerves? From not enough B vitamins? What hardships had this charming child endured? My worries grew. Her bare arms in her short-sleeved shirt were thin, not a wobble of fat as she bent to pour tea. I didn't know quite how to respond. Sit back on the leather couch far from her, as Hayun was motioning me to do? I watched Ellery adjust the teacups as she knelt by the side of the table. Perfectly mannered.

Usually, polka-dot shirts such as the one she was wearing made me dizzy, and this was no exception, but I did my best to look elsewhere. Her jeans were torn at the knee. I knew it was a popular style, but I wondered if she couldn't afford anything else. For her most recent birthday, I'd sent her a card and a calligraphy set. I should have sent her money, I thought right then. And her whole presentation was plain — no necklace or earrings. In fact, no jewelry except for a ring on her left hand, small. Certainly not an engagement ring. That was a relief.

It hurt me to see her look positively frail. Chipped fingernails. Rough hands, as if she did manual labor. Well, that's what restaurant work was. How had she chosen that career? I tried not to judge. Hayun should have convinced her to become a lawyer or doctor. I focused on her face. Beautiful arched eyebrows. My mother's high cheekbones. A few lines around her eyes. At her age, she needed to start wearing eye cream — stave off those wrinkles that were waiting to erode her smooth complexion.

Hayun interrupted my thoughts. "Sit, sit," she said, making her way past her granddaughter and then around the coffee table to stand right beside me. She pulled my wrist as she sat down on the vanilla couch, so we both sank into the slick cushion. Did I have enough strength to get up again? One shouldn't be so physical with a woman my age, but

I accepted her enthusiasm after I saw my great-granddaughter look on with such a beam of warmth in her eyes.

Ellery poured me tea. I changed my mind about the eye cream. She was lovely just as she was; she didn't need a thing. "You've been such a good family friend to us all these years, Mrs. Cha," she said.

From her, *Mrs. Cha* seemed too formal, and *friend* stung a bit, but I couldn't offer her an alternative. I smiled at her. I wished there weren't an ocean between us or I would have seen her more regularly. She was a dear, dear girl. I said, when I regained my breath, "These apple slices are excellent, very professional-looking. Such talent you have."

"Oh, apples!" Hayun laughed too loudly for the distance between us in this room. "She can do so much more than cut apples."

I choked on the tea going down my throat, and Hayun patted my back as if I were a child. I waved her away.

"Can I get you something else, Mrs. Cha?" Ellery asked.

I swallowed and said in a voice still hampered by the coughing fit, "No, no, just give me a moment." I picked up an apple slice by a toothpick and took a tiny bite. Chewing that tart crescent and then swallowing it calmed my throat. I gave her an approving smile. "You'll make your husband a very fine wife."

"How did you know I was getting married?" she said in a startled voice, her eyes blinking rapidly.

I had meant the future, in the future, a husband in the future, but I saw now in her face that I'd come upon a secret, and my stomach twisted.

In such matters, it's best to blame someone else. Even if she and Hayun had thought I would not make the trip from Korea, I would have liked to be invited. They had offended me, and I was indignant, fanning the flame of sudden alarm. A wedding? It felt like an ambush. Joyce's letter flashed before my eyes. Could she be engaged to — I stopped myself from thinking of the possibility. *Don't jump to conclusions,* I told myself. *Don't even think his name right now.*

"That's big news," I announced to the room. "I would have liked to have been told." This last was directed at Hayun.

"It doesn't matter — he's broken it off," Ellery said; her hands were clenched together on top of the coffee table.

My patience was rewarded. So the young man was not as enthusiastic as she was. I understood that. Feeling calm again, I reached over and patted her hands. "It'll be all right."

She jerked them away without looking at me, her head lowered, a posture that reminded me of my son. The whorl on top of her head eerily similar to Gwangmu's, though not as pronounced.

I wanted to tell her love wasn't worth the anguish.

"You'll find someone else," I began and didn't get to continue. She jumped to her feet and left the room.

Hayun and I both looked in the direction she'd run.

"I'm sorry about Ellery. She's been like this for months now, poor girl." Hayun let out a loud sigh, then looked at me strangely. "Are you all right, samonim? Would you like more tea?" She held the spout over my cup, which was half full.

"How can you even think about tea at a time like this?" I said.

Hayun retreated with the teapot, saying in a quavering voice: "I wanted to tell you, but he's been so sick. You can't imagine how worried she's been for him."

"What do you mean, *sick?*" The dread returned. Over a million Koreans in America. What were the odds?

"That's just it. No one knows. The doctors can't find the cause. He told her to pursue her dream of having a restaurant someday, and he's right, she can't sit by his bed for weeks on end," Hayun explained.

"Of course she can't, but you're not making any sense. What's happened with her job?" This was all too confusing. I struggled to keep my fears from making me flee this house.

"Oh, samonim, Ellery was fired from the restaurant here in

California because she took so much time to be with her fiancé in Ohio. Her bosses at the restaurant have been terrible, though who could blame them — she hadn't been there for very long. But I tell you, even this job was strange. You know they were up for the same position. He was late for his interview. If he'd arrived on time, they would never have met again — I forgot to tell you they were friends in Oberlin. But then at the job interview, they saw each other, and she said it was instant love. After that they were inseparable; she flew there, he flew here, every day off she got. And then he became terribly sick a few months ago."

Oberlin. Again. The college in Ohio. Ohio, where Joyce and Jordan lived. Hayun looked away and arranged the abandoned teacups on the tray. She bit her lip, looking everywhere but at me, like the teenage girl I remembered from years ago. Why my son had found her attractive, I'd never know.

"Be still. Sit down," I commanded, pointing to the couch. "What's this man's name?"

"Oh, why does it matter now? She's different than Jiu. Ellery wants to start a family right away and she is so good around children. A wedding and a family — Ellery had so many plans."

"His name. Tell me this fiancé's name," I repeated. My mouth was dry; my heart knew before she said it.

"Jordan. Jordan Ko."

Three hundred million people in America, and Seona's great-grandson and my great-granddaughter had fallen in love.

"But the engagement is canceled?" I asked.

"You saw her face. It's over, but Ellery can be stubborn, she'll find a way."

"Listen carefully. Do you remember what I said about Seona?" I asked.

"Ellery isn't anything like Seona. She'd never elope like your sister, and it's Jordan himself who doesn't want to marry her." Hayun wiped tears from her eyes.

First off, Hayun was wrong. Anyone could run off; Ellery was no different. Second, Hayun was missing the more obvious point. "Oh, be rational for once! Jordan is sick, he's right to call off the marriage. Let's be honest."

Hayun's chin quivered. Ellery had inherited her tearful, emotional high-strung disposition from her grandmother. If I was going to get anywhere, I'd have to soften my tone.

"Hayun, Seona's descendants live in Ohio. Her granddaughter married a man whose name is Ko. Think about it."

"Could they help Jordan?" Hayun exclaimed.

Last names obfuscated the matter, I had to admit. I was going to have to spell it out. "Jordan is my sister's great-grandson."

Hayun pulled her chin back as if she'd smelled something offensive. "Samonim," she sputtered. "That can't be right."

I nodded.

"Well, I have to tell her right away, right now." She rose to her feet.

I stood up and held her arm. "And how would that work? No one in my family knows about your indiscretion with my son."

Hayun's face blanched. "But Ellery has to know."

"You must promise me you won't tell her," I said.

"But, samonim —" she began.

"You of all people know that romantic love doesn't last," I said, hating myself a little for bringing it up, but I had to. She couldn't spill the secret now. Not after all this time and the many sacrifices we had made.

Hayun's face changed as she remembered how I'd forced her to leave. "My brother said the same about you and him," she said.

I was prepared, as I always was when I was cruel, so the arrow she'd aimed at me penetrated only so far. She'd known about my own feelings for her brother, Siwon. Hayun and I had both ended up alone. I took a deep breath and exhaled in a loud display of acceptance. *Touché, Hayun.*

Now we could focus on the work at hand. "The engagement is off, as you said. Call her back here. We have to convince her to move ahead without him but we can't tell her the real reason. Promise me you won't tell her."

Hayun nodded, her mouth in a tight line, and left the room. I paced about until Hayun returned. She held a Kleenex to her nose and was sniffling.

"She says she needs to sleep; she apologizes, she's very tired," Hayun said.

"Well, that's not good enough. I'm leaving soon." Hayun just stood there and clasped and unclasped her hands, looking to me for help. "All right, we don't want to push her," I said. "She might convince Jordan to change his mind and run off and elope with him." I hated saying his name aloud, but I had to.

"She won't do that," Hayun said in a reprimanding tone, her posture suddenly straighter, as if I were obtuse to think it. "She's been interviewing for jobs all week — it's been very stressful for her. She thinks if she can work again, she'll at least send Jordan some money for his medical care."

"She needn't concern herself with that," I said, although I didn't disclose my plans to go to Ohio and handle the money for his treatment myself. *Jordan will get better and forget all about Ellery.* The wheels in my mind were turning. I could send her off on a dazzling tour of Asia and then afterward, who knew? She might want to live with me in Korea. That fantasy beckoned from the horizon. I could see it. Distance was the answer for Ellery and Jordan. I'd sent Hayun and Jiu away once; now I'd bring Ellery back to Korea.

Hayun looked skeptical. "Ellery will want to work," she said.

"Well, I'll offer her money to go on a grand trip of Asia with me, then. I could pay her — I'll think of something."

"You'll have to convince her yourself, that's all I'm saying," Hayun said in a miffed voice.

"Fine. There's plenty of time tomorrow. We'll make it work. I'll call her in the morning. Give me her phone number." I picked up my purse, which was on the couch, and took out my phone. It took me a moment to understand what was on my screen. I'd never had so many alerts before. The phone's cover photo of a purple hibiscus in full bloom was marred by a barrage of texts and missed-call alerts from Chohui and Mina. Silent alarm bells sounded around me.

"Text me Ellery's phone number, but right now, take me back to the hotel immediately," I said.

CHAPTER 11

The drive back to the hotel seemed much longer than the drive out. I returned the calls from Chohui and Mina and texted them, but there was no reply. What did this mean? I tried Aera too, but no answer. Chohui's and Mina's texts simply said, **Where are you?** and **Call me.** I texted back rather nonchalantly to Mina, **Out for a walk. See you soon.** To Chohui I was more direct: **What's the meaning of this?**

My head was down, and I was peering at the phone closely, so I hardly commented on Hayun's wild swerving as she drove. Whatever got us there fastest, I told myself, but then she sped up, as if the silence between us was unbearable to her.

"Watch out!" I ordered as she entered an intersection without minding the stop sign. I closed my eyes as we coasted through without incident. "You're a terrible driver," I said, letting out one long exhale. She ignored the comment.

"So much traffic tonight," Hayun said. "I can't stand it when Ellery is upset."

I sympathized and took two full cleansing breaths. Of course she was rattled by her granddaughter's response. Still, I didn't want her to think she could go off the rails again. A stop sign was a stop sign. How far away was the Fair Hotel? The lights of the city looked to me like

106

erratic lost sailboats on a windy sea. I was feeling nauseated from the worry. I tried calling Chohui four more times. Still nothing. What was the meaning of all these calls and text messages, and why wasn't anyone answering?

Several minutes later, we turned onto the street of the hotel. The traffic snarled out of lanes; a police officer directed cars away from the block. I told Hayun to let me out so I could walk. Something terrible had happened, I was certain of it.

She said it was too far and didn't reduce her speed. I had to bite my tongue to keep from haranguing her. I was a captive in her car. We circled the block again, and this time I saw from the other side of the street a gurney being rolled out of the hotel, and I saw Mina chasing after it in a white terry-cloth robe with both hands flailing above her head, as if she were shooing away mayflies. I told Hayun to stop and released my seat belt.

"Samonim, it's not safe," Hayun said in a frantic voice.

"I mean it, stop this instant," I said and unlocked the car door. She swerved and halted behind an SUV three vehicles from the traffic light.

"That is an ambulance and that is my sister. I'll call you. Goodbye," I said. The night air was cooler than when I'd gotten into the car. I looked both ways because that feeling came over me again. My mother's admonition to be wary of fate. The warnings were out there. Traffic. Mine was to watch out for traffic.

Why did Mina look frightened? Why was she outside in a bathrobe?

I was crossing the street when a car horn blared, and I startled away and stepped in front of a minivan, which braked with a screech.

"Samonim!" It was Hayun honking her horn. Silly woman. Nearly caused me to expire right then or, at a minimum, require another ambulance to be called to this confusing scene.

I waved her away. And then I raised my voice and said in Korean, "Go, go on."

"I'll make sure you get inside," she shouted.

"I'll call you tomorrow, go," I said. And then I hurried to the hotel, dodging between another pair of cars pushed on by a police officer to Mina, who was staring at me with her piercing eyes.

"Whose car was that?" she snapped.

I couldn't help myself; I looked over to see if Hayun had driven off at last. She hadn't, of course, and waved when she saw me glance her way. Ignoring the wave, I turned to Mina, fully expecting Aera and Chohui to be nearby.

"What's happened?" I said.

She pointed her chin toward the rear doors of the ambulance, where a figure wrapped in a white blanket was lying on a gurney, strapped in with wide belts. Did she mean Chohui? Was that Chohui?

"Is Chohui hurt?" I shuddered even saying it.

"What? Of course not — it's Aera, her stomach," Mina said. I took a few steps closer before a policewoman raised her arm and kept me from going farther. And on the gurney, yes, I saw my second-oldest sibling's thick dyed-mahogany hair, her face turned away from me.

"My family," I told the official in uniform and pointed.

She peered into my face, and I hoped I didn't look like a criminal, though her appraisal made me think I must have appeared to be one. Then I realized I had spoken in Korean. She mumbled something into the walkie-talkie on her armband and waved me on. I pulled on Mina's robe sleeve, and she stumbled after me.

The medics were counting in unison. "One, two —" They raised the gurney, collapsed its metal legs, and slid the stretcher into the vehicle.

"Aera, we're here, we're here," I called to her. My second-oldest sister didn't respond.

"What is it? What has happened?" I said in Korean to the para-medic. He ignored me.

"She was retching so much she passed out. You weren't in your room," Mina replied. "Where have you been?"

"Food poisoning?" I asked.

"Whose car was that you were in?" Mina's bad breath had intensified.

"Just tell me, is Aera all right? Mina, is she unconscious?"

"How should I know? That's why I called Chohui. You weren't answering."

"Then what happened?"

"Chohui phoned the front desk. They called the ambulance. We didn't know what happened to you. We thought you'd been kid-napped. You were missing and I thought all kinds of things."

"But I'm fine."

"I didn't know — how could I know? You've been acting odd for days and now this disappearance," Mina said.

"I'm here, I don't know what you're talking about. Where's Chohui?"

As if on cue, Chohui appeared in front of me. "Saint Francis Memo-rial Hospital — that's where the ambulance is taking her," she said. She was wearing her coat over her nightgown, and her eyes were bright with excitement. "Samonim, you're here."

"Where else would I be?" I replied.

The ambulance made beeping sounds just then so we looked toward it. A paramedic motioned at us, pointed her finger to the sky, and climbed into the vehicle. The rear doors were still open. What did that mean? Did it mean Aera was about to leave us for the heavens above? I felt my knees weaken.

"Samonim, are you all right?" Chohui asked.

I snapped to attention. "I'm fine. You should know better, Cho-hui — did you raise an alarm about me?"

She blushed crimson and Mina said, "This is not the time, Jeonga." It was fine when she had been cross-examining me a few seconds earlier. Another paramedic shouted something to us.

"Only one can go in the ambulance," Chohui translated.

"I think family should go," I replied and looked at Mina.

"Who, me?" Mina was flustered and looked around to see if I meant someone standing next to her, as if Aera would appear there, although we knew well enough that she couldn't possibly.

"One second," Chohui said to the paramedic and I marveled at how casually she spoke. With hardly any accent. Then she turned to us.

"I'll volunteer," she said, a squeak in her voice.

One of Chohui's favorite shows was a medical drama. Good thing for us that she didn't mind going, because I certainly didn't want to catch whatever Aera had.

"Go ahead, Chohui," I said. "Wear a mask. We'll meet you at the hospital."

Mina agreed. "Yes, go, and don't let those people harm her, don't you think?"

In seconds, Chohui was inside the ambulance. The back doors closed, and the vehicle pulled away from the curb. It took several more minutes for the other emergency vehicles to leave us. The lights and commotion conspired to make it harder for me to grasp what we needed to do next.

"There's that car you were in," Mina said, pointing.

In all the time it had taken for us to settle who was going to the hospital, Hayun had barely inched forward. She saw us looking at her, rolled down the window, and shouted in Korean, "All okay, samonim?"

Mina's jaw dropped. She stared from her to me and then back again.

"She worked for me eons ago," I said to my sister, then called to Hayun, "We need a ride to Saint Hospital!"

I sat up front to give Mina the luxury of the entire back seat but also so I could squeeze Hayun's leg to warn her to watch her words. I explained about Aera and Chohui and the stomach illness.

"You look familiar," Mina said. "When did you work for my sister?"

"It was a long time ago. You wouldn't remember," I said.

"I have an excellent memory for faces," Mina said.

Hayun jumped in. "I was very young at the time and was the sister of —"

I pinched her leg to deter her from disclosing anything more. Then I told Mina, "I wouldn't expect you to remember everyone who ever worked for me."

In the car, Mina asked question after question of Hayun, and I answered all of them.

"What sort of work did you do for my sister?" Mina began.

"Housework, the usual," I said.

"Are you married?"

"Never married," I replied.

Hayun made a sharp left turn to keep up with the ambulance.

"I see. And you happen to have bumped into my sister this night?" Mina said.

"Hurry, we must go to Saint Hospital," I answered as traffic suddenly cleared.

"You mean Saint Francis, samonim," Hayun said.

"That's what the paramedic said, I don't know," I replied. Should I know? This was Hayun's city, not mine.

Mina was silent for a while. I knew she was estimating Hayun's age and counting backward, cycling through her memory. "When did you move to San Francisco?" she said after a pause.

"Oh, here we are at the hospital. Thank you, Hayun. Very nice to run into you. Take good care of yourself."

"I hope we see you again, samonim," Hayun said. "So glad you called."

Mina had just gotten out of the car, and she stopped in her tracks with the door open.

I didn't know what had gotten into Hayun. "Yes, well, whatever, goodbye," I said. I got out and slammed the door closed.

Hayun said through the open car window, "Please, if you could see us again, even tomorrow, I could drive right over. I'll arrange it. I mean, I hope your sister is well soon, but if you have the time or need anything, I will come right over."

"Yes, thank you," I replied, urging her to leave with my curtness.

"Call tomorrow, samonim," Hayun pleaded.

I didn't make any such promise, but her words stayed with me. I said, "Mina, get going. Close the door."

How rude. Simply rude. If I hadn't needed a ride, I would never have risked that conversation. Well, now Hayun had shown me she wasn't trustworthy. But still, she hadn't spilled the beans about the fact that even with one million Koreans in America with nine million square kilometers of land, my great-granddaughter Ellery was engaged to be married to her third cousin Jordan. A bizarre coincidence I couldn't deny.

I was able to breathe a sigh of relief when I looked back and saw Hayun's car departing. Without Chohui, Mina and I didn't know how to find Aera, but lucky for us, Chohui appeared from the hallway and beckoned us to follow.

"How is she?" I asked.

"They're running tests, samonim," Chohui replied.

"Well." Mina released a huge sigh. "That means she's well enough to have tests run on her."

This made no sense to me. "Will they discharge her tonight?" I asked Chohui.

"Oh no, they have to watch her overnight. She's got an IV for fluids," she said, the last three words in English.

"Just like Aera to worry us for nothing," Mina said.

"We'll see her and come back in the morning," I announced. "They'll release her then, won't they?"

Chohui shook her head. "Actually, they won't say. Come fill out some forms," she said. "I tried my best, but I didn't have all the information."

"How long will she stay? Is it necessary?" Mina blanched. "We have a flight the day after tomorrow."

"Her age is the problem," Chohui replied.

I looked at Mina, who was fidgeting with her robe's belt and holding a handkerchief over her mouth. Her chin was lowered. My confident sister seemed cowed by the American hospital. "We'll divide and conquer. You handle the change in flights," I told Mina. "Push it forward. Surely for a health emergency — we can get the doctor to sign a form for the airlines — they'll waive change fees. Use your most persuasive voice. And I'll talk with the doctors."

That seemed to give Mina reassurance. She knew how to handle business affairs and the tickets had been booked by her son, after all. Good for her. I loathed being on hold with those airline people. I also knew Mina was phobic when it came to germs and hated to be in the hospital, even for Aera. I raised my scarf over my mouth and nose and directed Chohui to do the same. "Lead the way, Chohui," I said.

Despite the energy Chohui had displayed in front of the hotel, she seemed like she was about to collapse now. She kept sighing. After we talked to the doctors, I'd get her some tea in one of the awful hospital cafeterias I'd heard about. And honestly, I could use one myself. The jet lag was threatening to overwhelm me. I'd have a strong cup of tea and think about what to say to Ellery tomorrow. Watching Chohui ask a white-coated person in the hallway for directions, I thought how wise we had been to bring her. Clever Chohui. Mina's or Aera's aide wouldn't have been as resourceful.

CHAPTER 12

O nce Aera was admitted to the hospital, the doctors insisted she would have to stay for at least two days as a precaution. Mina and I became suspicious — if they wanted to keep her that long, then maybe what she had was contagious and she needed to stay a few more days in isolation. In Korea, we were very respectful of containing infections. Mina and I spoke to the doctors by phone and decided not to set foot in that hospital again. Chohui, being the youngest and healthiest, would visit her each day. When it was time for Aera to be discharged, we'd have Chohui escort her to the hotel. Aera was confused on the phone, but she agreed we didn't want to transfer viruses back and forth to each other. One time was enough, she said.

Caution is the secret to a long life. It got me to the age of ninety-five, the year I thought would be my last. And then I was suddenly on an upswing and felt stronger each day. Pushed away sad thoughts. Get to ninety-five, that's my advice. You have a second wind then. Acupuncture was my secret weapon. All three of us sisters saw an acupuncturist three times a week. So now, at over one hundred, barring mishaps with a food item, which could happen to anyone of any age, we were sturdy and capable. Also determined.

I had to get rid of Mina and Chohui. My thoughts churned all night about how to succeed. Turned out that being free of them was easy. Mina didn't come down to breakfast the day after Aera was taken to the hospital. When I called her from the restaurant in the lobby, she said she'd suffered nightmare upon nightmare of ambulances and car accidents.

"You were the one," she said. "It wasn't Aera, it was you in the ambulance."

"Aera's your favorite, I know. You must wish I were the one in the hospital right now instead of her." I chuckled.

"Stop that, of course not," she said with genuine upset in her voice.

"I'll have room service bring you tea and toast, you'll feel better," I said.

"Mostly I'm tired."

I had to keep her away from me. "Maybe you caught what Aera had —" I began.

"Do you think?" she exclaimed. "I hardly slept, so I thought it was just fatigue and jet lag. We're not so young anymore."

"I feel fine, so it must be something else," I replied.

"You do? But we were up late last night."

"I really am fine. You were with Aera more than anyone."

She gasped. "You're right. What should I do? Should I go to the hospital right now?"

I only needed a day with Ellery. "I wouldn't go to the hospital if I were you. And get germs from sick people on top of what you already have? Just stay in bed and get some rest. Your body can fight it off if you relax."

"But this is the room Aera was in when she got sick. I used the bathroom she used. I shouldn't be here at all."

"That is a very good point. Shall I call the front desk and move you to another room?"

"What about Aera's things? I don't want to touch them — what if they're infected?"

"I'll have Chohui help you — she's tougher than all of us — and just in case, I'll stay well out of your way."

"You mustn't get sick, Jeonga. In my dream, they were taking you away in an ambulance and wouldn't let anyone ride with you. I offered — I did. Chohui wasn't anywhere in sight, though I looked and looked for her."

"You told me already. That was Aera, not me."

"My dream wasn't about last night. And Chohui went with Aera, remember?"

"All right, then, let me call the front desk and send Chohui over. Do the windows open?"

"How would I know? Chohui will figure it out."

"Remember to stand far away from her. Other side of the room. Maybe even the hall."

"I know what to do. Call me when I'm supposed to switch rooms."

I went to the lobby to get a new room and card key for Mina, then I instructed Chohui on how to move Aera's things and help Mina get situated in her new room. After that, I told Chohui she was free to go sightseeing. She perked up at the thought of an entire day without three old ladies.

Almost too easy. Almost as if it were meant to be. Everything clicked into place to allow me to spend time with my great-granddaughter. No reason to make that leap, but I remember thinking it. The way everything fit together, moving me toward something I was fated to do.

And then I encountered a glitch. When I called Hayun, she said Ellery had left and she didn't know where she'd gone.

"But you told me to see her today," I said in shock. "She'll be back soon, won't she?" My watch said it was ten o'clock. Where would a young woman go at this hour when she didn't have a job?

"I'm as surprised as you are, samonim. She could be taking a walk. I'm sure she'll be back soon. Shall we call you then? Or would you like me to pick you up and you could wait for her here?"

Oh, that word — *wait*. I certainly wasn't going to *wait* for her any-where. In fact, that could very well be what Mina saw in her night-mare last night. I would die in Hayun's car. I was sure of it. Hadn't she rolled right through a stop sign? I was determined never to be held captive by her again.

"Don't you have one of those tracker things on her phone?" I said.

"She's almost thirty years old, samonim, not a child."

"Give me her cell phone number," I said.

"Sure, but why? I can pick you up and —"

"Please, the number," I repeated, cutting her off.

She read it to me slowly while I typed it in. We went over it several times to be sure I had it and then I said goodbye.

I was still certain I could manage to keep Ellery away from Seona's great-grandson in Ohio. The engagement had been broken off, after all. I was just going to make sure it stayed that way. Not difficult.

She didn't answer her phone, though the voice mail indicated that I had reached the right number. I texted her slowly to be sure I had the correct grammar and spelling, which the phone helped me with, offering me an array of choices. People's carelessness did come in handy for those of us learning a new language. While I waited for a reply, I headed back to my room.

I bumped into Chohui in the hall. She seemed uncertain as to how to use her time off. She explained that Mina had transferred to a new room and all of Aera's items had been moved as well. "That was fast. Well, go on and enjoy the day," I said.

"I don't know what to do," she said.

"Just walk outside and explore. There must be something fun — what about Fisherman's Wharf?" I said.

"I'm sorry, samonim, but that looks boring. It's just shops and things for little kids. Where are the museums?"

"Look on your phone," I said in exasperation. "I'm surprised at you. Go make some friends."

I was irritated because Ellery hadn't returned my numerous voice messages and Hayun still had no idea where her grandchild could be. And I had not anticipated that Chohui would give me any trouble.

"It's not what I expected," she admitted.

"That's jet lag talking. Get some fresh air."

"Is that what it is?"

"Here's the free time you wanted. And don't forget, you won't have it for long. I want you to check in on my sister at the hospital later. I'll want a full report. No need to return for dinner. Eat out by yourself. Tell your friends about the restaurants in San Francisco. I think some are famous. I'm sure I'll just eat something here and turn in early. Don't say I never let you have any time off — it's what you wanted, remember?"

"You're right," she said and headed for the elevator, purpose in her step.

What a relief. I returned to our room alone. I needed a moment to think. I plopped into a chair.

Tomorrow Mina would be in better health, and I'd lose my chance. My head spun with worry. How could Ellery keep me waiting like this? I was old. How much time did she think I had in this life? Just at that moment, Hayun's name appeared on my phone's caller ID.

"Hello, where is she?" I said.

There was silence before Hayun started speaking.

"Calm down, I can't understand you," I had to insist.

"They're called bars here, samonim. I'm so sorry. This is not like her at all."

"Does this mean she's hurt?" The sound of Hayun's voice led me to believe there was something harmful about winehouses.

"No, she's very upset, and now I'm upset. She feels she can't come home."

"Well, I told you she was showing all the signs of someone who would run away. She hasn't flown off to her fiancé, has she?" I said.

"She's in a bar on Powell Street."

"Where is that?" I asked.

I heard her muffled voice call to someone. And then she returned to the phone. "Sorry, I have a plumber here for our kitchen sink." Her voice wavered and I thought she was going to cry.

"Well, give me the exact address and I'll go to her."

According to my phone's GPS, she was nearly a kilometer away. I thanked Hayun and told her to attend to her sink. How terrible for it to be broken at a time like this.

It was now 1:30. The day was going to be over soon. My goodness. I was glad to be able to walk. The thought of being inside any vehicle did not appeal to me. Nothing with wheels, I decided, unless absolutely necessary. As it turned out, the weather was lovely, and I was there in thirty minutes.

It's true, even in America, that when an old woman walks into a bar, people move aside for her, as if their own grandmothers would disapprove of this place where they're hiding. A respectable bar would be different, but I'm talking about a hole-in-the-wall. A place without a sign. A place that didn't want a lot of customers. Not that it was sleazy, just that it was spare and in need of sun and cleaning. But it was the way everyone there liked it, the dust, dirt, and dimness.

Inside, I spotted Ellery talking to an old white man at the bar. They seemed to be the only two who didn't notice me. Her chin was tucked down, eyes on her shot glass. He was too close, I thought. But then I thought, *Perhaps this is good. Let her forget Jordan.*

The bartender didn't even ask if I wanted anything. Looking at me warily, she wandered down to the end farthest away from the two of them and busied herself with touching the tops of bottles.

The man with Ellery waved his arm toward the bartender. "Another," he said. But the bartender didn't respond. I took a seat on the other side of Ellery and waited for her to notice me. Good thing I was present. Too much alcohol and she could stumble and never get home. And this codger, what did he want from Ellery in the middle of the afternoon? Up close, I could see he was too old to be a possible romantic interest even if in my day those were frequent pairings. Even if he could take her mind off Seona's great-grandson, I could not have him be an alternative. Not in this day and age. We'd made progress. It was the kind of progress I was pleased about; there were many other changes of which I wasn't as accepting.

Ellery was dressed in the same clothes she'd been wearing yesterday. Maybe she'd been wandering all night. *Hayun should keep better track of her grandchild*, I thought.

"Go to him, that's what I say," the man said. He picked up his empty shot glass and put it down again. "Remember the love," he said.

She shook her head, but a smile began on her lips. For a moment, I was certain she was sober.

The man leaned in. I worried it was for a kiss, so I glared at him, a concentrated stare.

"No," he said, lurching back. "I can't believe it." He pulled at the hair just above his forehead and gaped at me.

"Are you all right?" Ellery asked.

"Don't move," he said to her solemnly, still staring at me. "We mean you no harm," he said in my direction.

I glanced around but no one was near me.

"I saw them when I was a kid but not since then. What do you want?" he bellowed. He looked at me and then off to the side of me and then still farther to the side of me.

I took a step forward and he slid off his stool. Slowly, as if he was afraid I'd do something drastic to him, he backed away. His eyes darted to the side of me again, as if someone accompanied me.

"I don't know what to do," Ellery said and then she started laughing as if her own voice were the funniest thing she'd ever heard, and in that laugh I remembered something of my sisters and me.

"Shhh, quiet, don't get them mad," he said and continued to retreat. I saw the bartender look in our direction and shake her head.

"I'm not mad," Ellery answered, bubbles of laughter still surfacing. "It's absurd."

"Not you — the ghosts."

She still hadn't turned in my direction, but her body stiffened.

"Are you okay?" Ellery said.

"Hey." His hands were raised in surrender. "Good luck." He put one hand into his pants pocket, drew out some bills, threw them down on the bar, and exited without looking back.

"Hello, Ellery," I said.

She noticed me at last. "Oh, he thought you were —" And then she laughed again. "Mrs. Cha, he thought you were a ghost," she said.

CHAPTER 13

allowed myself to giggle and she joined me. *Ghosts, what a concept,* I thought. Americans were either foolish or wise — I didn't know they believed in ghosts. It seemed too ancient a concept for such a fast-modern place.

"I thought you left," she said, her voice struggling to stay crisp. "Did Halmoni tell you where I was?"

Her hair fell into her eyes as she tried to focus. I wanted to brush it back and tell her everything would be all right. Feeling suddenly like my mother when she tried to comfort me when I'd felt forgotten by my father and Seona. Only Ellery was not so little. The drink on the bar in front of her reminded me of her age. What she needed was fresh air and sunshine. I wanted her sober and paying attention to every word I said.

"I heard Fisherman's Wharf is not far from here. Shall we get some lunch? I'm famished," I said in a bright voice.

"I'm really not in the mood, Mrs. Cha. I'm sorry. Go ahead without me," she said, appearing to dig in. She was not going to leave this place unless I changed tactics. People in love had to talk about the object of their passion. They suffered if they could not. It was an additional suffering on top of their anguish. I knew this from experience.

"Do you have a photograph of your fellow? I'd like to see him for myself," I said.

She complied grudgingly, but I sensed her interest had been sparked. Holding up her phone, she clicked on the screen, then turned it toward me.

It was a photo of Ellery and a young man with their arms around each other. He had dark wavy bangs across his forehead, covering his eyebrows, like that singer in BTS named Min Yoon-gi who went by Suga now for some reason. Chohui was a fan, of course, and had played BTS songs in the car and pointed out who was who in the videos when we stopped at a traffic light. I took Ellery's phone to get a better view. He was a few centimeters taller than Ellery, who stood with a smile on her face in the photo. She appeared carefree, languid in her stance, while this man stared hard at the camera lens with a grim look.

"So serious," I said.

"No, he's not. He was just sad because I'd driven him to the airport — that was the end of our first date. I like it the best because it's the only picture of us together before he got sick," she said. "He's the most honest person I've ever met. He can't lie about anything. What you see is what you get. I love that about him. He's a hundred percent, whatever it is. He can't pretend or change the way he feels." Even though her voice lowered at the memory, I noticed that she held her head a little higher.

"Jordan, is that his name? Your grandmother mentioned it," I said.

She confirmed that it was. "Here's a better picture of him." She offered me another photograph on her phone. This time Jordan was smiling, clearly smiling at Ellery, who must have been behind the lens. I noticed that Jordan's eyes crinkled into crescents the way Seona's eyes used to when she was young. I heard Ellery sniffle and I worried she was going to request another drink, so I said, "Tell me how you met."

As expected, Ellery began to talk, and as she spoke, I signaled to the bartender to bring us tall glasses of water, which Ellery downed in earnest between long descriptions of that fateful day in Palo Alto. I could picture her waiting for her turn to interview with a chef whom even I had heard about. She'd walked around the block twice because she was early and collided with someone at the restaurant entrance, a man who was late for his interview because his flight had been delayed, who had run two and a half miles because his rental car had gotten a flat on his way from the airport, who was sweating from the heat (it had been an excessively hot day). She'd felt so sorry for him that she'd told him to take her interview time even before she recognized him from Oberlin College, which they'd both graduated from. They had mutual friends.

"You learned all that in the first few minutes of meeting him?" I asked.

"He recognized me right away, even though we'd both been out of school for a few years by then. He has an extraordinary memory, Mrs. Cha," Ellery said. "He's good at everything. I would have given up if my flight were late."

I was skeptical. "Or called and explained and rescheduled. And I'm sure you're more skilled than he is. But why did you give him your spot?"

She shrugged. "He came all that way from Ohio. I figured I could reschedule mine."

"You've got a good heart," I said. "Don't let people take advantage."

She shook her head. "He'd never do that to me. I offered but he refused to take my place. He's not that kind of person."

My estimation of Jordan rose. "Well, glad that worked out." I made a big show of looking around the bar. I had to get her outside. With her generous heart, she'd surely come with me once we left.

"Could you at least point me to a place around here where I might get something to eat?" I asked.

She nodded and slipped off her stool.

Once we were out in the sunlight, I asked her again about Fisherman's Wharf. "Which way is it? I'm terrible with directions," I said.

"Too crowded with tourists," she said. "Oh, sorry — did I offend you? If you want to go, I'll show you."

"I hate tourists too, though I guess I'm one here," I said. I realized I'd been speaking to her in Korean all this time except for the last three words, which I'd said in English. "I didn't know you knew Korean so well," I said. We made our way down the block.

"Halmoni made me go to Korean school. Also, I love watching K-dramas, but mostly it's talking to her. I wish I knew it better," she said as we walked.

"Knowing Korean expands your job opportunities," I said.

"I suppose," she replied. "Well, I should go back to Halmoni's now. Thank you for this talk, Mrs. Cha."

I stopped to look at the menu taped to the window of a Thai restaurant. My plan was to keep her with me as long as I could. "So many dishes," I exclaimed.

"If you're hungry, this place is pretty good," Ellery said, gentle girl that she was. She wiped her face with the back of her hand. She had completely sobered up.

"Perfect," I said with a grateful smile. "Come join me."

She held the door and said, "They have really good spring rolls here."

The smells from the small restaurant made my mouth long for food. No need to pretend anymore. The woodwork, the quiet rich-blue-painted interior — Chohui would like this place, I thought. It had not been on Mina's list, I noted with smugness.

We ordered a few items from the menu, and after the waiter brought our food, I turned to her. "There are well-paying jobs for a cook like you in Korea," I said.

Her mouth wobbled and I thought she was going to flee. Had I said too much, pushed too hard once again?

Ellery put her fork down. "That's kind of you, Mrs. Cha, but Korea is too far. I was hoping I could be near Jordan, even if he doesn't want me."

"Of course he wants you, dear. It's the illness talking," I said. *Tell her she should find someone else to love,* I told myself, but I couldn't stand to see her fall deeper into sorrow.

She sniffled. "I know, I know. He didn't actually say he didn't. Remember, he can't lie, but he said he didn't want me to put my life on hold for him."

"The important thing is you and what you need. We have to live our own lives."

"But I love him, Mrs. Cha."

"You threw your job away for him."

"It's my fault. Leaving them in the lurch. Jordan didn't understand; he was so angry at them for firing me."

"Let me help you. I know some restaurant people in Seoul," I said. "I eat out a lot, and they're my friends. They might have an opening. It could be temporary, of course, until you found something better."

"A job is what I need but to be all the way in Korea?" she said. "I can't do it."

"I understand," I replied, buying myself some more time.

Her eyes filled with tears and she sniffled again and then cleared her throat. "He has to get better, Mrs. Cha."

"I'm sure his mother is taking good care of him," I said.

"How did you know about his mother? Did I tell you about her?"

A misstep but I smoothed it over. "You did." When lying, keep it simple.

She smiled and wiped her cheeks. "Joyce is the strongest person I know."

"So he's in good hands," I said.

"I don't know how she's managed to pay for what she has up until now. She was so glad I was there — of course I would be, but she made me so comfortable and thanked me every day."

"Not every young lady would give up her job to nurse the man she loved."

She took her napkin and blew her nose. "You think I should go to Korea and send money to him that way?"

"Good idea, Ellery. You can work and help pay for his care, and over time, when he's better, you'll reevaluate your relationship."

"He will get better, Mrs. Cha."

I nodded. "Korea has all kinds of advances in medicine. Maybe you can find something there to help him. Look at you: You're a cook and very capable. And you're almost thirty years old, Ellery. Time to think about a family."

Her eyes filled up again. "You mean babies? We both want babies, we talked about it."

"You did? But you — you're too young," I stammered.

"You just said I should think about starting a family, Mrs. Cha," she said, and rather than being angry at me, she gave me the saddest small smile. "My mom didn't even want kids and then she had me. I'll love my kids. I want to be young enough to play with them and be there for them."

I had to think fast. What was it Hayun had told me? This called for more than my usual charm. I cleared my throat. "Ellery, you have plenty of time for babies. Building a life — you're a cook, so you must want your own restaurant someday, right?"

"I do."

"Then you have to focus on that first. One thing at a time."

She nodded. "I could work and send money to him, and I'll ask Joyce if she's looked into experimental treatments." And then she reached out her hand and squeezed mine. "Thank you, Mrs. Cha. I need to work. Jordan's illness has taken all my focus. I can help him by sending him money. I've always wanted to go to Korea. It looks beautiful. It is beautiful, isn't it?"

I agreed it was. "Not as many people as here, though. Three hundred million in America."

"How many in Korea?" she asked.

"Fifty million in South Korea," I replied. "We must move on this quickly. Time is of the essence. How long have you been out of work?"

She told me it had been three months and then she explained what she enjoyed doing as a cook, and I made her type it into the notes section of my phone. She also wrote down her e-mail.

"I'll send you my résumé and references. I might still hear from one restaurant in Dayton," she said. "They were going to expand, and they'd need more cooks. I just don't know how long that would take."

"Talk of expansion is not reliable," I said. "The question is if they'll even grow. Businesses can't take risks these days."

"You're probably right," she said and looked down at her hands.

"Seoul has a variety of high-quality restaurants," I told her, and she looked at me, hanging on my every word. "You could stay with me until you found a place of your own," I added. "Just for a little while. I might even know of an apartment in my building that's available." I knew how young people wanted their own space. I chattered on about how Bogum could suggest some rentals near me if she preferred a different style apartment, how I could help her get furniture. How in the future, her grandmother could visit her.

"And don't worry about your flight. I have frequent-flier points I haven't used in years, and I'd be happy to apply them to your ticket and your grandmother's as well," I assured her. "At my age, I don't imagine I'll ever get a chance to use them. Besides, soon you'll be making enough money to send her a ticket yourself, and one to Jordan, when he's feeling better."

"That's all too much, Mrs. Cha, thank you, you've been such a dear friend to my grandmother," she said.

Could I jump for joy or would that make her suspicious? I was thrilled she'd move to Korea to work. Who did I know who owned a restaurant? Mina and Aera surely would have contacts. And Bogum too. And all my nephews and nieces and their children. I'd have to word my request in the most persuasive way. Who could I say Ellery was in relation to me? Grandchild of a dear friend? Grandniece of a man who had been in service to our family for decades? I was in such a good mood, I decided to indulge this young woman who had been so agreeable. I wanted to celebrate. We had some more tea, and talking more about Korea seemed to raise her spirits.

We finished up and she said she had a surprise for me. It was nearly five o'clock. I ordered a few dishes for her to take home, and I took the spring rolls for Chohui. She liked to have late-night snacks. Not a good habit, but seeing how cooperative she'd been this entire trip, I thought she'd enjoy this. We had Thai food in Korea but this one was indeed excellent across the board.

Ellery called her grandmother. I heard her say, "I'm fine. Don't worry, I'm sorry, I should have called you earlier. Okay, yes, I'll Uber back. We did, we ate. I'm bringing some Thai — it's okay, it's not a lot, I'm bringing your favorites. Mrs. Cha paid for all of it. I have so much to tell you. Probably in an hour, all right? Thanks, don't worry."

My plan was to spend more than an hour with her. I had to be certain she wouldn't end up flying straightaway to Ohio tomorrow if she could and then the engagement would be back on. With our bags of food in hand we strolled down steep streets to the harbor. My goal was to cement a bond and I felt I was on my way.

In minutes we were in a crowd.

"Fisherman's Wharf, just like you said you wanted to see," Ellery said, holding out her arms.

There were stores and restaurants, dogs on leashes held by people walking in groups. I didn't know where to look; shouting and laughter filled my ears. I stumbled and Ellery caught me before I fell.

"Is this what you wanted?" she asked, pointing to the sights around us.

I almost said, *No, get me out of here*, but she seemed relaxed and I wanted to keep her with me. "I love this place," I said. "Thank you for bringing me."

"You're not like other senior citizens," she said with a laugh.

Pretending for her was a joy I hadn't known in many years. I was so convincing, I fooled even myself. The arcade was my favorite, although it was dark inside, filled with a swarming stream of people, teenagers who pushed and dodged in front of me. Ellery had her hand firmly on my forearm and navigated us down one aisle of strange machines that burped and beeped. Old wooden arcade games I recognized from movies and posters were side by side with new-fangled ones that had digital numbers that flashed and whirred. I oohed and aahed at them all.

I requested another walk-through because I saw that this was a place many young men seemed to congregate, as opposed to other parts of the pier. This time I stopped by an Asian man about Ellery's age and his Black friend, who was hitting a pinball machine with his hips. It reminded me of one I'd played once when I was visiting Siwon in Colorado. We were at a carnival and we both tried this game. I'd done quite well at it and he had admired my skills.

"This one is a classic. I know it," I said to Ellery. She looked distracted by her phone, but I asked the Asian man some questions in English. "Where did your friend learn to play so well? Is he the pinball champion of San Francisco?"

He was patient at first until he seemed to get bored and returned to cheering on his friend. Ellery whispered to me, "It's not that hard."

"My friend here could play better than you," I announced. Challenges were my forte.

Ellery blushed, but I saw that both men understood what I'd said. The man playing paused, and the silver ball slipped down the middle and into the exit hole. "No!" he exclaimed but he had a smile on his face when he turned to us and didn't seem to hold us responsible.

"Want to take a turn?" he asked Ellery. He had a warm smile and seemed curious about the pair Ellery and I made.

She pushed me forward. "She's the expert," she said.

Under normal circumstances I would have refused, but this was for Ellery. I was bold. "How about five American dollars I can beat your score?" I said to him.

The three of them looked at one another. Exactly what I wanted. Pull them together in camaraderie. Let them be astonished by me.

"How about we bet one dollar," the friend of the man who had been playing said. I noticed he gave Ellery a wink, and she gave him a grateful smile.

With as much verve as I could muster, I stepped up, asked how to start the game, pulled back the lever, and off I went to defeat the machine.

I was completely entranced by the obstacle course before me and was hardly aware of anything else but preventing that orb from falling down the middle to its demise. I'd always been captivated by games.

Small plastic flippers sent the ball up to the top of the machine again and again. Bells chimed and dinged. The marble slipped into pockets that yielded points and then landed in the middle of a paddle so I could send it back through the maze of lights once more. I forgot I was in an old body. I forgot Ellery was beside me and that I was in San Francisco. I was in a space that consisted only of flashing lights and this little silver orb traveling down a ramp of traps and treasures.

Ellery laughed. I looked up to see her; was she flirting with one of the men? A groan went up around me that carried me like a wave, and I lost track of the ball for a millisecond. It went down through the center to the exit and vanished.

To say I was devastated would not be an exaggeration. My knees began to buckle, so I leaned against the metal edge of the pinball machine. "Give her some space," I heard Ellery say.

A small crowd had gathered around us. I suddenly felt shy.

"What are all these other people doing here?" I whispered in Korean.

Just then the crowd cheered as my score lit up the screen. "You beat his score — you won," she exclaimed. And then she turned to the men whom we had spoken to earlier. "Hand over the dollar," she said and held out her hand, palm up.

The man who had been cheering on his friend took a bill from his pocket and placed it in her hand.

"We need a rematch," his friend said.

Ellery looked at her phone. "Another time. I've got to go," she replied. As much as I wanted the day to continue, the food that we'd put on the floor by the pinball machine was getting cold. And I'd accomplished what I'd set out to do. Better to stop while I was ahead.

"Thank you, good match," I said in English and hooked my arm through Ellery's. "We make a good team," I told her.

Ellery smiled. "Korea, here I come," she said.

I held up my hand with the pinkie finger extended. Such an old craggy hand, but I held it up anyway.

She hooked her pinkie around mine, and we shook them.

"Promise?" I said.

"Promise," she replied.

CHAPTER 14

My heart was decidedly lighter after that. Back at the hotel the next day, I called some restaurants in Korea I frequented and spoke to the managers. Chohui made plans with a friend of a friend of hers to walk around Berkeley. She still seemed disappointed in America, which worried me because Ohio was certainly not going to be more exciting.

Without Aera between us, Mina and I had a lovely day together. We shopped, we ate, we spoke to Aera on the phone; she was spending one more day in the hospital. Since Ellery had already taken me to Fisherman's Wharf, I was an excellent guide when I showed Mina the popular tourist attraction. She insisted I take photographs of her in front of signs indicating famous sites. I agreed not to take a selfie of us so Aera wouldn't feel she'd missed out. Mina didn't want to go into the arcade, which was fine with me. She had never liked games the way Seona and I had. The weather was pleasant, so we strolled in and out of shops, then returned to the hotel for an early dinner. I told her about Ellery's quest for a restaurant job, referring to her simply as the granddaughter of an old friend, and Mina seemed vaguely interested in helping me.

That night, Chohui wore a sleep mask she'd saved from the plane and didn't stir in her slumber. A rising urgency told me I had to be able to call Ellery with details of a job before we flew on to Ohio. Any day now, that restaurant in Dayton she'd contacted could reach out to her, and she'd accept the offer; I was fearful of it.

With the time difference, I was able to make calls throughout the night to people with whom I'd done business in the past, and I had a lengthy conversation with Attorney Kim. Surely he would know of someone who needed a cook? Also, I directed him to modify my will. At the moment, Gwangmu's children in Chicago were the main beneficiaries. They were my official grandchildren. Ellery was a beneficiary too, along with Chohui. Ellery was receiving a sizable amount, of course, but I asked Attorney Kim to add more for her, now that I knew she needed financial support, and include a small sum for her mother and grandmother as well. I relished the vision of Ellery's face when she learned of my actions. As for Joyce Ko and her son, I was beginning to reconsider the amount of money I'd specified in my letter. Mina and Aera would pay their share for Jordan's medical expenses — Mina had said so when we were planning this trip — but had they set aside anything in their wills for Seona's heirs? Mina and Aera had many children and grandchildren and seemed myopic in their attention to them. Joyce's letter haunted me, I had to admit. She had brought up the disinheritance. Joyce would receive a portion of the sale of the family home, as Mina had mentioned, but shouldn't I do more for my favorite sister's family? I sent Attorney Kim a message asking him to add Joyce and her son to my will too. Balance it out so Gwangmu's son and daughter inherited a little less, I told him. Only then was I able to sleep, a peaceful sleep I had not had in years.

The next morning, Mina wanted to see the Golden Gate Bridge, but I was determined to make more calls about restaurant jobs in Seoul. We stood in the hotel lobby and argued.

"It can certainly wait until we return," she said when I asked her to call her children for additional restaurant leads, which annoyed me.

"This granddaughter of my old friend has been out of work for six months," I said, knowing I had to exaggerate for her to respond to the urgency of the matter.

"Are you still talking about that cook?"

Mina's terrible bad breath had worsened with the American food we'd been eating. I stepped back but not before her spittle landed on my cheek.

"We must do our best to help the younger generation," I said to my sister, then found a tissue to blow my nose and wiped my face in the process.

Chohui had been standing there idly listening to us. She too seemed curious about my obsession with finding a job for Ellery.

"Samonim," she said, her brave face on. "Your friend's granddaughter can work for you instead of me."

"What? No, she went to college, much too qualified," I said.

Her face fell and I realized I'd hurt her feelings.

"Come to think of it, you're just as talented," I said, ignoring the disdainful look Mina threw me. *Why are you propping her up?* she seemed to say.

Chohui blushed and said her interests lay elsewhere. She wanted to go to design school. A little lie to cover up her embarrassment, I thought, and no doubt she was aware of Mina's judgment. I should have reinforced my comment, encouraged her to believe in herself, but I didn't have time for such indulgences. Now when I look back, I know I should have insisted she go to college. She had a good eye for design, an awareness of people's needs, and I wasn't going to be around forever.

"You may accompany us today, if you wish," I told her to make her worry less about her significance in my life. Chohui begged off, saying she wanted to ride a trolley car. She promised to check on Aera and escort her back to the hotel when she was ready to be discharged from the hospital. As she breezed through the revolving door with her head lifted higher than she held it when she was by my side, I thought how she could be any young woman in America — she'd blend right in with her hopeful outlook.

"Now, what about your restaurant connections?" I asked Mina.

"She's not family, Jeonga," Mina said.

"She's a good girl," I said.

"Aren't they all, don't you think?" She was patting her hair. "Speaking of family, I hear you haven't been in touch with Gwangmu's children," Mina continued.

"Young people are busy these days," I said and was careful to maintain a distance now. "I might make some calls upstairs in my room. Attorney Kim insists he'll have news for me. What about going sightseeing after lunch?" I said.

"I'll never understand you, sister. You have actual grandchildren in America — they're your blood," Mina replied, then she aimed herself in the direction Chohui had gone. "Come along."

A chilly dampness permeated the lobby just then, as if the air-conditioning had been increased, but I pushed it away by following her outside.

"I know a wonderful street full of restaurants that we didn't see yesterday," I said upon joining my sister. "I'll write to Gwangmu's children when I return to Seoul, don't worry."

"It's really about patience; we don't have any patience. Gwangmu could have educated his children better about reaching out to their grandmother," Mina said in a rare show of compassion for me. Though she was wrong about my feelings. "You've been so far away in Korea, you've forgotten how to be a grandmother. I should have kept in better touch with Gwangmu. I remember how Bogum and Gwangmu played so well together as children."

My first response was to remind her how good I was as a tour guide to her and how much fun we'd had yesterday. I didn't want to think about Gwangmu, though it was true Bogum had supported him when Aera's children bullied him at family gatherings.

She prattled on, ignoring me.

"The cutest American names, Ned and Pam. Did you know Pam moved to Singapore? She divorced her husband. Ned seems all alone. Bogum said he's been calling often. Family should stay in touch no matter the distance, don't you think?"

"They're very busy, I'm sure," I replied. I didn't even know if my grandchildren still lived in Chicago. Ned had never called or written. Neither had Pam. With an American mother and a dead father, why would they be interested in me?

"But you agree that family is important. We should make an effort to visit them."

"Family is, I agree," I said.

"You do?"

"If the occasion arose, I'd be happy to see Ned. So, what about your daughter-in-law's contacts at restaurants for Ellery? She seems like a very social individual," I said.

She wrinkled her brow for a moment. "Ellery? Isn't that the name Joyce mentioned in the letter?"

I took the initiative to ask the bellman to secure us a taxi to the Golden Gate State Park. She was terrible with American names, I reminded her.

Finally, the morning came when we set off for the airport. Aera looked thinner but otherwise her old anxious self, pulling at her gloved hands. We had to transfer planes in Chicago to land in Dayton. I didn't understand why this was necessary, but maybe Bogum saved money this way. This was the reason I didn't doubt our layover in Chicago.

I tried to explain my nervousness away. Chicago was where

Gwangmu had lived. I was feeling jittery because of his death and, to be honest, how he'd treated me before he died. Those years when he had lived in Chicago.

Short layovers always made me nervous. An unforeseen delay, and you'd miss the connecting flight. Plus, Aera was slower than us, having been weakened by food poisoning. I didn't want to hear from Mina how her son would have to change the reservations again if we missed our flight, so I hurried everyone as much as I could, warning Chohui to unbuckle her seat belt as soon as we landed and be ready to keep the aisle clear so Aera could walk out. The flight attendant admonished Chohui for jumping ahead of people and made her let others pass as a penalty. I could have told that man it was my fault, but he was intimidating in his snappish way, so I was paralyzed for a moment and had to exit the plane without Chohui. She caught up with us at the line for the women's restroom in the terminal.

I first suspected I was being duped, and brushed it aside, when Mina said, as we waited for our turn, "I've never seen Chicago."

"We can't see much from the airport," I said as a woman with a young girl walked by. "How long until our connecting flight?"

"Maybe I'll get to do some sightseeing here. The Chicago lake, I think," Aera said.

"We're going to Dayton, Aera, and it's Lake Michigan, not Chicago lake," I corrected.

"Top of my list is the Art Institute of Chicago," Mina said.

"We don't have time for any of that. This is only a layover. We're going to Dayton," I said. I saw several people stare at us and then look away. The airport was full of travelers from all nations. I heard Japanese and French, German and Spanish, floating through the air around us.

"We might as well enjoy it while we're here," Mina said.

I threw up my hands, still clueless. My sisters were both very confused, I decided.

"This way to the baggage claim," Mina directed.

"Why would we need to go there?" I asked, halting my steps. "Shouldn't we be looking for our connecting flight?"

"Bogum made the arrangements. We fly to Dayton tomorrow," Mina replied.

I expressed my consternation at such an inconvenience. Again, that was him being the cheapskate that he was.

August in Chicago wasn't cold, but it was windy. The city had an appropriate enough nickname. Mina's floral silk scarf blew off her neck, and Chohui ignored us when all three of us called to her to chase it along the line of cabs in front of the airport.

"We're not eating first, are we?" Aera said.

"What else would we be doing?" I said with a laugh, looking at Mina to join me. It didn't always have to be the two of them against me. Mina and I — we could join up against ridiculous Aera. Our time in San Francisco without her was becoming a more and more pleasant memory. I expected Mina to agree. She was rather disciplined about her eating. No snacking and never eating unless four hours had passed between meals. Aera was a big snacker. I'd caught Mina rolling her eyes as Aera asked for more pretzels from the flight attendant. *No wonder you get sick from eating,* Mina's eyes seemed to say. She hadn't looked at me, but if she had, she would have seen the amusement in my eyes.

Instead Mina said something I wasn't sure I'd heard correctly. The wind carried away half her words: "First we see Jeonga's grandchildren and then —"

"Seona's grandchildren are in Ohio," I corrected but Mina was busy showing a piece of paper to the driver of a car that pulled up, and now she was opening the door and motioning for us to pile in. She slid into the back seat first, clutching her handbag to her chest, as if someone else would look after her large rolling suitcase, which she'd abandoned on the sidewalk. Of course that someone was me because Aera launched in behind Mina. Meanwhile, Chohui was wrangling Aera's suitcase along with her own in the direction of our taxi. This left me to manage my suitcase and Mina's.

I resented their inconsiderateness, my sisters. They thought there would always be someone to take care of the practical matters, someone to look out for them. Even if that someone was taking on more than she could handle. Did the thought occur to them that they could afford it if that person failed? Was everything replaceable?

I rolled my suitcase to the rear of the taxi and handed it off to the driver, who stood by the open trunk. Once my suitcase was secured, I decided to leave Mina's on the sidewalk for Chohui to handle. Sliding into the back seat, I heard my sisters chatting, heads bent together, oblivious to me. I had to insist they move over to make room. They claimed to care about me, but look how involved they were in their conversation with each other.

I looked back through the rear window and saw the driver heave Chohui's bag and then Aera's bright red suitcase into the trunk. Chohui stood beside him, her head lowered to her phone. Again with the phone! What was so important that she couldn't pay attention to her job?

Just then I saw Mina's Louis Vuitton suitcase start rolling away from the spot I'd left it in. Chohui was still engrossed in something on her phone's screen and seemed unaware. As if it had a mind of its own, Mina's suitcase began to pick up speed as it headed away from us on the walkway down the slope. I was about to shout to Chohui because I knew I'd never hear the end of it if Chohui let Mina's suitcase disappear when a woman appeared out of nowhere and stopped the suitcase. She steered it to Chohui, who had run toward the wayward luggage by this time. I watched her thank the stranger. I'd have to speak to her about this later. Mina would be merciless, and Chohui would never be able to work for anyone in Seoul again if disaster had indeed struck.

I glanced at my sisters again. Mina had no idea how close she'd come to having to buy new clothes and whatever else she had in her bag. My sisters were still engaged in deep conversation. I might as well have traveled alone. It would have been less painful all around. I was at the mercy of these two. They chattered on about their children. Well, I focused on what I needed to do. In truth, I would have liked to ask Aera about her restaurant contacts. She might know of a job opening. Her children had vast social circles, but how could I broach it without Mina chiding me for obsessing, as she had in San Francisco?

Our taxi driver got into his seat and started the car. Chohui joined him up front. I tapped her on the shoulder, but she ignored me. She seemed peeved at me, of all things. I didn't lean back because I assumed we'd be at our destination in a few minutes. It took a while, but as the car turned off the highway to lush green lawns, I realized we were not going to a restaurant. Later, I learned that Mina had deceived me. Bogum and his mother had planned an extra stop in Chicago for their own reasons.

CHAPTER 15

Seeing Mina give the driver an address at the airport should have tipped me off right away. I thought it was the address of a restaurant because in San Francisco she'd let Chohui give instructions to the driver. The massive tree-lined streets should have warned me. Why would a restaurant or hotel be in a residential area? But I suspected nothing. As we turned down yet another street with large-porched houses and empty sidewalks, Mina leaned toward me in the taxi and dealt a blow to my chest as surely as if she'd taken her hand and smacked me. She caught my eye to be sure I heard her.

"Remember our conversation about family?" she said with her eyebrows raised.

And then I knew where we were headed. The realization swept over me like it does in a nightmare. I had to get out of the car at once. I wasn't going. Mina couldn't make me.

"Chohui, tell the driver to stop immediately." Chohui whipped her head around, then turned back to the driver and said something in English, but he didn't acknowledge her.

I tried my own version of American words. "Mister, stop now," I said. My heart was attempting to escape from my chest. To get his attention, I tapped on his shoulder.

"You're squishing me," Aera shouted.

"Mister," I repeated.

"Please, can you pull over," Chohui said. As if those were the magic words, the car moved to the side of the road and stopped abruptly.

I opened the car door and hauled myself out. My back twinged. It often gave me trouble. Sometimes everything gave me trouble. I heard my sisters protest behind me, calling my name.

Down the street I rushed. Down the long avenue with its tall trees, branches arching over but just short of touching their partners on the other side — cruel how they tempted each other. The wind rustled the leaves in a menacing way. Whatever Mina and her son and Aera and Chohui, whatever they thought, I did not care. I doubted Chohui had been in on this scheme. She was guileless.

"Samonim, samonim." Chohui's voice cut through my thoughts. I had collapsed on the sidewalk and was struggling to catch my breath. Arms encircled me, patted my back, and eased me to the cool grass. Luckily, I was wearing my linen pants, so I didn't scrape my knees.

Oxygen flowed through my airways again, and I pushed Chohui away. "I can get up by myself," I said to her. "You made me fall, chasing after me that way." Probably not true but I was humiliated.

Chohui apologized at once, which made my sisters sympathize with her and call me ungrateful. A surprising turn of events. I got back into the car.

"Why did you jump out like that?" Mina asked.

"You tricked me," I said.

Mina breathed out heavily and Aera fussed with her gloved hands. It was clear she was feeling guilty.

"Oh, Jeonga, you're really becoming senile," Mina said. "Tricked you? You said you wanted to see your grandchildren. Ned is expecting us."

I didn't reply, because what was the point? We had arrived.

The house was a large brick one with a porch in that Frank Lloyd

Wright style that Siwon had shown me in photographs. He'd admired American houses.

"This isn't Gwangmu's house," I said. This house was in stark contrast to the one my son had bought for himself and his new wife after their small civil ceremony to which I had not been invited.

"This is where Ned, your grandson, lives," Mina replied as she motioned for me to get out of the car.

Of course. I felt foolish for making such a remark. Why had I thought this was Gwangmu's house? I was having trouble tamping down my memories of him now that I was about to meet one of his children. He'd sent a photo when the first child was born. His house had not been as grand and sturdy as this one. It had been small and naked-looking. A shed, really. The house had white plaster on it and a black roof. The photo showed my son with his handsome thick hair standing outside in the glaring sun, holding an infant in his arms, his new wife beside him with a hand shielding her face. At least she was protecting her eyes. I couldn't see much of her face that way, but I thought she was clever, while my foolish son was not — and the baby shouldn't have been in direct sunlight either. He wrote in an accompanying letter that the baby's name was Ned. I read the name several times and asked everyone to pronounce it for me.

"Ned?" Siwon asked when I told him over the phone. He spoke to me from Colorado. "Are you sure?"

"What's wrong with it?" I asked, becoming alarmed.

"Was it Ted, as in Theodore? Theodore Roosevelt was an important president. Maybe it's a T?"

I studied the Hangul that Gwangmu had written along with the English. "No, it's definitely an N."

"Well, then, there must be a good reason for Ned," he'd said, and my sisters agreed that there was no need to fuss.

"Simple and clear," Mina said. "Most American names can be confusing. Take Sylvia, for example. Why did that actor take that as her American name? And why couldn't she spell it Silbia? No, Sylvia is the spelling. It makes me feel as if I'm losing my mind."

They all said I should not seek a Korean name from the naming shaman. Gwangmu told you the baby's name, they'd said to me. *They* meaning my sisters and Siwon on separate occasions. Remember how sensitive your son is to you, they'd said. You're always fighting.

I felt very alone during that time.

Which is the reason I'd caved. I decided to forgo a battle over the name and focus on the sunlight in the yard. I told him to plant a tree. I wrote him a long letter. Not a peach tree, I told him. But some sort of tree. Not too big or else it will fall on the house. Something to give your child some shade. I made the argument for the child's sake because I knew if I said it was for his sake, he'd ignore me. He always did. Once he'd cried out that I thought he was a weakling, that every time I spoke to him, I was saying he wasn't strong enough to handle what everyone else did. Which was not true. I thought he was quite strong. What was a mother supposed to tell her child if not how to protect himself?

So I told him to plant a tree for his child. Let him play under the shade of it in the yard, I'd written. And if you don't have a courtyard (because the photo didn't show any more of the house, I didn't know how far it was from the road), then build some sort of wall or fence. I'd heard stories of children being run over by cars or horses or other people. To which he wrote back: *My wife and I hope you'll visit us soon.* That was it! Such a reply after my lengthy, carefully presented argument. His note was terse and aloof.

Mina pointed out that I should appreciate that he'd written at all. "It's lovely that he wrote to you in his beautiful handwriting," she'd said. She'd always admired his penmanship. I attributed it to the lessons with Siwon.

But I said he was too cheap to call his old mother on the phone. How I wanted to hear his voice. And she said he called Bogum all the time. They talked regularly. And it wasn't her son who was the caller. She'd been at his house when a phone call had come from my son. "Dear good friends as well as cousins," she'd said arrogantly. I say *arrogantly* because she seemed to imply that my son cared more about her family than he did about mine. "And," she added, "I know for a fact that your son thinks you don't want to talk to him after the last time you spoke."

I said that was only because he'd surprised me with the marriage. He hadn't prepared me. All in one short phone call. He'd spoken in a rush of words: "I'm married. We went to the courthouse, that's how they do it here in America. She's not Korean."

"What is she? A palm tree?" I joked.

"Mother," he said.

"Too bad, I hear palm trees are stunning. So many in Hawaii — why don't you move there? Tall and majestic."

"Mother," he repeated, slower this time, frustration seeping through.

"Let me guess. If she's not Korean, what is she?" I burst out laughing.

He hung up.

We used to joke. He used to laugh. But inside I was crying. I had not been informed about his engagement. I had not been asked to attend his wedding.

"Why does it matter?" Aera said. "You know once they go to America, they're American anyway. Your son is no longer Korean. Don't kid yourself. They're your blood, no matter what."

I could see the logic of that. My son goes to America, stays in America, therefore he's American. He would change his citizenship to American. In fact, I believe he did. But he'd always be my son even if his wife poisoned his and his children's minds so they'd cut ties with me. It was easier to imagine she was the villain, though I knew nothing about her.

No more complaints, no more arguments. No more calls. He'd sent me a brief note and that was all. That photograph. And then, after two more years, another photograph. No accompanying letter. I checked the envelope in disbelief. In the photo, he was standing in the same spot in front of the same house. Again, no tree. Again, no shade. He was holding another baby this time and there was a child at his knee. The boy Ned. Tall for a two-year-old, with his father's same thick hair. This time his wife was not in the picture, but the boy at his knee had his hand up to shield his face, and I thought he was quick-witted like his mother. A little imitator of his mother. My son, on the other hand, had not learned. It was difficult to tell, but I thought he looked thinner, his pants hiked up a little higher on his waist and his cheeks gaunt, but maybe it was because they were darkened by the sun. In his arms an infant with limbs extended. Why wasn't she swaddled in a blanket? What about sunburn; what about insect bites? The dangers were everywhere.

We had a girl! We named her Pam! he wrote in Hangul and English on the back of the photograph. Nothing personal to me. It could have been sent to a thousand people.

I wrote back and told him Pam was a beautiful name. I didn't say I thought it was ridiculous. I'd seen enough American movies to know that was no name for a proper young girl. When I told Siwon, he didn't believe me. "You must be wrong," he said. "I have a student named Pamela — Pam is just a nickname."

I wished I could say he was right.

I also wrote that I wondered where his lovely wife was. Why wasn't she in the photograph? I said I wished to know my daughter-in-law.

Wasn't that a gracious effort on my part? I didn't criticize him. I didn't mention the tree; I didn't mention how thin he looked or that the sun was giving him skin cancer or that an infant should not be held out to the elements that way. I offered to pay for plane tickets if he wanted to bring his family for the New Year celebrations. I told him I understood if traveling with his young children might dissuade him, in which case he could come alone. I told him I could visit him if that was more convenient.

He didn't write back.

You could see why it wasn't a fight that time. No reason for estrangement at all. I was grateful for the scraps of news that Bogum passed on to me through Mina. He took my son's side — as if there were sides and we were at war. Which we weren't. I just didn't visit. I couldn't tell you why. Bogum wanted me to go, I could feel that, but if Gwangmu couldn't even call me to say hello, how could I just show up? My son didn't call even on Chuseok or Independence Day or any of the holidays that he knew were important to Koreans. I figured he wasn't Korean anymore, so why would he bother?

I realized in those days how I'd misjudged my own mother. When Seona eloped, my mother had seemed indifferent. "She has to make her own way," I heard her say over and over to my father. I'd interpreted her subdued tone to mean the loss hadn't affected her as deeply as it had the rest of us, but now I know she had been holding herself together and her quiet voice had been a dam she created to keep back more sorrow than the rest of us felt. Probably even more than my father did. For all his wringing of hands and pacing, he hadn't given birth to her, hadn't nursed her or disciplined her. Mother had only tried to give Seona everything she ever wanted. I found myself doing the same things she had when I was raising my son and seeing reflected in his face the same expressions I had turned toward my mother.

Even Mina and Aera commented on how much I resembled our mother when I was a new parent.

I wondered if my mother had loved my father, had known a great love, even. Those were the thoughts later in my life after Siwon left for America. Would I wish it had never happened so I could be as content with my life as my mother had seemed to be with hers?

CHAPTER 16

Now I stood in front of my grandson's house. Gwangmu's son's house. I looked more closely at it, allowing the others to go ahead. Sons weren't supposed to die before their mothers. Joyce had a chance to save her son. I had not. The wide porch was made of dark wood, and gray stone supported a dark slate roof. I paused on the walkway. Siwon would have liked this house. I was reminded again of one of the last times we spoke.

We were writing less and less by then, arguing more and more on the phone. It seemed I had a talent for disagreeing with everyone. I said I didn't like any of Frank Lloyd Wright's houses. He said I didn't appreciate quality. Did it matter? I asked. He said it mattered and hung up the phone. In the past he used to be amused by my disagreements with him and seemed to see them as opportunities to tease me and show off. But I knew it was because I had stopped visiting him in America. Everyone was going to Colorado without me.

That was the past. Now Mina was already on the porch, at the door, and was waving to us to hurry. The taxi driver was piling the suitcases on top of one another on the sidewalk behind me. When I made it up to the porch, Mina, Aera, and Chohui were nowhere to be found. I considered sitting in the large rocking chair by the formidable cypress front door and waiting for them. Let them visit with my family. How much effort had Mina and Aera made over the years to get to know my grandchildren? Did they know anything about my grandchildren's children? That thought pulled me up short. I wondered how many great-grandchildren I actually had. I couldn't recall ever hearing about any births. Had Bogum said anything about Ned or Pam having children?

I was settling into the rocking chair when Chohui opened the door and stuck her head out.

"What are you doing there, samonim?" she asked.

"If you're coming to get the suitcases, don't bother," I said. "I'll keep an eye on them from here."

"But samonim, everyone is waiting for you inside," she said and headed down the steps. This was new. An impudence. Did she think she knew better than I did about such matters? When we returned to Korea, would she challenge every direction I gave? Bringing her to the United States was going to prove to be a thorn in my side for years to come. Or so I thought.

"Chohui, don't make me repeat myself," I said.

She halted on the stairs and pivoted back to me. "I could put the suitcases on the porch."

"Do you see anyone about?" I waved toward the street. "This is not a place where people come and snatch your belongings. And besides, we're leaving very soon. It would be a wasted effort on your part." That last I added because she had started to slump.

"If you're sure," she said and walked back up the steps to me.

I nodded. "What are they doing inside?" I asked.

"Lunch," she said. "Ned bought Korean food."

"What kind of Korean food?"

"All sorts," she said. A rumbling sound came from the direction of her person and I realized she was hungry.

"Go on, then." I waved her to the door.

"Not without you, samonim," she said.

"I'll be in soon," I replied.

She didn't seem convinced, lingering at the door. Maybe because I'd dashed off earlier.

"Surely insects of all kinds will enter the house if you hold the door open that way," I said.

She promptly shut it and stood examining the porch, looking all around, but she was as startled as I was when the door opened again and Mina stepped out on the arm of a man. Aera followed. I could see her out of the corner of my eye, but I was entranced by the man. He had a handsome face beneath a beautiful head of dense, dark hair. He was certainly in his fifties, based on his leathered complexion — which a dermatologist in Korea might have corrected — and had a trim athletic form that gave him the air of a man of leisure. Probably played a great deal of golf. If Gwangmu had lived ten years longer and eaten well, he would have been the spitting image of this man.

"Where is she?" he asked Mina in English, looking toward the sidewalk.

Mina pointed to me, and he turned and said, "There you are, Grandmother."

I didn't have the strength to stand. Gwangmu's son, Ned, was in front of me.

"Charming — you must see the food," Mina boomed in Korean in my direction.

He waved to the doorway, which Aera was fully occupying. "Shall we go in? I'm sorry I don't speak Korean," he said.

His lips curled in on themselves. Resentment or simply uncertainty? So much of my son, even in his expressions. I expected a similarity but not such a complete duplicate. Where were signs of his white American mother? I braced myself.

"Where's your mother? Your sister?" I asked in my best English.

"My mother passed away last year, in her sleep," he said. "She was eighty."

"Too young," we all chorused.

And then I added, "We'll head to the cemetery, don't worry. I'll make sure she has a clean, well-maintained burial area."

"It's really okay," he said with confusion in his eyes.

"She's buried beside my son?" I said.

"Right, yes, that's where she is," he said. "The money you sent paid for two plots."

Burial sites were cheaper in America than in Korea, it seemed. Good news, for once. "So tell us about Pam," I said, warming up to this replica of my son and preparing to stand. He stepped forward, dropping Mina's arm, and extended a hand to me.

"Pam is — we have to sit down together for a long time to explain that one," he said.

"At my age, every story is a long one," I replied. Even his hand looked like his father's. He laughed, and even though I could tell Mina and Aera didn't understand, they laughed too. Chohui gave me a big smile.

"Oh, come inside, Jeonga," Mina said in Korean. I didn't hesitate another second. I placed my hand in my grandson's. It took me several tries, going back and forth, to rise from the rocking chair, even with Ned's help.

"Will the luggage be all right if we leave them, Ned?" Chohui asked as they waited for me to get to my feet.

I told Chohui to shush; why trouble Ned when I'd already given her explicit instructions? Didn't she trust me?

When I was at the door, Ned dropped my hand and bounded back down the stairs to the clump of luggage. For his age, he moved with ease, hauling each suitcase up to the porch in no time. "They'll be safe here," he said, catching his breath. Well, apparently not in as good shape as I'd first thought.

Inside the house, I noticed that the dark oak paneling and heavy curtains were not inviting, nor was the dampness. Had any window been opened in years? Still, the lunch was indeed a pleasant sight. He hadn't made any of it but he'd ordered in from a Korean restaurant, he explained. I didn't stop him from telling us this. It seemed to be his form of an apology. The effort was admirable, and I applauded him for it. After many days in America, I missed Korean food. My sisters and Chohui joined me. Ned seemed to take delight in our response. Between bites, I looked at the photos that covered the walls and were set up in frames on many surfaces throughout the dining room. So many that when you picked one up, you saw another one immediately behind it.

There weren't many photographs of my son. Most were of Ned and Pam and their mother and other strangers. When I returned to Korea, I decided, I would send Ned photographs of his father as a child to add to this collection, to make him matter as much as all these other people in this house did.

Mina had her bartering voice on. "My son, Bogum," she said in English. "My son telephoned you, yes?"

We were seated around a large dining table, Mina right beside me. It was crowded because there were too many pieces of furniture for the space.

Ned smiled broadly. "Bogum, yes."

"Uncle," Aera said with her chopsticks raised.

Ned seemed perplexed.

"She means you can call him your uncle because he's older than you. He's your —" Chohui paused to ask me about the relationship, and I confirmed it for her. "He and your father were cousins," she said.

Aera nodded.

"Yes, Uncle Bogum," Ned replied.

"This is your grandmother," Mina continued, jabbing me in the side with her elbow, then breaking into an embarrassing giggle.

What was her point? I wondered. We'd already been through this on the porch.

"I know," Ned said after a pause.

I had to grab hold of this conversation before Ned believed us all to be fools like Mina; she sentimentalized these sorts of relationships, while Ned clearly did not.

I picked up a photo that was close to me on the credenza, a woman holding a book in front of a small child. "Yours or Pam's child?" I asked.

"Neither," Ned said between bites of room-temperature beef. I wanted to ask Chohui to heat it up for him, but it would point out that he wasn't being a thoughtful host, so I said nothing about it.

To break the awkward silence, I said as loudly as I could, looking straight at Mina, "Family is important."

His shoulders relaxed at my words. Setting his chopsticks down, he filled us in. Turned out that the child in the photograph was a student of Pam's in her kindergarten class. He explained that his sister hadn't been able to have children of her own. "She's past the age now for it to be a safe option," he finished, wiping his mouth.

"Jiu had a baby when she was an older woman," I said without thinking.

"Who's that?" he asked.

Everyone stared at me.

"I'm sorry about Pam," I said.

Ned patted my hand. "It's all right, Grandmother. Pam has a long history of health problems. It's not a secret, but it has inspired me to look into a family mystery."

My heart picked up its pace, reminding me of my own secret.

CHAPTER 17

E ven when she was a child, she was always sick." Ned began to tell
us about his sister. He gave us a tight-lipped smile, which helped
when I couldn't understand his fast English. He was going to deliver
grim news, no doubt. Sitting here in this house in Chicago, I ordered
myself to compose my face. Mina and Aera were watching me. I saw
their eyes sweep the room and then pause on me occasionally, as if my
response would help them comprehend his words.

Ned continued, "Adoption was what they should have done to
begin with, but her husband wasn't interested. Anyway, that's in the
past — she has a teaching job, and in Singapore she can have a new
life without reminders."

"Excuse me, what reminders?" I said.

"I mean miscarriages. She had seven that she knew of in all the
years she tried."

"Seven," Chohui echoed.

"Your English is not so good; he must mean two," I said to her.

"She's right, you're wrong," Aera said to me in Korean. "I'm good
with English numbers."

I blushed. "Since when do you know English better than I —"

"Did they try IVF?" Chohui asked. "I've read about it."

"Yeah." He nodded. "Anyway, Pam's problems with pregnancy reminded me of another time when she was very ill," he said.

A family mystery, he'd said. Well, this was of the medical variety. He wasn't any closer to finding out about Hayun and Ellery after all. I'd been wrong to worry.

"Surely this is from your mother's family, a health problem inherited from her side," Aera said in Korean.

Chohui translated. Ned paused a moment and then said, "It's not about blame, I assure you, or even tracing exactly who might have been sick with what." His cheeks were flushed, and he wiped his hands on the tops of his khaki trousers. Another reminder of Gwangmu. The same gestures. My boy.

"What was she sick with?" Mina asked. Chohui translated again.

I was glad for my sister's nosiness because I wanted to hear Ned's answer too. I imagined Gwangmu's anxious face as a father. His head down. His precious child ill and what could he do about it? Did he worry about fate's role in possibly losing a daughter after he had let the other one go to San Francisco?

Ned cleared his throat. "So, when we were kids, Pam was diagnosed with leukemia."

We collectively gasped. Cancer.

Ned nodded. "Well, back then they were just starting to do bone-marrow transplants. This was 1973. I remember my parents arguing one night. I was going to be tested to see if I could be a donor for my sister, but it hadn't happened yet, and my parents were nervous. We were all nervous. I didn't understand everything, but I remember I was sent to bed early but I crept out because I heard them arguing in their bedroom. From the hallway, I heard Dad say if I didn't turn out to be a good match, he had one other person we could try but it had to be the absolute last resort. You see, he'd always told us that there weren't many people with the last name Cha in Korea."

We all nodded. A common fact in Korea. Hak and Cha were the smaller clans among all the other families on our peninsula nation and had to be even more careful than others in who they married.

"Go on," Mina told my grandson.

"My dad used to say it to show us how special we were."

Everyone sighed but Ned, who wryly smiled. I recognized his smile as my own.

"Not a good thing in this case, of course," he continued. "So my mother begged him to tell her who it was. She asked if it was his mother." He paused then and looked at me. My sisters and Chohui regarded me too.

"I would have done it," I said in a shaky voice. Why hadn't Gwangmu asked me? He'd shared nothing of his daughter's illness. Just those two letters, one when each child was born.

Ned sighed. "No, it wasn't you."

His curt reply stung. The matter-of-factness of his tone. But Gwangmu still should have told me. The burden he'd borne without me wasn't fair to either of us.

"Then who?" Mina asked.

The image of teenage Gwangmu holding a baby in his arms in Korea flared up in my mind's eye. Ellery's mother, Jiu, of course. Gwangmu suspected his firstborn could have been a donor. The realization made me stand up from the chair. Everyone looked at me and I didn't know what to say. Thankfully, Chohui rescued me with her question.

"What happened to Pam?" Chohui said.

"Tell us," Mina urged.

"She lived, obviously," Aera said in a dry tone. "She's in Singapore, remember?"

Ned's face relaxed into a smile. "You're right, Great-Auntie," he said.

We all sat back. The air in the house suddenly seemed fresher. I felt compelled to mitigate my sister's rudeness.

"Well, I'm sure your father meant there would be someone who also had bone marrow that would work. This is America, after all, and they can help all kinds of people with cancer now, especially leukemia," I said. "With enough money, everything can be cured in America. We're on our way right now to help a relative."

"Indeed," Mina agreed. "Do you have cancer on your mother's side of the family?"

"What business is that of ours?" I replied. "Of course it's from her side of the family."

"It's good to know," Aera replied.

"Will you two stop bickering?" I said. I glanced at the bookshelves that surrounded us, offering a different tack. His name was on the spine of one volume. "Look here, Ned, how wonderful that you're a writer of books. I enjoy reading novels."

"Are you a medical expert?" Chohui said, studying the books in the pile on the table.

"No, but I learned so much just by listening to my parents and the doctors in the hospital. Turns out I was a match. If I weren't, then no one else really could have been, unless my parents had a child somewhere we didn't know about." He laughed at that point and my sisters and Chohui were so intent on his story that no one saw me clasp a hand over my mouth.

"But I remembered their conversation out of the blue one day, which is why I started this family-tree project. I don't even remember what prompted it — strange. So then I called Bogum — I mean Uncle Bogum — and he helped, but there are gaps. Let me get something to show you what I mean," he said, and without another word, Ned pushed back his chair and left the room in a hurry.

"He means well," Aera said as she picked through the japchae on her plate. "He looks exactly like Gwangmu."

"Not exactly," I replied, and my heart lurched. No one could be my son. Even if I saw a resemblance, I didn't want anyone else to. I got up and began to pace.

"Look at all these pictures. Ned's mother went overboard, don't you think? I hear that people do this to make themselves seem more important than they are. Ned must take after her," Mina said, getting to her feet too and peering at framed photographs. Her intention was to snoop. She even opened drawers. "So much clutter."

"He's not married. Something must be wrong with him," Aera said.

The duplicity was breathtaking. Only moments before, they had been fawning over him, and now they were ripping apart his character and rifling through his mother's precious keepsakes. My sisters' hypocrisy made me want to throttle them both. How they would have fanned the flames of local gossip if they'd known that Gwangmu had fathered the child of a laborer in my house. I was astonished to see my suspicions confirmed. They pretended I should be in touch with my grandson when all they wanted was to find material with which to gossip — the nerve of them. I felt a familiar rage. They said these things aloud in front of Chohui, who was invisible to them, being from another class. I looked at my aide, who was concentrating on the screen of her phone, a frown on her face. My sisters had been relieved when Seona ran off to elope. I remembered Mina and Aera thanking our father for standing firm on blocking Seona's relationship with the man she said she loved for the sake of their own new marriages and unblemished reputations.

"They're already married off," I'd cried to my father. "Why does it matter who Seona marries?"

"Their in-laws are looking for even a small stone to throw at our family. It's human nature. They'll use it to justify their superiority over your sisters. They'll make them suffer in large and small public ways," he had replied, the only time I could remember that he'd given me his full attention. "Don't ever be like Seona. She thinks she can live outside society's judgments."

The swinging door to the dining room yielded just then to Ned's back, for his arms were balancing a tower of files and notebooks. Chohui moved glasses and dishes from the dining table to make space.

He thanked her, placed his load down, and wiped his face with his sleeve, just like Gwangmu. The pang in my chest cut straight through my middle. Again and again, the reminders.

With nervousness, I peered at the piece of paper on top of the pile to which he pointed, my hand over my mouth again, tamping down the nausea that was creeping upward. Sea garbage, that's what it was, wave after wave edging toward my throat.

"Samonim, are you all right?" Chohui said to me in a soft voice.

I nodded in a brisk fashion and shushed her with a finger to my lips. I needed to study this work Ned had done. If I opened my mouth, I might hurl vomit. The question I was focused on was: Did he know the truth about Ellery?

I went right to the bottom of the diagram, the most recent descendants. Several small boxes with names in English filled in were connected by lines to other boxes above. Ned pointed to each branch, beginning with the top.

To my eyes, the diagram was correct except for a few omissions. I thought about how Siwon would have admired my grandson for his diligence as a scholar.

"You're a wonder to embark on this in English," Mina said in Korean, which Chohui translated.

Ned beamed. "You're too kind." Then he turned to me. "So this project started because of the next book I'm writing. The thing is, I can't really shake the thought that my father was speaking about someone else in the family when Pam was sick. It's a leap, I know, but I can't quite explain it. He said other things during those years. I was a child, of course, but it's the only explanation that makes any sense. I've been wanting to ask you — I'm doing research on my father's generation and I've come across some documents. I believe you have an entire branch of the family that no one knows about."

The room disappeared. I had tunnel vision, seeing only the piece of paper with the diagram of the family tree.

In the distance I heard Aera say in Korean, "What does he mean?"

Chohui's voice floated through. "Do you mean illegitimate?"

I was there in the room, listening to them contemplate the existence of someone who I knew very well did in fact exist, when my phone vibrated in my pocket. As if in slow motion, I took it out and saw a text message from Ellery. I read it over three times to be sure I wasn't misunderstanding what it said.

Thanks for all your help, Mrs. Cha. I wanted to tell you right away that I just got offered a job in Dayton. I'm flying out tomorrow. I will visit you in Korea after Jordan is better. Thank you again!

In the background there was the swirl of more conversations. I deleted the text and put my phone in my pocket.

"Well, there are those ancestry tests for that. We could find out," Mina said. Her disembodied voice circled like water emptying into a drain. "The other day, my daughter said that in America people are finding relatives of all sorts through those kits. Who knows what your father might have engaged in? Our family is pretty straightforward. Our sister Seona, of course, she eloped, but we know from her son that she only had two children."

"No," I shouted. The room zoomed back into place. I could hear everything again as usual: the scrape of the chair against the wooden floor as Mina adjusted it, the swish of Aera's gloved fingers as she rubbed her thumb against her pointer finger. "Absolutely preposterous, no such thing happened, not ever. Your father was an honorable man, honest, caring, gentle, the most thoughtful man who ever lived."

Chohui was up and by my side, restraining my arm. "Samonim, Ned is not saying he wasn't that. He's asking if his father —"

I struggled to free myself from her grasp. "Get away from me."

Desperation can lead us all over the cliff.

CHAPTER 18

I pushed past Chohui and my sisters, who had stood up to lunge for me, so many hands trying to hold me to the living in that house in Chicago. If only I'd let them. Instead, I fought as if they were death itself. How wrong I was. How can we know whom we should battle? We have only the lessons we've learned up until that moment, partial wisdom with the arrogance to believe we had the complete view.

Deep in my ignorance, I scurried along the wide American avenues until I reached a busy intersection with stores and bumper-to-bumper traffic. Across the street, I saw a shimmering bench. It looked like a lifeline — the irony of that notion, when even strangers tried to alert me, their voices raised together: "Bus! Bus!" I thought they were call-ing to the driver for themselves.

I was wrong. They were calling out a warning. The Chicago transit system vehicle squashed me. I died at that intersection in America.

"Jeonga," a voice called to me.

I looked about. Orange mist all around. I was alone.

"Jeonga," the voice called again.

I looked down. Dressed in a hemp hanbok and white sneakers in my one-hundred-five-year-old body, I was in an orange, persimmon-scented afterlife. It took a while for feeling to return, for sensory awareness to connect me again to this form of a body that I had, different but oh too similar to what I had lost on that street in America. Why couldn't I have a younger body if I was to prove myself in this strange place?

"Jeonga." This time the memory of my sister Seona emerged from the cloudiness of my consciousness. Strong enough to last. We were sisters. That fact alone released a flood of images from my past.

"Jeonga, your turn," she'd said to me decades earlier. "Remember the song."

I recalled being with my sister in the town square in Korea long ago. Clumps of old women crooned a song: *My love has gone, who asked me to live together for five hundred years, compassion nowhere. I cannot go on. Geureochi, amuryeom geureochi. Five hundred years.*

They sang about love beyond life, beyond death. I remembered the love. That remained, the feeling of love; everything else you forget. I remembered my sister's love, which filled me, even in this afterlife, with hope. I wanted to see her again. I walked forward, stumbling every few steps with my old-lady feet. My sister's voice beckoned, and I followed, my hands outstretched before me into the damp orange mist. But something pulled at me from behind too. Which way to go? Something on the periphery in the distance over my shoulder, the weight of dread, expanded behind me like a cape. I walked into the colored mist, away from it, but it pursued me.

Remembering Seona made the problems I'd left in America fully reveal themselves. All at once, I remembered everything. I can't tell you how — it just happened. A film sequence of years ago. Seona had gone away and left. She'd left and never written to me. Not ever. The memory frightened me, as final as it was. How could I have forgotten? Other memories from our childhood emerged: Her face with the sesame-seed mole above her eyebrow flushed with anger. I knew she was leaving our family forever. And beyond those came the ones that took my breath away. I winced in pain. Gwangmu's head lifting from where it hinged chronically downward, his chin on his chest: "Why, why, why did you send her away?" The beautiful whorl of hair on top of his head.

Sobs welled up in my throat — all the regrets had followed me into the afterlife. I knew I'd brought this upon myself. I was sorry. I'd said I was sorry. How many apologies could one person make to fix mistake after mistake? Would I suffer forever? From the time Seona left our family, I'd kept secrets and made decisions to keep more secrets, to keep people apart. Seona, Siwon, my son, Seona's son, their children, their children's children. All for what? To protect our family's reputation? Now the entire world would know, from Korea to America. And everyone would think I had done nothing to fix these mistakes. I'd died an old woman who had learned nothing and done nothing to avert the biggest disaster of them all. Why did the small dangers matter when they led to the disaster of all disasters? The family was doomed.

The fear kept rising in me. The great-grandchildren — they would find out; they'd discover the whole story. Everyone would talk; everyone would know, and they'd despise me. Ellery would hate me. And it was all my fault. I had failed. Ned and my sisters with Chohui at the dining table in Chicago, America, scrutinizing Ned's charts. The family tree had been incomplete, the way he had drawn it. It had blank squares. But I knew they were close.

I had to do something to get back to them. But how? I searched my mind. Seona was calling to me. I knew her voice. She must be my guide here in the afterlife. Folklore told us after we died, we were in a holding place for forty-nine days, and a guardian would guide us through. I must be in that place. Even movies said so. Chohui had told me about them. It was the only explanation. I looked around for Seona. Only orange-shaded persimmon mist around me, but she had to be here somewhere. Why else did I hear her voice? This probability brought me a mixture of sadness and relief. If she was my guide, it meant she had died before I did. My chin sank to my chest as a deep sorrow pooled there.

Just then I heard my sister's voice again, this time close by, near my ear, a whisper: "Jeonga."

Whipping my head about, my arms extended, I searched as if I could grab hold of her. "Where are you, Seona?" I called. I walked, arms outstretched, and stumbled. This time, I lost my balance and found myself on hard ground, on my bottom. The pain was a shock. I cried from helplessness. Why didn't she answer? I called her name over and over.

From my eighties on, I'd had trouble with my tear ducts. Tiny openings in the inner angles of my eyelids had narrowed with age, causing blockage of tears. A minor irritation that had prevented tears from releasing when I was alive caused tremendous backup now. My eyes welled up but only a few tears actually surfaced to wet my cheeks. I realized I had hardly cried in the last few decades of my life. Wailing was still possible, even in a low-timbered croon.

I'd begun to doubt my ears when I was startled out of my despair by a thud at my knee. My sister's favorite fruit, its orangish-red plump shape with the wide green cap, lying on its side in the light orange dust; it had rolled into my leg. When I held it up, I could make out Seona's teeth marks as clearly as I had seen them a century ago. The front-left-tooth imprint was crooked while the right one was straight. My pulse accelerated and I got to my feet.

"Seona, I know it's you. Come out. Come out," I called, shaking the persimmon at the air.

In response, another persimmon appeared a few meters ahead, this one to the side, again with just one bite taken out of it the way Seona used to test persimmons in the bowl on the table of our childhood house because she thought another in the bowl must be sweeter than the one in her hand.

The thought lifted my spirits. Surely this was a communication! Seona was orchestrating this game, the way she had all our childhood contests. There was a certain satisfaction in remembering. I left the fruit on the ground and continued on my way to the next persimmon, trusting. Seona would answer all my questions soon — she must be waiting for me.

As in our childhood, I knew it was futile to try to change her mind; she would not appear until she was ready to appear. "I'll play along," I called.

The orange mist cleared at a fork in the path, but I saw another abandoned persimmon down the trail of the left branch, same teeth marks. A wind gathered around me, but I pressed on, following it around a curving bend.

"I see what you did, Seona, I can keep up," I said, hurrying.

This time a scattering of several persimmons materialized ahead, and I despaired at how far I had to go. Still I trudged on. She wanted to have her fun before helping me. That was the sister I remembered. Persimmon after persimmon with indentations.

After what seemed too long a while, I wanted to give up. I remembered this had been the case in our past too. I was often worn down by Seona. Surrendering might bring compassion — if I collapsed right here and didn't move, would she finally show herself? I stopped in my tracks, my hands on my hips, challenging her.

This time a persimmon appeared out of the mist in front of me, rolled, and hit the toe of my sneaker. I bent down and felt its heft in my palm. I ran my hand over its unblemished smooth skin. Seona hadn't taken a bite out of this one. It looked delicious. The flesh of the fruit gave when I squeezed it. A good sign. Just then, I heard a rippling click overhead, like geese returning in the spring, that rose in pitch.

Not any sound that was human. I peered up. It frightened me. And then I breathed a sigh of relief: Fear was another tactic I remembered my sister had used. I waited until the mist shifted and swirled and the sound stopped. Another persimmon lay ahead. I could see the dark small globe in the path, but I was suddenly thirsty like I'd never been before. The juice of the persimmon in my hand would quench that thirst, I knew it would. I could almost taste it before I put it to my lips. All mine. I would eat one persimmon. What was the harm in that?

I plunged my teeth into the fruit. Too eager. Suddenly, the sting of its unripeness tore the roof of my mouth. I threw the persimmon to the ground. Seona's laughter sounded from somewhere to my side. No mistake now. Full-throated glee. I should have known better. If she hadn't eaten it, there was a reason.

"Not fair," I shouted. When no answer came, I called to her again: "Stop torturing me." I'd said such things when we were children. Rarely had she given in and come back. Why had I ever believed she cared about me? I swerved left and right, ignoring each persimmon, afraid to touch another one. No choice before me but to continue. I stumbled forward. The fog deepened but I pressed on, branching paths off branching paths, following the orange globes along the trail they made. Seona was selfish. Mean and selfish and I should have known better than to follow her. I stumbled and fell. I got up again and walked on. My childhood anger revived, I stomped with each step the way I had long ago, but the hurt cut deeper than it ever had in the past.

I trudged along, growing weary. My pinkie toes hurt as they rubbed against the inside of my sneakers. The persimmons cruelly dotted the path ahead of me. "Seona!" I shouted. "Stop." She must know, of course, that I'd failed to preserve our family's reputation, that I'd cursed the generations to come. Why else was she tormenting me?

The horizon looked the same — just a thin dark orange line in every direction. I walked slower as the persimmons stretched ahead in greater intervals. And then they vanished. I doubled back to make sure I hadn't missed one. No matter how hard I looked, none appeared. The path dissolved. I was in a vast field of orange mist. I trudged forward.

Over time I wondered if I was going forward or in a circle. Why did we humans think we knew what it would be like to die? Pure arrogance. I was hearing things because I wished for them to be so. My heart sank. The arches of my feet hurt now too. I gave up again, this time in the middle of the field, and collapsed.

"I give up," I shouted, but it sounded like a squawk.

I put my head in my arms and cried. "I'm sorry," I sobbed, rubbing my eyes surging with trapped tears.

"What are you sorry for?" came a reply. It was my sister's voice; I'd know it anywhere. I wasn't imagining it. I raised my head, wanting to tell her everything in that moment in a rush, but I wasn't ready; something in me held back.

"Seona, show yourself," I said instead.

"What are you sorry for?" she repeated from somewhere I still couldn't see.

I stood up, turned all around. "Sister, help me," I said, sobs arising unexpectedly again.

"Silly, you never surprise me — all these years and the same silly willful Jeonga. I am trying to help you, but maybe you don't deserve it."

"Of course I deserve it. Why do you say that?" I felt a rage rise in me. "If you show yourself, I'll explain."

"Oh, you're telling me what I ought to do?"

I sputtered and then I stopped. "I said I was sorry. What more do you want?"

"You didn't make it to Ohio, America," she said. "One hundred and five years you lived, and you didn't make it."

I dabbed my eyes — a few droplets had made it past those clogged ducts — with my long skirt. "It was our sisters' fault. They came with me to America and then made us go to Illinois. If they hadn't done that, I would have helped your great-grandson. I was on my way to him when they delayed me."

"Could be true." Her voice came wafting over my head. "Silly Jeonga, come this way."

A path appeared ahead of me. "Why should I? It's over; I failed. My whole life was a failure and now all the generations to come will suffer because of me."

"Why are you giving up?" Seona's voice floated through the air to me.

"What can I do?" I wailed.

"Just like you to quit," she said.

"It's not my fault," I blubbered on. "I'm dead."

"So?" she said.

"So!" I threw back at her.

"You're always putting up walls."

"I'm dead. I failed."

"True, but that doesn't mean you're finished," she said.

CHAPTER 19

I shook my head back and forth. "No more. I've been following your persimmons and you've given me no answers," I said and refused to continue. I was done being tormented by my sister, even in the afterlife.

There I was in the middle of an orange field with a walkway in front of me, and I was making demands. I couldn't help it. My feet hurt. It was my old role to talk with my sister like this, and hearing Seona's voice gave me comfort and courage.

"Weak character. Appa said it and he's right," she said. "Quitter."

I wailed louder.

"Do you want to see Eomma and Appa?" she said.

I looked up and nodded slowly. "And you," I said. "You too, Seona. I want to see you."

A wind whipped up around me. I covered my face with my hands, coughing, and my eyes and nose filled with orange sand. A roar pummeled my ears. And then in another moment there was quiet. The cyclone had dissipated. I shook my head, rubbed my ears, blinked, and rubbed them again. Thick sunlight of monsoon season beat on my head and shoulders. I shielded my eyes with my hand and stared without comprehension. A solid wooden structure was before me. And then I knew what it was, my eyes able to focus. Ahead was the gate to our childhood home, solid old wood in large planks marked by three

rows of iron rivets. The surface was varnished in clear protective fin-
ish. I stood and ran to it, touched the smooth wood and raised mounds
of the joints. I didn't care how I looked; I wished I could wrap my arms
around it. Instead, all I could manage was to spread my arms and press
my cheek against the surface. Home.

All I wanted was to be in my mother's arms again. To be young,
before everything went wrong. The gate was heavy, but I pulled it
open. There she was — my sister Seona as a young child, her back to
me in the swept-dirt yard. She was hunched over beside the seesaw I
knew well — the long wooden board perched on a rolled straw mat.
I'd made it in. I was home. Eternity could come and I would be safe.
Farther ahead was our house with its long wooden porch and curled
eaves, the hibiscus in full bloom, purple and pink varieties. I breathed
a sigh of relief and focused on my sister. No one else was about.

"Seona," I called to her. "I'm here!" My voice sounded like a croak.
I touched my neck, felt familiar loose skin. There was no mirror for
me to verify it, but I could see that my hands were still more than a
century aged, with their hideous liver spots in big disks on my raised
veins, my bones with their deep ridges, the knuckles knobby and scaly.
They looked worse here in the afterlife. How could that be? Did we
keep aging forever? How come I wasn't young like she was? I wanted
to step on the board and jump with her, first me, then her, teetering
together like when we were children.

My sister's response was to look up at the sky. I looked too — bright
sun and the wings of something red. A cardinal, exactly like the
strange one that had appeared outside my apartment in Seoul when I
was working on Joyce's letter.

I wet my lips with my tongue and swallowed. Cool water to drink
would help. "Sister, don't you remember me?" I asked and approached
her, but the long skirt over my old-woman legs rustled and hin-
dered me.

Her eyes were squinting, and her bird lips opened, and I saw that I was wrong. She wasn't five or six years old. She was younger than I'd ever known her. And her song — I didn't understand the words. Did we lose language after we died? Did she not understand me or I her?

She didn't show that she was aware I was with her in any way. She gathered dirt in the palms of her hands and let it fall through the spaces between her fingers. In case I scared her off, I stopped a few steps away and hunched over on the ground so I was at her level, listening to her made-up language of *ahs*.

"Seona, are we dead?" I said as gently as I could. My sister had her head bent over and the stubborn zigzag part clearly showed above her braided hair. Her eyes narrowed as she concentrated. Even in play, she was focused intensely on the task at hand.

In response to my words, she jerked her head toward the house instead of in my direction. But it was another voice she was attuned to, and now I heard it too.

Our mother's voice. It was calling, "Seona, our Seona, where are you?"

I watched with my heart in my mouth as my mother appeared from the side of the house where I knew the kitchen to be and walked toward us. What would she say when she saw me? I imagined her face relaxing into calm joy. She had a way of nodding when she was elated, as if she had believed in the arrival of good news and was now vindicated when it was confirmed.

I rose as she glided down toward us, as firm as the trees in our yard but in motion. Her forehead was smooth with eyebrows that never required shaping, slender winged arches. Straight and strong, she was walking with one arm outstretched and the other on the top edge of her maroon hanbok's skirt where it met the cream-colored jacket and I knew in that instant that she was pregnant with me. I was in two places at the same time, in the yard but in her uterus too. The ground

beneath my laced modern sneakers was solid and yet I felt the buoy-
ancy of the fluid that I was suspended in slosh about as she walked.
Here but aware of being there too; I occupied both places at once. As
she drew near, the feeling of being in her womb felt more real than
what my eyes presented to me. Was I going to vanish now? Return to
being a fetus? I suddenly objected to it. I wanted my memories. I
wanted to face her now as an old woman.

"Eomma, look, I'm here," I said. As I spoke, the immediacy of the
ground beneath my feet returned and I was no longer aware of being
in her uterus. I took that as a sign. "Eomma, help me," I said.

She didn't pause or turn her head. She was leaning down toward
my sister. "You can't hurry your sibling's arrival with songs, our Seona.
Appa wants you to have dinner with him," she said and Seona leaped
to her feet and sprinted past her. How rare, the privilege of eating with
Father.

I went with them toward the house to see for myself, grateful that
my old woman's body didn't fail me. "Eomma, I'm coming," I said as
I followed.

"I need your help," I added, but neither of them glanced back.
Seona had scrambled up and into our old family house with its sliding
rice-paper doors, its tiled curved roof. I knew the smooth wooden narrow porch that skirted the entire building. How her feet abandoned
her shoes before she stepped up to that same porch and then inside.
Before she took off her own shoes, my mother looked over her shoulder in my direction, and my heart stopped. Here was the moment she
would recognize me and wrap me in an embrace. *How long it's been,*
she'd say. *I've missed you.*

Instead, she remained calm, and I knew she couldn't see me. Her
eyes swept over the yard and then she turned and went in. But she
made an uncharacteristic mistake — Seona had slid the door open, of
course, and left a gap for Eomma, but Eomma didn't close the door

all the way after she disappeared inside. She left a space and I knew it was for me. She must have sensed me here, and it felt like grace.

"I'm coming in, Eomma," I called. I had to bend to get my sneakers off and it wasn't easy. Why had I agreed to wear these new bothersome things? Better grip, so you don't slip, the advertisements had said. Well. All the laces. They didn't tell you about that. My mother had placed her upturned rubber shoes neatly next to Seona's small ones and a few others that I didn't stop to study. Maybe we had guests.

It took me two tries to get up onto the porch, but then I felt the uneven texture of the well-worn pine through my white socks. I used to sit on the edge and dangle my feet, my legs too short to reach the ground. I remembered swinging them, slicing them through the air, no worry in the world. Time, just time, to cut up like that.

The temptation was too great, I crouched down and ran my palms over that wood I remembered so well. And then I stood up, ready to join my family inside. My hand gripped the edge of the bamboo border of the sliding paneled door and I marveled at it. Just held it there a second. How I used to curse it, how I welcomed the new high-rise apartment when the time came to move, and now, the regret. Except some of this wood was rotted by then and accompanied by insects and robberies. There came a time when I had to move. But this moment, Seona and my parents, I wanted to be with them again forever.

The sliding door stuck, and I couldn't budge it beyond a hand's width, reducing me to spy from outside. Little Seona was in Appa's lap, her head lowered. That was my spot, but she was eating rice with our father's long spoon out of the overturned top of his metal bowl's cover. Eomma was across from Appa, and my older sisters who should have been on either side of her were missing. It made sense in my mind when I remembered that Mina and Aera were still alive. This was family who had already died. Well, then, I belonged there, with them.

Myself as a child — those were the memories I treasured most. Simple life. Simple loves. Playing with my sister. My mother, my father, the smell of meeuk guk, my favorite soup, which reminded me of the sea even though we didn't live close to it. I smelled it now coming from the house. My father must have brought it back with him from a trip.

My mother's voice permeated the air — not a sound, but I heard it all the same in my mind. She was spooning soup into her mouth, but I heard her voice. *When you were sad, I was with you.*

"Why don't you look at me?" I asked.

Look back but go forward, she replied.

"Seona is playing a mean game," I said, and I knew this was an old pattern. I'd said this to my mother many times when we were alive.

Is this what you want to do with the time you have left? she asked.

I felt piercing sorrow rise in my chest. "Help me." I waved my arms around.

Just at that moment, Seona looked right at me. Her eyes met mine through the small opening, no mistake about it. She shook her head back and forth and held up Father's long spoon like a wand, and some force — I swear I didn't see anyone rise to do it — some force slid the door shut.

Immediately I attempted to slide the door open, but it didn't budge.

I called and then knocked hard on the wooden frame. Nothing. I peered close to the paper windows of the door. Was anyone going to help me? Would Eomma come to me? We'd just had a conversation, hadn't we? I couldn't see any shapes. I pressed my ear against the paper window and listened. Any sounds? Nothing. They must not know the door was stuck closed. I took hold of the edge of the frame and shook it back and forth. I refused to accept what I'd seen. Seona had not magically shut the door. I moved to the side of it and peered in again, cupping my hands to shade my eyes. I pressed my ear to the paper again and again. I searched the other side of the house, as far as the porch would allow, skirting around ceramic pots of kimchi on the edge.

This was not the way it was supposed to be.

At first, I didn't notice the wind, so intent I was on making myself heard. But then my skirt billowed out, the house porch shook beneath my feet. I looked out to the yard, where the ground began to ripple and then move as if carried by a river beneath it. Like lava, the ground swirled, packed dirt flowed around the house and became a series of rows of undulating dirt and stone and grass converging in one direction, heading into a whirlpool to the side of the house. The house and trees, the gardens, the ponds, those remained; only the ground was drawn in.

My hair, short bob that it was, blew over my eyes. "Help," I called. "Help me." I pounded harder on the door. "Let me in! It's Jeonga, I'm here." But the ground continued to swim about me, and the wind seemed to be taking something from me. All sides of me. My hand blended into the paper wall — in horror, I pulled it back and rubbed it. My hand, my old woman's hand, but it was mine. My stance widened; I took a step away from the house.

The sound of sand running through an hourglass sizzled around me and I heard a deep rumbling coming from below. An earthquake in the afterlife?

"Eomma!" A screech from inside my chest spewed from my lips. "Let me stay on the porch, at least. Eomma, what's happening?"

Suddenly, a bigger gust blew through and I lost my grip on the porch. It moved me to the very edge. By some miracle, I managed to pivot and embrace a large fermentation pot. The hard surface was ice cold against my cheek, but I held on despite the ache in my arms. I called to the air.

The wind was fiercer now. I watched the plank that was our seesaw sucked into the center of the whirlpool, and the straw mat rolled after it. Small earthenware jars on the porch fell with loud thuds to the ground. Dust rose all around, so I had to close my eyes, but still I held on.

"I'll do anything, just make it stop," I whispered, my cheek still pressed against the cold ceramic surface.

CHAPTER 20

The motion of the ground began to subside in time. How much time? I didn't know. I wept and held on. And then all around me the sound and feel, on my skin, of one great exhale of air. Beneath my knees, I felt the feet of the house settle again to the ground and I was able to release my grip on the clay pot. From the sheer effort of holding on tight, I collapsed on the porch. It was quiet except for the sound of the flowing dirt, that slithering noise of sand falling through an hourglass. But to my eyes, the whirlpool of dirt in the center seemed to have vanished. I covered my ears, but the sound persisted, penetrating my skin. I returned to wrapping my arms around myself. Was the whirlpool within me? Was I dissolving?

"I'll do whatever you want, don't let me disappear," I pleaded, closing my eyes.

"Follow me." Seona's voice came from ahead of me, at the gate.

Relief flooded through me and anger too. When I opened my eyes again, the house remained, and the seesaw and everything was back in its place. My sister's voice came from the gate again, and this time it was her older voice. Gone was the high lilt of childhood. I was sure it was her voice, but something about it was different. Had I forgotten it over time? What kind of game was this? How had she gone from the house to the gate? The large gate creaked open and a young woman walked in from the road. I blinked repeatedly. A mirage?

It was Seona. She stood in her going-to-work clothes, a navy-blue skirt suit, her hair held up in a chignon, pale blue eyeshadow beneath her eyebrows, red rouge on her lips. Makeup on her face, which Mother thought was risky but Father was proud of. He had recently begun wearing suits himself. Seona looked to me to be the age she was just before she left us.

"Run fast, like a fox," she urged, motioning with her hand for me to follow.

I looked to the house and all around, but I was the only one on the porch. It made sense that she would be talking to me. But she'd never called me a fox before. She had many nicknames for me, but none of them had been that.

"You never called me a fox before," I said.

"You dare to question me?" she shouted.

A sound like a wood chipper crushing tree branches crackled the air behind me. I glanced over my shoulder and watched the wall of the house tilt away. More? I couldn't handle much more. Seona was ahead, waving to me from the open gate.

"I'm coming," I called as I grabbed my sneakers, which had miraculously remained intact beneath the house, and charged for the gate faster than I had thought possible. The sound of wood hitting wood increased as I ran with one sneaker in each hand toward Seona and the gate.

I picked up my pace as I passed the urns, which seemed to be on a conveyor belt heading in the opposite direction I was going. The hard dirt hurt my socked feet.

I paused and looked back at the house. Where was my mother? My father? They were nowhere in sight. The house slumped into the ground that was funneling down, indeed like an hourglass's sand sinking through. The shock of the house disappearing gave me a jolt. I turned and started running again, but I stepped on my hanbok, lurched forward, and fell on the ground, dropping my sneakers. My knees stung; my palms were bleeding.

"I can't go on," I called to Seona. I watched as the expression on her face changed — something of an old woman in the scrunching of her eyes and nose and cheeks so that skin gathered in tiny pleats in the lowest dips where all joined.

Her hand was on the gate, preparing to close it. "Not enough," she said.

Leaving my sneakers behind, I lumbered toward her. I felt the vast emptiness expanding behind me, but I didn't dare lose a second of time. To be left alone for eternity could be my fate. She began to close the gate behind her, the opening reduced to a sliver, but then she hesitated. I reached out my hand and saw her flinch as if she thought I was going to touch her.

The air behind her shifted, and her hair seemed to bleed into the sky. I didn't dare take my eyes off my sister's face. "Seona, we're sisters," I said. "Why are you torturing me? You tell me to come, but now you won't wait for me, now you're going to leave me in here?"

At the sound of my voice, she seemed released from a minor pain and then she did it, she began to shut me in, and I leaped forward — I was astonished but I didn't question it now. How could I leap with my old-woman legs? But I leaped anyway, and I was through to the other side just as the heavy gate creaked shut.

My beautiful young-adult sister was only a few meters ahead on the road. Our old childhood-home road. Wooden gates between stone walls. Seeing her on the road at the age she appeared to be now sent sharp points of pain through the bottoms of my feet. An old memory threatened to overtake me, on the last day before she'd eloped with her love. Painful tears stuck to the rims of my eyes.

I picked each foot up, flexed my toes, and put that foot down again. I became intensely aware of the road beneath my feet. Pebbles, pricks. I lifted the skirt of my hanbok and stared at my dirty-white-socked feet.

Feet age in the worst way. They swelled and became sensitive, as if reminding you how much service they'd been to you all your life, and now that I was one hundred five, my feet were rebelling. The sinking of sand through the earth had quieted, so I returned to my childhood home and tested the gate, which gave with a little push. Did I dare retrieve my sneakers? I spied them overturned in the middle of the now calm yard. If I ducked in quickly, I could be back out on the road in seconds. I couldn't possibly walk all the way to Seona in my socked feet. Here was my opportunity.

I dashed in, leaving the gate ajar. I gritted my teeth and suffered the pain of running on pebbled dirt. Once inside, I swept up my sneakers and ran out again. In my haste I almost collided with a figure on the road. Seona had returned for me.

"Why didn't you follow me?" she shouted. She had her arms raised and I thought for a moment she was going to hit me.

This was unacceptable. She was the one who had walked on ahead. I had so many questions and she was the one who was playing these games. How dare she be angry at me? To be in front of her now as she had been back then just before she left us to elope with a stranger. I launched into everything I had been thinking for years and had longed to tell her and then some.

I said to her: "All these years. All these years you've forsaken us, and you're angry at me? How dare you? Have you no idea how much you meant to me, to our parents, to our whole family? I've needed you — so many times over the years, I wished you were somewhere I could reach you. Just to talk to you and get advice. That you could be so far and not even in touch by mail — why couldn't you have just sent me a letter? Did you ever wonder about me? The borders between North and South Korea weren't always closed this way. And even during the Korean War — when you heard of the fighting, did you wonder if I was even alive? Surely somehow you might have tried to find out.

"Was your life so full, so wonderful that you never looked back? Was it so full of love that you thought about our parents only with hatred, and that hatred shadowed all of us, even the love you once had for your sisters? Or maybe you just didn't care."

Seona's mouth quivered and I thought I'd finally made an impact. But she didn't reply so I tried a different tack.

"You have to understand, Seona," I said. "I refuse to believe you changed that much. Whatever it was that kept you from writing to us, I know you have thought in the years since that you should have. I know this to be true. It must be. So that morning that Aera knocked on my door, I didn't let her in, she's right. But I imagine you're the only one who would understand what happened to me that morning and all the years since. Since love is what you chose. Love is what you left behind and ran toward. All you'd ever known. Over me, our sisters, our mother, our father — you chose a stranger over us and I didn't understand how you could have done it until my own stranger arrived. You'd understand why I made the mistake of choosing love. Would you understand what I had to do to make up for that mistake?"

Was Seona blinking back tears? She turned her head too fast for me to know for certain. She pivoted on her heels and tossed over her shoulder, "You think you know everything. That's why you've given up," she said.

"Well, what can I do? I would have liked to have stayed with Eomma and Appa in our house, but they disappeared, and it seems that you made them disappear, didn't you?"

"You think you know everything about me."

"No, I don't. I'm asking you why you never came back, why you never wrote, didn't you hear me?"

"I'm supposed to teach you how to move through this place, but you don't want to learn."

News to me, and with her muttering, I nearly missed it. I put my hand out to make her slow down and nearly touched the fine silk material of her blue suit. She yanked her arm away and faced me.

"You care only about yourself."

I took a step back, shaking my head. "That's not true, I've cared about everyone. I've taken care of everyone. I sacrificed more than you did. I did everything for everybody, and all they did was leave me. I loved too much."

"Too much? What about your husband? Did he die with too much of your love?" she said in a snide voice.

"What?" My hand covered my mouth. I was startled. My husband? He'd died years ago, an entire lifetime for some. Well, this was all wrong. She had it all wrong.

"You weren't there," I said. "In my defense, he never loved anyone. He wasn't capable of it. And how would you know? You were gone before I married him. Unless —" I looked around. "You know things in this place you didn't know when you were alive..." My voice trailed off.

Seona shrugged. "I know enough," she said and leaned in menacingly. I lurched back. Why was she threatening me? And then she straightened and dusted off her hands. "You have to trust me if I'm to teach you how to move on."

"You've been nothing but terrible to me, why should I trust you?" I pouted. I knew I had only her in this place, but I felt, as I always did in Seona's presence, like a young child.

"For instance," she said and took a step toward a gate and then backtracked and went to another. "Yes, this will do." Then the strangest thing happened; even in this bizarre place, I was still surprised by what I saw. Seona proceeded to dip her shoulder into the stone wall and the rest of her body followed, her head too, and then she pulled back and the rest of her body emerged back on the road again. "Come on, you try it."

I put my sneakers on, walked to where she stood, and touched the wall. It was solid stone. "What games are you playing?" I said.

"Find out. See you on the other side," she said with a laugh. Not a laugh I'd ever heard from my sister. I doubted for a moment it really was her. This might be a test. She might be a gwisin, a demon sent to fool me. I hugged my arms around myself. Oh, so much danger. I didn't know what to do. I sat back down on the orange dirt of the road. I wasn't following her anywhere. Not when there could be another whirlpool of dirt that would suck me into who knew where. Why had I ever thought Seona would be kind to me after death?

I'd barely settled myself in for a long sit when Seona or the gwisin or whoever poked her head through the stone. "Go through the gate if you can't figure out how to slip through the wall. You'll see you knew nothing when you were alive," she hissed and then her arm emerged from the stone and the hand at the end of it gestured toward the gate.

I shook my head.

"You didn't know everything about your husband," she said.

"I don't care," I said.

"You think he was incapable of love, isn't that what you said?"

I shook my head again.

"Come, Jeonga, you think you know everything about love. So much so that you've made yourself an expert, haven't you?"

I looked up.

"Tell me," she continued. "Come in here through that gate and give me your advice about this one. It might surprise you."

That was a curious thing to say. Surprise me? I'd seen all of it. I'd seen love hurt and destroy; it alienated and faded away. I picked myself up, brushed off my skirt and sleeves and hands, and found the gate was unlocked. I went inside.

CHAPTER 21

Seona stood with her back to the wall and her head cocked to one side, studying me. I ignored her and focused on this yard in front of me. It wasn't my childhood home this time but my husband's home. An odd taste entered my mouth just then. Have you ever noticed how walnut tastes like mold on a sweet rice cake? There's a moment when that white hairy frost of a mold appears — not creeping in but sprouted when you were not looking. So many things a walnut can be made into. Walnut sweets, walnut breads. My mother loved walnut cakes the most; I'd never cared for them.

Here we were in my in-laws' yard. It looked like my own home, though it had fewer rooms and no seesaw. Why was I in my husband's family's courtyard?

A sound from the house made me look over. A door slid open and out walked a young man. I would know my husband anywhere. He must have been, from the acne constellation on the skin of his face and the hair that has been trimmed back for high school, just about to be engaged to me. How young he was. Namgil, my husband. I hadn't seen the resemblance to Gwangmu before. The same thick hair, which our son had inherited. Why had I not noticed it when my husband was alive? When had I stopped seeing him without disdain?

"Is he real?" I asked. "Are you showing Namgil to me or is he actually here in the afterlife with me now?"

Seona shrugged again. "There are souls who left some of themselves here so I could call on them. A library, if you will, of souls. The rest of them have moved on."

I was astonished at her words. He'd loved me enough to leave a part of himself to wait for me. And then I realized that was true for Seona too but she'd left more of herself, more because she was my sister. "Can I see others? I'm sure they waited for me too," I said.

Seona scowled at my words. "Always thinking you know everything," she said. "Pay attention." She pointed to my husband, so I did as I was told.

Namgil had a persimmon in his hand, and he sat on the porch and began to devour the fruit. Then he winced. Silly boy; he'd bitten the inside of his mouth. Something he'd done often when I'd known him. He let out a yelp as he raised a hand to his cheek. I laughed, and he looked up, which made me wonder if he'd seen me. Had he? But then he went back to eating the fruit. He wasn't going to grow much taller than he was now, 172 centimeters, I thought as he stretched out on the porch with his legs to the side, his arm bracing his head.

Suddenly, my stomach plunged with a squeamish wobble, making me double over. I had the sensation of bones knocking into the back of my calf. *Whoosh* — I felt something come through my knee and saw a dog appear in front of me and run toward the house. And just as abruptly, the feeling was gone, and I could stand again. The dog launched herself up to the porch and licked the juice of the persimmon off his face. He sat up and rubbed her ears, and she settled into his lap.

For some reason, the love that dog showered on my young husband produced a despair in me. The sight of the dog frolicking, belonging to that boy, made me grieve for what I had never experienced. Had I ever had that kind of devotion in my life from anyone?

Seona's voice came from behind me. "It's just a dog," she said. "What are you sad about? Are you feeling sorry for yourself?"

"You weren't there," I howled.

"I'm glad I wasn't if you acted like this every time you saw him," she said.

"I tried to love him, I did," I said and covered my face with my hands. Shame draped its arms around my head. Why did I feel as if I'd wronged him? Because his soul had waited for me? Because I wished someone else had waited and not him?

Some might have considered him a poet. But he didn't know how to write poems or draw or sing or compose music. He sank into gloom like a trough in the yard and bathed in it and never paid any attention to me, as if all that mattered were his feelings.

Back when he was alive, he was quick to cry. Even if that were acceptable, no one knew how often he cried, and people misinterpreted why he was crying. He cared only about himself. He cried not for the death of a parent or a sibling or a friend who was dear to him. No; he cried when leaves fell from the trees in autumn, at the thought of leaves dying, as if they were separate, sentient beings. "Disintegrating," he'd say. And he would blame me for not understanding and he'd turn away and go off to carouse with his friends and drink too much rice wine, and later he'd complain of terrible nightmares.

"There's more," Seona said, interrupting my thoughts. "I hoped we could skip all this, but it seems you need to go through the steps. Did you feel the dog run through you?"

I nodded in misery.

"You let yourself feel love for your husband," she said.

"I didn't love him. He didn't let me love him," I said.

"I think you loved him more than you admit, but maybe you're right — maybe he didn't love you."

I wiped my nose with my skirt, which I hated to do. Where were handkerchiefs in this afterlife? This was not her business and not important. I was glad to have the subject changed to the dog. I had to focus on practical matters; they helped me when my husband's emotions threatened to drag me down. How had that dog run through me the way Seona had gone through the stone? "How does the dog know more than me?" I pointed at the wall.

"Who's there?" my young husband shouted, and I knew in that instant that although he couldn't see me, he had sensed my presence. He stepped off the porch, slid his feet into his shoes.

"Can I talk to him?" I said.

Seona put her fingers to her lips in a signal for me to be silent. "Here's the thing. Isn't it odd how we care about the creatures that have a voice? I heard about the cricket you saved and took outside when it was dying in your house," Seona said. "You'd stomp on an ant or a spider. But the cricket, ugly creature, it had a voice. I'm not blaming you; I'm just saying when something has a voice, we have compassion for it."

"What do you mean, you heard?" I whispered. "You were there, you helped me."

Seona pointed to the sky, where a red-winged bird flew in a wide circle overhead. But I couldn't watch long because the gate opened at that very moment and in ran a young woman.

She was dressed in a high-school student's clothes — a plain dark skirt and white jeogori — and her hair was cut to her chin. I was certain this was a younger version of myself. Who else would run to my fiancé in his yard? We had been friends once. I remembered I'd enjoyed his company in the early days of our relationship, before he withdrew from me.

I never knew I was as graceful as that when I ran. Or that my hair had such bounce. I always hated how my hair lined up to my chin, how thin it was. It was why I was impressed with my husband's and our son's hair.

She ran in and I marveled at how lovely I appeared from this vantage point. I'd had no idea back then. So much enthusiasm radiating from my body. I wasn't aware I could be as lithe and joyful in expressing my desire for life, but I must have been. When had I been as happy as this? How beautiful I was.

My husband and I were both naive about all matters of romance. We were too young to have had any real-life experiences, protected as we were by our families. I don't remember being carried away like this. I had never had such an aura of lust around me. Our relationship had been innocent, denuded of passion entirely. But I looked to the world at this moment, my young self, as if I wanted to procreate with him and him alone — the flash in my step, the spring of my hair; my body was full of hope.

She stood close to him, without any modesty. And he made an attempt to kiss her while she dodged him with coyness. Where was the chaperone? Something was wrong here. Did I dare engage in such immodest behavior out in the open? I knew emphatically that I had never, never, never touched him that way before we were married. And, if I were to be completely honest, even after we were married, we had never kissed. Sex had been awkward and frightening.

Had I ever felt such young love? Why hadn't I held on to that feeling instead of turning bitter through the years? Except I knew why — you can't change the way you feel, can you? You can only change the way you act, and I'd done that. Later, when I felt my own true rush of love with Siwon, I'd believed it was new. Still, the sight of this young version of myself appearing this enamored made me doubt my memory of our time together. Had I remembered incorrectly? Had I wanted to love him and given him the impression I did? I couldn't have been as good an actor as this. Seona said I was always terrible at pretending.

I rushed up to the young couple, circled until I could get a better view of their faces. They'd both stepped back now and were gazing at each other, into each other's eyes. Their attachment was clear. And so was the fact that this girl was not me. Never had been me.

My hand was up to my mouth in a gasp. Again, like on the road, I was wrong. What were these tricks of the eye?

He looked in my direction. The impudent girl turned his chin back to her and said, "No one is there, silly, no one can see us."

Her voice was shockingly similar to the voice of a girl in my class, someone who lived three neighborhoods over. It couldn't be. I looked again at her face, and in the middle of my inspection, she let out a squeal because he reached for her waist. She leaned away.

"You're still promised to Jeonga," she said. "Why can't you do something about that?"

"Am I?" he said and kicked at the dirt.

"Stop that," she said. "Rumor is you are."

"I told my father I love you," he said.

At his words, she leaned toward him again, but he bent backward this time and they both blushed and laughed. I'd never seen my husband as in love as this. The two of them, these children, inched their way toward each other once more.

I tore my eyes away; it was a private moment between them. I knew what it was to feel this kind of love. I wouldn't have wanted anyone to witness me in that state. The thought brought a sharp pain in my side as if I'd been stabbed, and I stumbled and fell to my knees. How many times can I be knocked down? Each intake of breath brought on another stab. A memory flickered like a flame: "I love him, Mrs. Cha," my great-granddaughter had said, sitting across from me in a Thai restaurant in San Francisco.

"Make it stop, make it stop," I pleaded. Why was I the one to suffer here?

"Admit you were wrong about him," Seona replied.

"Admit what? He was the one who never loved me because he already loved another," I threw back at her. "Why did he agree to marry me? It's his fault we were miserable, his fault." The injustice of it all billowed up like smoke; I could hardly catch my breath. I had never had a chance. He hadn't been unhappy about trees losing their leaves in the autumn. He'd been missing the woman he loved. I understood all of it now.

"He stays in this place to be with her?" I whimpered.

"Something like that. I don't know all the details — only what you have to do to get out of here," she replied.

Then Seona disappeared through the wall and when I touched it again, it presented itself only as the solid stone wall it seemed to be. I hurried to the gate and walked out without looking back.

I was alone again. I chose a direction and walked, my hand on the stone wall. No sign of my sister anywhere. Somewhere in this maze of roads, I got pebbles in my shoes and I took them off. In frustration, I flung one sneaker at a wall. It bounced back. Not directly but the way gravity usually works. *Thud* and then down to the ground at the base of the wall. I threw the other shoe at the wall too. Who cared about old feet anyway?

I was reduced to wailing on the ground again. How long? Let's call it forever. Trudging on, only to thrash on the ground — that was my fate. Dust and dirt on my face and the long skirt used as a handkerchief to wipe my nose.

"I refuse to believe I'm here to be tortured by you," I said and sniffed. "I didn't know about my husband's first love. How could I have known? That doesn't prove I think I know everything. Show me the reason. Show me why I deserve to be in this afterlife."

No answer came. Nothing happened. I got up and paced back and forth in the dirt and wondered why my stomach was quaking with hunger. How wrong we humans were about what happened in the afterlife. As if everything in life was repeated in death.

Waves of despair washed over me. I didn't deserve to be here. I had observed every filial piety tradition. I didn't do anything but what our parents wanted, and I'd gone to pay my respects at their burial sites faithfully. Why was I here?

With my hands, I pounded the pebbly dirt. I didn't care how snot ran down my chin, how I blubbered and fussed. At my age, the body produces fewer liquids of any sort. But the ache was the same if not more.

The sight of my husband and his girlfriend reminded me of something else. The flash of lights on a pinball game. The tug of love. My great-granddaughter Ellery needed me. Ellery was in love, back in the world of the living that I'd been ripped from to land here. And now this.

How could I help her? I threw my head back and studied the orangish murky sky above me. Seona had left for love. What could I do to get her to help me?

CHAPTER 22

S eona, you're the one who doesn't know anything," I shouted at the vast strange mist above me. And then to the wider landscape and wherever my sister was hovering, "You left us, you never called me a fox, and now you're leaving me again. How could you?"

In an instant, Seona was in front of me. I startled and leaped away. But she was there again right in front of me with fancy-young-woman work clothes on and she waved her fists at me, but I scrambled away, ducking my head in fear of feeling the force of a blow from her.

"You have to think about someone other than yourself," she shouted. "I'm never going to get out of this place until you admit you don't know everything."

I glared back at her. How dare she scream at me? "You were right, back there at my husband's house. I didn't know. Okay? Is that what you want me to say? I don't know everything. I didn't know everything when I was alive." And then, despite my intentions, I found myself pleading with her. "Don't leave me here with these walls — there's something I'm supposed to do."

Seona sighed. Tension seemed to leave her figure. "What walls?" she asked.

I looked around us. Along either side of the road was a ten-foot stone wall as there had always been in the past on our street.

"If you can walk through it, you can go," she said. And then she lurched at me and I thought she was angry again and jumped away and collided with the wall, except *collide* wouldn't be the right word because I found myself falling into the cold surface. Into a curtain, solid but giving. My arm went through the stone up to my elbow. Horrified, I tried to right myself and pulled my hand back but I lost my balance and fell, infinitely falling through gray cloth and a plush murky substance that reminded me of foam.

No pain. Intact. My hand was still attached to my arm and broke my fall. Down to the ground I went. But I was on the other side of the wall. Inside a courtyard. I scrambled to my feet and tentatively touched the wall again, and again it was cold but not resistant. A tap with my finger, and my hand followed it into fabric like before. I pulled back my hand and the fingers looked the same, though I noticed a slight smoothing of the skin, and when I flexed my fingers, the ache in the joints was gone. Well, now. That was something.

I looked at the wall again and pushed my hand through, the stone like the cheapest polyester fabric. I plunged it farther, making sure my feet were braced, but it was the same, just more material; I couldn't find a separation. I was in up to my shoulder now, yet it was more material. I knew it couldn't be so — the wall was not that thick. Here's the thing about this discovery: What did it mean? I could walk through walls? What other powers did I have?

Tentatively I entered the wall with the rest of my body and emerged on the other side. Such an odd sensation to walk through a solid mass. I felt a resistance, a stretching of molecules, but I was dead, so could they be molecules?

Seona stood a few meters away on the road, looking at me with disgust. But something was wrong with her face — it undulated when I stared at it. "Finally, you get the point." She smirked.

To test my powers, I traveled through the wall again and returned to the road faster this time. Seona was nowhere in sight. There I went again — instead of listening, I had to see for myself. What good was I? I sat on the ground and pounded my fists on it.

Suddenly, I heard a rustle of cloth and the crushing of tiny sand and pebbles. A cheap black cloth shoe appeared by my folded leg. My hopes rose. Seona was back, wearing shoes she'd never worn, but who knew what was possible in the afterlife? I looked up to find a middle-aged woman whom I'd never seen before observing me.

She was wearing a simple, boxy, unattractive watery-gray pantsuit of sorts and black cloth shoes. Similar linen — rough with stitching that was large and announced itself.

I scrambled to my feet. She was my height. A tuck in the waist, a hemming of the sleeves and the pant bottoms, a little makeup would have done wonders for this woman in front of me. I didn't respond right away. She had a persimmon in her hand. What could I say? Did she follow persimmons too? Was Seona orchestrating our meeting? I would have asked but my hesitation was due to the grim expression on her face. A permanent single wrinkle straight across her forehead. Her hair was held back by a simple bobby pin, which showed me the part in her hair that was exactly like Seona's. And the same sesame-seed mole above her eyebrow. "You found me out. Your powers are increasing." She sighed as she reached a hand up and rubbed the beauty mark off.

A crushing realization made me take several steps back. "It was you. You're a ghost," I said, gasping for air. How terrible it was to hurt people like a gwisin did in the stories I'd heard. Always destroying. I'd been tricked.

"All this time," I shouted. "Pretending to be Seona. I knew it. Back at my house, with my parents, you were pretending to be — Seona never called me a fox. It was you." I pointed at the persimmon in her hand. "You left those on the path for me. But the teeth marks?"

She laughed — or *cackled* would better describe the sound that came out of her throat. "Oh, Youngest Aunt," she howled. "My mother said you were sharp, but it took you a while to figure it out." Her head was tossed back, and she slapped her thigh with her empty hand. As her mouth opened, I saw she had the same crooked front tooth that my sister had. Coincidence. What a fool I'd been. And how I had been tricked. The dusty ground around me absorbed a spray of her saliva.

This was Seona's daughter, calling me Youngest Aunt. This was how she really was, without the magic or whatever she'd fooled me with. I pitied her for her clothes and then admonished myself for criticizing this woman. She must have grown up in the Communist north; she could not help but wear what was available. How superficial I was, even in the afterlife. She had some pretty qualities. I let up on my critical eye. It had been a harrowing stretch of time between the bus and me and this place I'd arrived in. After a paralyzed moment, I finally found the will to speak.

"You're Taeyang."

"Daeshim told you about me?" she asked.

I nodded. "And how you and your mother were left behind in North Korea."

She looked at me with steady eyes. "It's not me you should pity. I hoped if you thought I was my mother, I could teach you what you need to learn faster, Youngest Aunt."

"Teach me what?"

"How to move through this place, for one." She kicked at the pebbles. "My mother told me so many stories from her childhood, it was easy to fool you."

"You should have just said who you were," I said.

"You felt too sorry for yourself to listen to me."

"Not true," I protested. "Where's your mother?"

"Busy." Taeyang pouted.

"Too busy to see me after all these years?" I sputtered.

"I used to hate her too," she said. "It's why I'm supposed to help you, guide you. It's my only way out of here."

"You've been no help," I said.

She kicked more pebbles at her feet, reminding me in that moment of myself. She muttered without looking up, "You can move through walls now; if you open up yourself, you can move through anything, reach anyone."

"What good does moving through walls do if I don't want to be here?"

"You should know she was miserable all those years after she left you."

I gloated when I heard this. She couldn't be bothered to come help me herself in the afterlife, so I was glad she had suffered. But I had always thought she had love in the midst of her suffering.

"Serves her right," I said and then caught myself. Was I truly glad?

"You should know she was unfair to me too," Taeyang said and she unleashed a flood of words and I listened. What else could I do? She was the only one who had shown herself to me, and somewhere in the accusation was sympathy. I knew it. She went on to describe Seona as a mother in a way that astonished me. I listened with the knowledge that children could be terribly cruel to their parents. Had my son said awful things about me too?

"My mother used to tell me stories of your life in the south. I know she missed her family — you," she said, studying my face, and I knew I looked eager. "Yes, you and your father and your mother, so much I couldn't bear it when she talked about all of you. I was jealous because she sounded as if she preferred her life with you to her life with me. She'd talk so much, her mouth would open and close as if she were speaking, but hardly a sound would come out, and I knew from her eyes that she was close to crying. I'd direct the conversation away from you and ask her about the house she grew up in. This part always made my father stomp away angrily. My mother would look at his back and sigh. 'Not comparing,' she'd say in his direction, but I didn't blame him. What could it be but comparing when we had such a simple home?

"She said her house had special gardens we'd never seen — that was the way she talked, always how it separated her from us. It was a house we'd never seen, a garden we'd never walked in — would never walk in — how did she know that? I did go to Pyongyang. I've walked in grand, beautiful gardens that Dear Respected Leader walked through, that were blessed for those who believed in his good grace. Her childhood home could not be as magnificent."

My breath caught in my throat. Seona had missed me, missed our family, had regretted leaving us for that man.

"I'm sure she only meant to share memories of her life so you'd understand where you came from," I said with a surge of compassion. Seona had remembered me; that much she had shared with her daughter, shared enough for a child to be jealous.

She spat at the ground away from our feet. "You think you're better than me, like she did," she said.

"No, no," I hurried to assure her. But she detected my lie and I caught myself. "Who is better than whom here? Aren't we all dead? I was just thinking how ghosts are everywhere. Even among ghosts, there are ghosts of another level, ghosts who haunt ghosts?"

She shrugged.

"Please go on," I urged. "You said you were teaching me how to leave this place, and you want to leave too. How do we do that?"

"Did you really have tall towers of sweets?" she asked.

I could picture her in that moment in miniature, this grown woman who was Seona's daughter. I saw her as a child, looking up at her beautiful mother, thinking how she didn't have her to herself because of her memories of us. "We had feasts. So many holidays and festivals. Your mother had the biggest sweet tooth. Has she been reincarnated? Is there such an option?"

"No," she replied. "That's not what happened to her."

"Then where is she?" I said. "I demand you tell me. Is there no one who can help me?"

She shook her head as if I were a hopeless case she needn't bother with. "I'm trying to help you — if you want to believe me, that is. Not many would try."

I don't know why it hurt to hear her say I had no one who cared about me. Was it true?

"What about my son? What about Gwangmu? Is my son here too?" I looked past her.

"He's paid his dues," she answered.

I was in disbelief. Even in the afterlife, he hadn't stayed to see me. I felt my shoulders slump. *After all we did for our children*, I thought. But then I remembered Eomma's voice at the house. "My mother spoke to me," I said desperately.

She said, sadly, "Your mother left ten percent for you. That was her voice you heard."

"But why you? You had nothing to do with me during my lifetime."

"We're not so different, you and I," she said. "Even though I didn't look like you, my mother said I reminded her of you. And she neglected me and abandoned you. That's what ties us together here. It's why, if I help you, I can go beyond."

"Beyond? Back to the living?" I said, and Ellery's face appeared in my mind's eye.

"I'm not going back there. Who would want that? I'm going beyond, out of here."

I started to pace. "I have to get to the living. I need to save the children. Do you know about that?"

"Who cares? Remember, you have to let yourself learn in order to move through what your eyes are telling you is in front of you. You have to know that you don't know everything — understand? Like my mother's forgiveness."

I decided I didn't like her at all. "Maybe you're leading me in the wrong direction," I said. "I don't want to go beyond, to whatever you call the beyond. I have to go back to the living."

"All of you capitalists are spoiled, just like she said you were," she scoffed.

"You're brainwashed, I'll forgive *you* for saying that," I said.

"You're not even worthy of being a worm," she said, the skin around her eyes tight. "I know about everything you've done."

How quickly the shame deepened. How much did she know? Anger rolled off my tongue. "I don't trust you," I spat and I moved to push her as I spoke. Her clothes were dusty. I hadn't seen the dust before, but she jerked away from me, and dust puffed off her as if she'd thrown herself on the ground many times. She kept her distance but with a steadiness that unnerved me. I turned my back on her.

"You have work to do if you want my mother's forgiveness," she said, almost a purr. "I also want something from you."

Now I'd hear her evil intentions. I should say nothing else to her. Who knew what I'd already said? Too much, too much. I looked around, frantic for help. *What can I do? How can I help Ellery now?*

Seona's daughter paused in kicking at the orange dirt and looked at me. "Why did my mother elope?"

CHAPTER 23

I found resistance in my throat even as I started to tell her. It should have been easy. It had been so long, but I realized it was the first secret I had kept to protect my family. We were told never to say that Seona had eloped. The official story was that she had gone to help my father's sick aunt. That night, my father stood like a door between Seona and her love. I saw her clench her hands. That last night I saw her, eighty-nine years ago, the night was a long one. Our father said Seona couldn't see that young man of hers anymore, couldn't go back to work at that hospital switchboard or meet him in the park or in the tearoom. I saw in her eyes such panic.

"I'm nothing without him, Jeonga," Seona had said, squeezing my wrists so tight, I squirmed. I was afraid for her. I thought she'd run outside and go right then. But Father blocked the doorway. I thought the trembling that overcame her at that moment would expand into every bit of her to the extent that she'd dissolve like sugar in hot water. I wanted to put my arms around her and hold on to contain her. I wanted to shout, *You are yourself, stay yourself, don't give up who you are,* but I didn't. I stood frozen in place and watched her shake with fury.

Father stopped her from leaving that night, but he had no other way to keep her with us and he didn't regret it, even if it meant his favorite child would hate him; didn't regret it because he knew, some-how he knew, he had to do everything possible to protect her when he could. He told her she would be dead to him if she eloped, that he would remove her name from the family records; he knew how much she cared about books and official forms. He said he'd cut her out of his memory. She would cease to exist.

I felt relief. She would back down now. When rhetoric was all one had at one's disposal, the words one chose were extreme. His sliced her heart. I knew it. She blanched and I thought it would be all right. She wouldn't go.

She didn't run at Father and try to fight her way past. Instead, she whirled, ran back to our room, pulled up the covers, and closed her eyes. How did she have the strength to be so patient?

Our sisters, our mother, they all went to sleep as if the incident were behind them, Seona's escape thwarted. But then, our sisters and our mother had never understood. In the morning, Seona was gone.

I stopped talking to Seona's daughter. Instead, I appealed to my sister, wherever she was at that moment. "I kept the family secret, but I also kept yours. I didn't wake anyone that night; I let you escape. I saw you and I said nothing to stop you. But I expected you would have kept in touch — at least with me. I was on your side."

Inwardly I was crumbling as I remembered how it was. A visit from her, just for a day, would have helped us all. If we could have seen her grief-stricken, guilty face, if she had returned, our lives would have been different. Father folded after Seona left. Just lost the will to live. He had pretended to be immovable, but I genuinely think he was caught by surprise by how much Seona's departure knocked the wind out of him; he was no one without her.

We were horrified by his decline in the days that followed. Mother would have called Seona back if she'd known where she was. Mother talked about it, especially in that first week. But Seona was gone. No one knew where she was. No one had heard anything. We asked at the hospital switchboard, spoke to her love's coworkers. I was sent to ask around; I searched for her everywhere. Father said there was no point. Seona was as stubborn as he was, and in the face-off, he had lost. We tried to help him. We tried, all of us, but it took just six months for him to die. How fast he went.

The day of Father's funeral, we had to support our mother. She couldn't make it on her own. Can you imagine? Our strong mother? She hobbled, despondent, not having been able to eat much the previous days from grief, but at least she drank some bone broth, drank tea at our urging. And we walked in our white hanboks, like the one I'm wearing now, everyone in the extended family following, and Father in his shroud.

The wind blew that day and we sobbed. All of us. Seona was gone and now Father was gone. How could he have loved her more than any of us? Even Mother? How could he have thrown away his life because Seona was gone? We couldn't understand it. My sisters were busy with their husbands and in-laws. It was only Mother and me after the funeral. Only us.

I was angry then. Angry at Seona. Seona should have come when our father died. Unreasonable, I know, but I didn't care if it made no sense. We all expected her to come running back and beg for forgiveness and give up that ridiculous man she'd chosen over us. A man she'd known for only a few weeks. That was lust, pure and simple. Among ourselves, we'd always believed that Seona had left for love, but it wasn't love like what one felt for one's family or even the love one had for someone that was built out of respect and years of working together for the good of everyone else. Not the kind of love where you put aside your own feelings and wants and thought of the greater good of the family.

I was also angry at Father and angry at Mother, who was not alive in the way she'd been before. Sleepwalking through the days. Why wasn't I important enough to make a difference in their lives? I think for Mother, it was less about Seona being gone. I think it was Father giving up the way he did that shocked her. Shocked everyone. I spread a rumor around the neighborhood then. I admit it. I told everyone that Seona was an ungrateful daughter. I told them she had not come home even though we told her Father had died. In truth, I had no idea where she was, but I pretended we had communicated with her and she had been too selfish to do her duty. The story that was spread was that she was disrespectful, callous.

Was that why Seona was angry with me?

"I made up those rumors. I'm sorry," I said. But I was not really sorry. Because even though I had lied about telling my sister about my father, she still had not come home. I'd hoped those rumors would reach her and she'd come home and redeem herself. Just for a day. How it would have helped all of us to see her. I knew she would have suffered knowing Father had died because of her, but if Seona didn't know, she would go on living happily with the man she loved. It felt unfair. Ignorance could not be your defense or shelter.

Taeyang's voice pierced through my memories. "You've made progress. Not enough, but it's a start. Now, about contacting the living —"

I came to my senses. I had to save Ellery. "Yes, how do I reach the living?" I demanded.

"You're just as pushy as my mother," Taeyang said.

"No, I'm not," I retorted.

"You might be worse than her, actually," she said.

"No one can beat your mother at anything."

"Maybe there's hope for us yet," she mused. "Were you ever open to talking to ghosts when you were alive?"

I remembered being frightened throughout my life on the rare occasions I wasn't on guard. After all, I couldn't have my head in a book all the time. Just before we left for America, I had woken up in the middle of the night and felt a damp dread permeating my bed-room. To combat it, I went to the kitchen for a cup of tea and turned on the television. My unease faded. Now I wondered: Had someone been trying to get in touch with me? But it didn't matter — I'd been afraid, that was true. And I hadn't wanted to know. I looked at my gwisin niece. "Can you reach the living?" I asked.

She knit her brow. "I tried with my mother — as if she even cared." She turned away, but I saw her eyes fill with tears.

"You died before your mother?" I exclaimed, not meaning to show such emotion.

She turned back to me. "Almost as young as Gwangmu. An acci-dent, just like him. She died soon after me. I couldn't keep her safe, though I tried."

"What year was this?"

"Well, I was forty. An accident at my job — the sorter took my arm and I bled out. Absurd how it happened. It's taken me a long time to accept it. My mother's death was easier to understand — at the age of seventy-five of pneumonia during a very bad winter."

"But how are you in the afterlife and your mother out of this place if you died before her?"

"I've told you how the afterlife works. It's not about time. Plus, she's not out of the afterlife," she scoffed.

"She's still here?" I said.

"We have to hurry. My mother is busy with that doomed couple," she replied, and I saw her not as the gwisin she was showing me but as someone much like her mother. I almost called her Seona.

"You know about them? But what can I do? I'm dead, it's too late."

"You have the ability inside of you to reach them."

"What do you mean?" I took a step toward her.

"This thing about Jordan and the generations to come" — she waved her arms — "all this has to be fixed by you and my mother."

"You're not making any sense at all."

"You still have more to tell me. Let me ask you: Why did you abandon my brother?"

I didn't want to have a conversation about Daeshim with Taeyang. I pushed that subject away. "Why didn't you and your mother come south with your father and brother during the war?"

"Become a puppet for the capitalist United States empire?" she said in a bitter voice.

"Did your mother feel the same?" I asked.

"She stayed with me, but I'll tell you, she was angry that you didn't take care of Daeshim. Why didn't you? How could you kick him out like that?"

I looked down, choking back shame. "It was a terrible time in my own life," I whimpered.

"You're pathetic," Taeyang said. I looked up and saw her rolling her eyes. "That boring man. Are you saying it's his fault you treated Daeshim so poorly?"

"What man?" An inkling of hope.

"You know the one I mean," she said with a laugh.

"Jin Siwon?" My heart dashed ahead. Was Siwon waiting for me here?

"Really, Auntie? Your son's teacher? I know you thought you were in love with him. Was he worth all that happened afterward?" she asked.

I searched the area around us. Nothing but the road, but beyond, I saw a hill. A hill and a rock and the figure of — it couldn't be. I headed for it.

"Where are you going?" Taeyang called after me. "You still have more to learn about reaching the living."

I didn't reply. Out there on a hill in the distance, I could make out the outline of a man. Taeyang had called him by name. Was it true? Could it be my old love Siwon?

CHAPTER 24

It was selfish, I admit it. How could I turn down a chance to have passion in my life again? I was still very much aware of my body even in the afterlife. I blushed as I hurried along, the pleasure he'd given me a live wire of memories I carried still. My niece's warnings rang in my ears, but I ignored them. She was broaching the subject of her brother and the way I had treated him, and I couldn't face that yet. Couldn't I have this moment to see the man I'd loved, had risked so much for? I'd tell him everything and he would help me. I couldn't resist the opportunity to see Siwon again.

I veered off the road and waded into an even thicker mist that darkened at my knees like a swamp. My socked feet sank into the muck like it was a field of rain-soaked reeds.

"You finally made it," a man sitting on a large boulder called. He waved a hand in greeting, American-style, then stood and walked down off that rock in my direction. I walked as quickly as I could manage, small hunched steps toward him. His gentle-timbred voice flowed through the mist to me as if carried on a breeze. I hadn't heard it in so long, not since his death. *Siwon, my heart.* I paused to wave back with eagerness and then resumed making my way to him.

He was farther than I'd guessed, but I kept going. And then a thought made me stop at once. Put my hand on my face. Though he was still too far for me to see distinctly, his posture didn't suggest an old man. I tried to stand a little straighter as I walked on, smoothed the top of my hair, then noticed my hands, thick and knobby, my fingers unable to extend all the way anymore. I'd given up on rings in my nineties as my knuckles swelled. Sometimes when my fingernails grew white rims, I saw my mother's hands. She wasn't vain except about her nails; she allowed herself that one beauty to make her fingers longer and I saw her inspect them when she thought no one was looking. Despite her, I'd kept my nails short after Siwon described the germs that could be caught under them. Science dictated my beauty standards after that. I realized I'd forgotten to clip them before I left Seoul, and the whites were longer in this light than they'd ever been, and I immediately hid them in the folds of my skirt.

I paused again. *Go, go, go to him,* my heart chanted. *But don't get too close or he'll see every wrinkle and age spot on your face,* my mind commanded. I stood still, unable to decide, but it didn't matter, he jogged the last steps between us, closing the gap.

His face had more hollows in it, around his eyes and below his cheeks; he had deep creases in his forehead and silver streaks in his hair, around the sides of his head. But there was kindness in his eyes as they crinkled at the far corners, a young man's grin on his lips. How unfair for him to look handsome.

I straightened the front of the jeogori self-consciously. If I weren't in this ridiculous hanbok, I could show him my good taste in my designer clothes and hide my flaws. I felt old in a way I hadn't since the last time I'd seen him, in Colorado. He had that effect on me.

Before I could worry a minute longer, he reached for me and I responded in kind. Just before we would have made contact, I picked up the smell of roasted chestnuts. His favorite from long ago. And then the scent vanished because he reversed course and increased the space between us. I was perplexed, but he seemed shy, toeing the ground with his shoe. I was surprised to find he was wearing the same shoes he'd had during our early days together, thin leather shoes, which struck me as odd when he'd had much better quality ones after he moved to Colorado. Maybe they had sentimental value for him.

My throat was dry, as usual, so I had to clear it before I spoke, swallowing and coughing a few times. I hoped he'd find the sound of my voice pleasant.

"Thought you'd be reincarnated by now," I said.

He laughed from his chest, a low-toned muffled laugh, with his mouth open wide, breathy like he was clearing condensation from a window. "I've missed you," he said in a rare admission.

"You should have," I returned.

He laughed again. He knew sarcasm when he heard it. He gestured to the field ahead. "After you," he said.

"No, after you," I countered.

"I insist."

"Then let's commence together," I said. Our usual banter, our usual way of being. "The rock makes sense — you always wanted perspective — but an orange marsh?" I said.

"You always set your sights high, so I figured it was the only way you wouldn't walk right past," he replied, his tone light and teasing.

"Then the rock should have been a skyscraper," I said.

"It would have taken me longer to get down to you."

"True, you took too long as it was."

"Noted. Smaller rock because I'm old now." He gave me a small bow of the head. I tried to squash the smile on my lips but didn't succeed. The joy of being attuned to each other like no other. Taeyang had not mentioned that this place could become my own eternal bliss. Perhaps she didn't have such a love to share the afterlife with and wanted to deny me this joy. Could you understand this kind of love if you'd never felt this kind of love?

As we continued to walk together, I observed that my feet felt no discomfort. A deep thrill in being in his presence pervaded my whole being. We strolled this way for hours, but I wasn't counting.

"It's just us now, as we always wanted," he said.

It was true. We had talked about this. I gazed at his dear familiar face, his eyes that sloped downward, that smooth square forehead. He'd let me sweep his hair back when a piece of lint had to be plucked out of it. I remembered how warm his complexion had felt, dry — never perspiring. I could be with him forever in this place. I deserved it, didn't I? I had lived for one hundred five years. I could rest now with him. My heart sang with a new tune. *You deserve to be happy, Jeonga*, it lilted. *The way it used to be, Jeonga.*

As we walked, he became even more sentimental. "My ultimate dream: talking and walking in the moonlight at the shore," he said.

I looked in the direction a horizon ought to be, expecting a crescent above us, but saw only the unchanged orange-colored mist fanning out far and wide.

"I remember we pretended we were at the beach at night after everyone was asleep," I said. "Is that what we're doing now?"

"Because we both loved the ocean. Hear the surf?" he said.

I strained my ears. There was only silence, but the ground beneath my feet yielded with each step. "We're on a beach," I said.

"This is my fantasy," he replied. "Only in my mind. The part I left for you."

"You're telling me I don't know what sand feels like?" I said.

Siwon had a way of making me feel adventurous, bold. I bent down and let a handful of fine grains of orange run through my fingers. "It must be my fantasy too," I said, picking up another handful of sand and bringing it to my nose. It smelled like mushrooms and chicken feathers. Ack! I threw it from me. "Why does it stink like my yard?"

"It's my fantasy, not yours," he repeated, watching my antics, but there was a sadness in his eyes. He'd walked on and was looking back at me. He didn't seem to be joking anymore.

His fantasy? Where was I in his fantasy? What belonged to me?

"But we're here together," I called as I hurried to catch up. I expected a reasonable explanation. Instead, I received a tremendous disappointment.

It happened in an instant, without thought. I stumbled by accident and reached for him and he put his hand out. Our hands should have touched. He should have caught me before I fell. But his hand vanished into the air at the point of contact. I landed on the ground once more. This was becoming too frequent an occurrence. My face flushed with humiliation and confusion. I pushed myself back up to my feet.

He averted his eyes, searching his hands, open before him. "Now you understand. That's why earlier I didn't pull you to me. I told you I left only a part of myself here for you."

Arrogant as usual, I had failed to hear everything he'd said. Still, I knew it now, and it was preposterous. It couldn't be true. I attempted to reach for him one more time but all I found was air. "But I felt you, I did," I sputtered as I swiped through his shoulder, his torso. He stood there, his mouth grim, letting me convince myself.

"But I could touch my niece Taeyang," I said and explained how she'd pretended to be Seona, how I'd run from her when Siwon had appeared on the rock.

"Are you sure?"

I realized that I'd never actually made contact with Taeyang, only felt the whirl of her form generate motion in the air between us. "Taeyang has not yet passed through this phase of the afterlife. Neither have you. Stay with me and we could be together like this forever," he replied.

But we could never touch? Ever? I refused to accept those terms. There had to be a way to solve this problem. I searched for an answer. It lay somewhere in the first moments of the afterlife I'd experienced. I had felt this before, running my hand through air until — the moment my body had become solid beneath my hands. Siwon was wrong. He'd never been wrong before, but he had to be this time.

"Listen, when I first transitioned here from that ridiculous bus accident —" I began.

"That's different. I've tried to ascertain the limits of this dimension, and there are some aspects that are immutable," he said, but I was still thinking about the way I hadn't even known my name when I first arrived in this place. "Change does take place, though. For instance, I've changed," he added.

"I didn't know who I was. And my hands — it took a while for me to be able to feel the rest of my body," I said. "With time, we'll get to hold each other, I know it."

"Nothing will change here between us because I left twenty percent of myself for you."

"Say that again? What do you mean by twenty percent?" I said. The orange mist seemed to undulate around us like oil in water that catches sunlight.

"The other eighty percent has passed through this place," he answered.

"You left so little of yourself that I can't touch you?" I stared at my beloved's face.

He nodded. "You don't love me with all of yourself either, let's be honest."

My mind was reeling from the fact that he had left me with a tiny fraction of himself, a remnant of Siwon, my love. If that was the case, maybe there was nothing I could do. I'd never be able to hold him or be held by him again.

I gazed at the endless hills like ocean waves all around us in this now sickening persimmon hue. All I had was one fifth of him forever in this afterlife?

"Why?" I was finally able to ask when I regained my equilibrium.

"I hoped you'd move to America after Gwangmu did," he replied. "If you had, we might have been able to revisit what we'd done to the family and found a way to reveal that your son had fathered Hayun's child."

I thought back to a time when I could have been with him every day. Gwangmu had started his graduate program in America. Nothing kept me in Korea. Siwon wrote me long letters about his colleagues and friends, invited me to stay with him. I'd hesitated because his world seemed too full to include me. Who did I know in Colorado, America, besides him? I'd be stuck waiting for him in an empty house while he went on with his career. No, thank you. By choosing to stay in Korea, I'd maintained my independent life. I'd never risked souring our relationship. But our relationship had never blossomed into a mature real-life union either. And I'd ended up lonely in an empty apartment regardless. Now I'd be lonely here in this forever land, unable to touch the man I loved.

"So this is retribution for my not changing my life for you," I said.

He considered that idea for a moment and then I saw him dismiss it. "You know me better than that," he said.

I had to agree. He wasn't the punishing type. He never held grudges. He was honest, and that meant that I had not mattered as much to him as I had imagined.

"We spent a short period of our lives together," I continued. "What about our letters to each other? Quality over quantity?"

"I've come to understand that I had reservations all along about our days during the war."

"So you never loved me. That was the reservation." Tears rose in my eyes, but because of those pathetic clogged tear ducts, they didn't make it down my cheeks. I swallowed and ordered myself to toughen up. Siwon was a scientist and philosopher.

"Twenty percent of excellent company is better than one hundred percent of dullness," he said, looking at his feet. "Touché about quality. I'll give you that."

The scientist and philosopher could be infuriating. As if he ever thought twenty percent could satisfy me. I decided I was not beneath making him envious. I didn't want quality after all. I wanted quantity. I hadn't been planning to mention my husband, but now it seemed appropriate to compare. I did want to wound him a little. Also, I wondered how Namgil and his love had been able to wrap themselves around each other.

"My husband and his first girlfriend were able to embrace in this dimension — what does that mean?" I said.

"Excuse me?" Siwon asked. "Your husband and whom?" His irritation softened my disappointment. He hated hearing about Namgil. That had been true back in our time in life together and was apparently unchanged.

"Taeyang showed them to me earlier. My husband and the first and only great love of his life. They're here too," I told him.

I could see Siwon searching his memory for all the instances when I'd spoken about Namgil. He had quite an astonishing memory. My husband, by contrast, couldn't recall what he'd eaten for breakfast or remember to pay a bill on time, but I'd learned in this afterlife that he had saved all of himself for the woman he loved. I had to admire him even if I didn't want to be the object of his passion.

Siwon was nodding. "Yes, I've heard of those. They're beings who left one hundred percent of themselves here for each other," he said. He closed his eyes for a long while and then opened them, looked steadily at me. "I'm sorry, I didn't think one hundred percent would have been the right decision for me, considering our relationship. The afterlife makes you reexamine your decisions, gives you a chance to redeem yourself. I don't know if they could still touch each other though. We're ghosts, remember."

"Well, I saw them," I said.

"I don't know everything, that's true. But I know we're limited, twenty percent or one hundred percent. We're dead."

Now he sounded like Taeyang. Unlike her, however, Siwon disarmed me with his sincerity. Obviously, I'd chosen logic over sentiment. I deserved what I had now. I had to accept that I'd loved a man who quantified emotion. I had a small part of him and I had to be satisfied, especially as I had been the one who had held back by staying in Korea. I'd tried to avoid being one of those pathetic old women in the town center and now I was just like them. Seona would be laughing at me wherever she was if she knew. She'd never accept such a fraction, and neither would I. Eternity with a man I couldn't touch was not a future I wanted. It had the noxious scent of a curse.

Thinking of Seona helped me focus. I couldn't touch Siwon and he didn't love me in the grand fashion I had imagined, but maybe he was right and I didn't love him that way either.

A cold splash of reality snapped me to attention. Rather, a cold splash of the facts. What was I doing here with Siwon? I had to reach the living. After that, maybe I'd let part of myself talk endlessly with this man standing before me. For now, I had to get out of this place. And he would be the one to give me information. I needed his intellect. He would know how to help Ellery and Jordan. Taeyang had confirmed there was a portal between the worlds of the living and the dead. When I was alive, I'd seen ghosts, so there had to be a way, now that I was one, to reach the living. Even at less than fully himself, Siwon would have some solutions to this problem.

"Let's walk," I said. He nodded and joined me. I saw him relax in his stride. He had never been one for any type of conflict.

I took a deep breath and began questioning him. "What do we control in this place? Should I just think of where I want to be — would that get me there?"

"I would say yes. While I've been waiting for you, I've been observing your grandson Ned," he replied.

I knew he'd help me. His admission almost made up for the tiny fraction he'd found worthy of our love. I held my arms above my head and said, "If I could hug you right now, I would knock you over with gratitude."

CHAPTER 25

That day in the afterlife, I could see why Siwon would be intrigued by Ned. My grandson had chosen to write about history. Family history was my particular problem. The irony of this was not lost on me.

"Aren't you curious why I picked Ned?" Siwon asked.

"He's the most like you," I replied.

"There are many ways that we pass things down besides our genes. Gwangmu was a dedicated student of mine," he said. "My best student. Seems reasonable that he would have taught Ned well."

I remembered my son's fondness for his teacher. No matter the other outcomes of the arrangement, Gwangmu had gotten a superb education during a time when such things were in jeopardy. Despite my desire to reminisce with Siwon, I had to return the conversation to how he'd looked in on Ned.

"How can you see Gwangmu's son from here?" I asked.

He tapped his temple. "You were on the right track. I use my mind."

"That's not an answer," I scoffed. "Do you pretend you see him, like you pretended we were walking on the beach?" It was cruel but he wasn't being specific enough for me.

"The mind is always the answer," he replied.

I kicked at the ground and then tried a different tack. Urgency wasn't his usual speed, I remembered. I had to remind him what was at stake.

"What about Ellery? She's your actual grandniece," I said. "She's in danger."

He shrugged, one of the habits he had when he was uncomfortable that I detested. "You're being dramatic, aren't you?"

Dramatic? I stomped my feet and refused to take another step. "You must know about Ellery, then. You must know we have to stop her from marrying Jordan," I exclaimed.

"I've already done my part," he said.

That gave me pause. What was he talking about? I pushed him to explain but he walked on in silence. Finally, out of frustration, I turned to spitefulness. "Oh, your part, looking in on family members here and there, watching what they're reading — is that what you mean?" I practically choked out the words. Here was the other side of our relationship: I made the bold moves and he took the path of least resistance.

"You sent my sister and her baby to the other side of the world," he said with reluctance.

"You helped me plan it," I retorted.

"I did, didn't I? I planned other things too. Tell me, how did Ned get so much information on the family tree? And what were the chances of Ellery meeting Jordan?" he said. His jaw was clenched.

"Well, but that was a coincidence, that was —" I stared at him. "That was you? How did you give Ned that idea?" I said in astonishment. I put my hands on top of my head and pulled my hair. "Ellery told me he missed his flight; he wasn't supposed to meet her again at the restaurant, except he did. How did you cause him to get a flat tire? How did you do that with your mind?"

"It was the least I could do," he said.

"The *least?*" I sputtered.

"We were wrong — did you ever think of that?"

"It was the only way to protect us all."

"Protect you and Gwangmu. Not me, not my sister."

"You're getting emotional. So you're angry. Now it comes out," I said. This was a side of Siwon I'd never experienced. My hands tightened into fists. Who cared if he saw my gnarled knuckles? We glared at each other. Good thing I couldn't touch him because I wanted to punch him flat.

Suddenly all the tension left his face.

"I'm only interested in the truth being known." His voice was calm and gentle. "Jeonga, the fact is that Hayun is part of the family. You should have put her in the family record."

"You made everything worse by orchestrating their meeting," I said, punching my fist into the palm of my other hand. "You should have left Ned alone too."

"If you know so much, what are you doing here with me?" he asked. There wasn't a stitch of recrimination in his voice, simply curiosity.

"Aren't you going to help me?" I sputtered. "Show me how to reach them?"

"That's your work in this phase," he said.

"Tell me how. How did you contact him? How did you slash a car's tire?" I pleaded.

He tapped his temple again. "Move away or toward. Open up. That worked for me. This is your last chance to think about your life." He began walking away so I lunged for him out of desperation. I failed once more, swiped right through his torso. I caught myself this time, then scurried ahead of him and blocked his way, but he walked right through me.

"You still think you know everything," he said as I spun around and raced to keep up.

"I'm asking you to help me. Obviously, I don't know everything," I

223

said. "You made everything worse and want to walk and talk as if we're not responsible for Ellery and Jordan."

"You didn't want to be responsible for them."

"But I do now," I protested. "Tell me what you know. What can I do? Show me! How do I use my mind?"

His chin was down, and he picked up his pace. I trudged on, helpless, waiting. Finally, he stopped, turned to me, and opened his mouth — a mouth I detested at this point — and his response stopped me in my tracks. "While you pester me, your sister Seona is trying to fix what you messed up. She's in Ohio now, in the hospital, at Jordan's bedside. Every step with me takes you farther from them," he said. Then he began to walk again.

"What is Seona doing? Why are you telling me this now? What am I supposed to do?" I called.

"Apologize," he said over his shoulder. "But you have to be ready to face the truth of your past."

"I said I was sorry."

"Did you? To whom? What about, exactly?" He looked forward again and continued to walk on without me, increasing the distance between us.

"That's not fair. Don't walk away," I wailed. It was pathetic, but what else could I do? I had to help my family.

The orange mist thickened around me. His form receded. My love was gone again. It was more painful to lose him this second time, knowing what I knew. I could have forgiven him everything he'd done — the twenty percent, Ned's family tree, Ellery and Jordan's meeting, all of it — if he'd just helped me understand how to get back to the living. The Siwon I'd saved in my idealized version of him would never have taken such actions. But that was just it: that Siwon had never existed.

The realization brought all my suffering to the surface. My feet suddenly ached again, I lifted the hem of my skirt to see my white socked feet covered in orange dirt. My shoulders felt bowed by an extreme weight. I shuddered.

I was a fool. I struggled as best as I could to go back the way I'd come. I had failed. One too many steps in the wrong direction, that was me. I'd been selfish and run to Siwon. All these years he'd resented me, plotted and planned to disclose to the world that his sister and her child and his sister's grandchild were part of my family. I'd also run from other truths. Siwon's facts; Taeyang's ugly last words echoing around me: *Why did you abandon my brother?* I couldn't tolerate the reminder. My mind shut down. I couldn't imagine a way forward, so there was none. In an instant I was falling.

All around me was water, like the center of an ocean, only it wasn't salty. Endless falling and I didn't know what would happen, which was terrifying. I thrashed. I fought for some solid ground.

My secrets would curse my family for generations and there was nothing I could do about it. My heart seized as water poured into my mouth and ears. There was nothing to hope for. I'd ruined everything. Our family name, my son's reputation — dragged through the mud, laughed at.

The gossips would say:

So this is what they were doing all those years ago.

I knew she was the worst mother.

Degenerates. Obviously, money couldn't even save them.

I could imagine our neighbors, old now, telling the younger generations, the younger generations whispering to their peers, even to their children. Everyone would point and laugh. And added to that, another secret: How I had treated Daeshim, my sister's son. Taeyang spoke as if she knew. And of course, she did. She knew, as everyone would know. I put my hands over my ears, but I couldn't stop hearing voices. They'd see how it actually happened. I squeezed my eyes shut but it was no use; the past was vivid in my memory.

225

A few weeks after Siwon arrived, another man with a teenager knocked on our gate. He told the maid to say he was an old friend of mine. What a thing to say. He was Seona's husband. I was shocked to see his face, see him standing in the courtyard with a boy who looked like him. I thought at first that my sister was dead. Why else wouldn't she be standing with them? Their clothes were torn, their faces dirtied by grime. "What have you done to my sister?" I said, circling them. I turned to look at the gate. Was she out on the road still? Even if he expected it, he looked taken aback when I faced him again. His mouth softened, went slack. "I've kept my promise to my wife — here's her son," he replied and pushed the young man toward me.

Seona's son said nothing, and I saw that he was a little taller than my own Gwangmu, but he looked so much like Seona's husband I couldn't see beyond that.

"But where is she?" I asked. Without waiting for a reply, I hurried to the gate and opened it. Peering out, I saw no one. Even so, I left the gate ajar in case she was on her way.

The confusion, the disappointment — the combination made me lose my balance as I turned back to the pair I least wanted to see in the courtyard. Siwon was there in an instant, keeping me on my feet, his hands on my waist. Our eyes met. I nodded, letting him know I was all right. Only then did Siwon let go of me. When I looked up, I saw Seona's husband's eyes register the intimacy of our interaction. I moved away from Siwon and addressed my brother-in-law with as much authority as I could muster.

"Why are you here, then?" I said.

He responded by addressing Siwon. "Are you the teacher?" Seona's husband sneered. "I heard about you."

I didn't give Siwon a chance to answer and stepped between them. "So what if he is? My son needs a tutor."

"Sons need food too," Seona's husband said and pointed at the boy who had returned to his side. It seemed crass, the way his hand was curled in a fist with only his pointer finger extended slightly, as if he would punch his son.

The boy flinched, as if he too predicted a blow from his father.

"You didn't answer me. Where is my sister?" I repeated. Something must be wrong. Why hadn't she come here herself? How did Seona live with such a barbarian? And a cruel one at that. Had she run away from him as soon as she could? Is that why she hadn't come home?

"You think she would ever come back to this house?" he said.

"But we're her family," I said in a voice I knew sounded weak.

He laughed. The ugliest sound.

"Is she somewhere in Seoul? In another city?" I asked, hope rising. I'd go to her if she didn't want to come to me.

"She'd rather stay in a battle zone than see any of you again." He flushed red as he spoke. And I knew I looked shocked and as crimson as he was in that moment because my hand flew to my cheek. The pain was sharp and radiated upward. He might as well have slapped me across the face. He hated me — which I didn't mind — but my sister, did she hate me, too? His tone said as much.

Siwon cleared his throat and then said, "Did she send a letter or any word for her family?"

My brother-in-law narrowed his eyes. "Her family? Her family kicked her out. She has a new one; she married me."

"Then why are you here? Why aren't you with her? What do you want?" I shouted. I wanted him and the boy to leave at once. I was done with this torture.

Seona's husband looked away and then turned back to me. "I don't want to be here, believe me, but the boy has nowhere else to go. I can't take care of him anymore."

"But he's your son," I said.

"He needs food. She made me promise to come here and ask for money. Unless you're too busy with the teacher. Unless you're feeding him."

He had no right to come to my house and make demands and insult me at the same time. We had very little — only enough for our household — and it was as if this man were the mouthpiece for all the horrible people my parents had worried about. How had they lost their daughter to one of them? I was speechless. What was I supposed to do? He said my sister would rather risk death than return to us, but she'd asked him to come here for help.

"That's no way to ask for a favor," Siwon said, taking a step forward as if to shield me from further upset.

"Are you the one who makes the decisions here?" He laughed, an ugly, haggard sound.

Hearing this man's words snapped me out of my disappointment. I wanted Seona to show herself. I wanted her to come here and ask for help for herself, her child, even her despicable husband, even if she hated me.

"You and your son are not welcome here without my sister," I said. "Tell her to come herself and I'll consider it."

"So the answer is no," Seona's husband said and spat on the ground. "I told her you would refuse. Once kicked out of the family, forever kicked out, I told her. You're to blame for whatever happens to her boy. I can't get a job anywhere; people are starving here."

"Tell Seona to show herself," I said, gritting my teeth.

The man scoffed. "It's too late, the fighting up north is too intense. You're ridiculous." He looked me up and down and then steered the child away by the shoulder, and they left.

Did it rain? It had been the rainy season because the humidity was broken for a few hours that morning. I remember thinking it wasn't winter, so Seona's child would be all right. His father would have to take care of him, wouldn't he?

228

The next morning, Siwon went for a walk, as he did every morning, and found Seona's son by himself asleep in front of the gate. He reported back to me that he was an astute young man named Daeshim who was the same age as my Gwangmu. He had been huddled along the curb, curled up, so at first Siwon mistook him for rubbish.

I agreed to let him stay if his father wasn't with him. Daeshim, who would in time become the father of Joyce, explained that his mother and sister had been left behind in a village in the northern part of the Korean Peninsula. When I asked again why his mother had not fled south with him, he said only that his mother wanted to stay. I looked for signs of Seona in Daeshim's face, but they seemed to elude me. "Did she say anything else?" I asked him.

He shook his head. "She didn't want to come." Hearing it again from her son was a blow. It had the ring of truth to it that I had to accept now. My sister had never written to me after she left. She'd had children and lived all those years and not wondered once about me and the rest of the family she'd left behind. Her husband and her son, they were the only links to her, and they said she didn't want to see me. I walked around for the next few weeks in despair. Why was she lumping me in with everyone in my family? I was her sister. Siwon comforted me through this time. He said I couldn't hold Daeshim responsible for his mother.

I tried to convince myself that Daeshim warranted my care and concern.

"Love," Siwon said. "Doesn't Daeshim deserve your love? He's your nephew."

"He could keep Gwangmu company," I said, the idea coming to me in a flash. It felt like a compromise. I couldn't admit that I was still hurting over my sister's refusal to see me, to even communicate with me. I obsessed over that detail. A letter, a telegram, something, anything after all these years. "She could have sent a note through her husband," I said.

"People change," Siwon said.

I didn't want to hear that. I focused on practical concerns now that I'd agreed that Seona's son could stay. There was the matter of which room Daeshim would have. I had the maid put Daeshim in a room next to Gwangmu's. They could be friends, I thought, and Gwangmu seemed to enjoy his company. I didn't give Daeshim the room Seona and I had shared because Siwon occupied it by then. It had a lovely view of the hibiscus bush, its flowers deep purple. Maybe it was a mistake, I thought afterward, when the teacher left too. The two people I'd loved who had deserted me had each slept in that room. What view did they have from it, beyond the flowers, that made them abandon me?

Seona's husband returned eventually. I remember there was a gap in days that was so long, his indignation at not being told where his son was didn't hold water with me.

"You should give me money now," he said.

"But he's staying with me. You should give me money to take care of him," I returned.

"I only need a small loan until I can find work," he said.

"Why did it take you so long to realize your son was missing?" I asked. "Or maybe you left him at our gate because you knew I'd take him in?"

"Don't you want your sister to reach Seoul? It's expensive to get her and my daughter down here safely."

"You said she doesn't want to come," I retorted, suspicious of his words.

"That doesn't mean she should be left up there!" he shouted.

I told him to return in a few days, after I'd sold the silk in my mother's trunk. Of course he had to try to bring Seona south. My plan was once he brought her over, I'd find a way to see for myself if she had changed. I was hopeful he would actually use the money to bring my sister to safety. He returned at the end of the week, and I gave him enough money to pay a guide, someone who was willing to go back and forth across the ever-changing lines of combat. It was the equivalent of two months of food for the entire household. Seona's husband actually thanked me. I thought we had an agreement. The waiting began.

Two weeks afterward, Mina and Aera started the trouble. They came with their children, curious to meet Seona's son. They criticized how I ran the household; they asked about Siwon, asked if he could teach their children if he was such an excellent scholar. I hated the scrutiny. I started to question whether Daeshim should be staying with me. I suggested my sisters take him to one of their houses. But during that visit, Aera's children were cruel to Daeshim, called him names, called him a liar. Gwangmu stood up to them and they were cruel to him in turn. Bogum played peacemaker, but it felt temporary to me, this détente. Gwangmu wouldn't allow his aunts to take Daeshim.

When my sisters finally left, I decided to send Daeshim out of our house and back to his father. I thought he could find out if his father was using the money to bring his mother and sister south. Siwon disagreed with me. Gwangmu became angry but I told him a son's place was with his father. Hayun made herself even more scarce, frightened of my proclamations.

I sent Daeshim away. I told him to return if he couldn't find his father. I packed him some food and a blanket and told him to come back to visit whenever he wanted.

"Your father will be glad to see you," I told my nephew.

Days went by. Gwangmu was despondent. He worried about Daeshim. I thought he would forget about his cousin as time passed. I hoped that when I saw Daeshim again, he would be with Seona and her daughter. How else could I make Seona's husband do as he had promised with the money I'd given him?

Could I have followed up with Seona's husband? Offered more money to make sure he brought her south? We were in a war. I knew not to trust him. How could I force him to do anything? He was her husband. That fact made everything feel impossible. Besides, I didn't know if she wanted to be found.

I couldn't forget that she hadn't written to me. If she'd given even one hint that she wanted to come south, I would have thrown all my efforts into helping her. I told myself I was doing what she had done when she eloped: focusing on love. During that time, I did little except relish my days and late nights talking about books and geography with Siwon.

This was the period when Gwangmu spent unsupervised time with Hayun. Weeks elapsed. After we learned of Hayun's pregnancy, Daeshim showed up at the gate again. He said his father wanted nothing to do with him, was living with a woman on the other side of Seoul. Daeshim asked to stay. He was terribly gaunt. Of course I allowed him to have dinner with us. But I was nervous that he'd find out about Gwangmu's indiscretion. It was logical that Gwangmu would confide in him. You should have seen the joy in my son's face when Daeshim appeared. But my heart was heavy with worry. There was too much out of my control. I felt helpless.

Daeshim was a reminder of his outrageous father and my silent sister. I couldn't bear to look at him. Not his fault, I knew, but I just couldn't understand why my sister had forsaken me. Plus, Mina and Aera were once more trying to meddle in my life. They sent word that they wanted to visit again. I was certain that Daeshim would learn from Gwangmu about Hayun's pregnancy and tell my sisters.

I couldn't just sit around and wait as tragedy unfolded around me. Action was required. One by one, I took the steps to protect my family's reputation. I did what I thought my father would have done in my stead. He'd refused to let Seona marry the person she chose; I would do the same with Gwangmu. My father had lied to our neighbors about Seona, saying she was going away to live with a relative, so I would send Daeshim away. Separate everyone — that was the answer.

I reached out to a Catholic church nearby, the same one I would contact later when Siwon wanted to go abroad, and asked them to arrange for Daeshim to get an education in America. I'd heard they did such things. To sweeten the incentive, I sold a few family heirlooms and donated the money to the church, making sure Daeshim would be well provided for; I also gave him enough money to travel to the United States and stay there, far away from us. Daeshim was a quick study; Siwon had said so.

Gwangmu was busy somewhere with Hayun so it was easy to tell him a few days after Daeshim left that his cousin had come to me only for money and that he did not want to be in touch. I told my son that Daeshim was just like his father and was trying to use us for our fortune. I said he had leaped at the chance to go to America.

Years later, the visit to which Joyce alluded, I saw Daeshim again and he thanked me for the boost I'd given him. Even though I demurred, he said it was more than even his own father had done for him, which was the truth. His regret was that Gwangmu had not returned his various letters and phone calls after he moved to Chicago. A lost opportunity to be as close as those initial days in Korea when they'd met.

"Gwangmu was very involved with his American family," I told Daeshim during that conversation. "He had no time for me either." I didn't tell him how I'd poisoned my son against his cousin.

"I only learned about his funeral from Bogum," Daeshim said.

I remember thinking as he spoke that he looked like his mother now in a way he hadn't when he was younger. Why had I thought he resembled his father?

"Silly to think it, but should I have kept you with us in Korea?" I asked.

"Don't give it another thought, Auntie," he said. "We all did the best we could." His hand was at my elbow as we made our way to my son's grave. My breath caught in my throat at his words. What a curious response. I had anticipated he would say, *I could not have achieved any of the things I did if you hadn't sent me to America and paid for my education.*

The best we could? Was that an insult? Or was it true? *Had* I done the best I could?

I could have done more for Daeshim. I should have done more. I'd seen who his father was, and I sent Daeshim back to him, and he'd slept in the street. More than that, I'd sent him away a second time and he'd been turned away by his father again. And even after that, to protect the secret of Hayun's pregnancy, I sent him to the other side of the world. Which was ironic, because soon after, my son and my love Siwon both departed for that far-off continent, and I was left alone in Korea.

CHAPTER 26

had caused a mess in my life on Earth — I admit it. I'd exiled both Seona's son and my granddaughter to America, setting in motion the sequence of events that would curse our family forever. A marriage could not take place.

I'd had more than half a century to admit my mistakes and I'd failed to do it. In this afterlife, I'd walked through persimmon-colored clouds and dirt in a white hanbok and sneakers and learned how to walk through walls, but I still didn't know how to reach the living to apologize, and I had turned my back on my niece who had tried to help me. Now she was refusing to return. Maybe it was time for Seona to help me.

"We were sisters, Seona," I called to the air, waving my arms. I was still tumbling down, but moving my limbs seemed to slow the speed. "Your daughter won't help me but I'm ready to fix my mistakes. You called me 'foolish Jeonga.' You were right. But I don't want to be anymore. How do I start?"

There was no response. I couldn't bear it. Waiting had never been a strong suit of mine. How did you measure time in a place like this? Maybe I was already too late.

Thinking of time gave me an idea. Korean mythology of the afterlife mentions trials. If I could go back in time, if one of my trials in the afterlife was to give up what I'd had, I was ready to do it. Was this air that felt like water around me a chance to wash it all away? Was that a clue? Would that bring Seona peace? If one decision led to another decision, one secret to another secret, could I go back to the beginning, before all of them, to a moment I could control? I could choose another way. I'd give back some of the secrets. The big ones.

I opened my hands, opened my arms, let all the memories go. The good and the bad. My memories that made me who I am. My life. Let all I knew go. *Forget. Wash it all away.* I wished for it. All the secrets I'd kept and protected with my actions. *Give me an alternate path, one without love.*

Closing my eyes tight, I repeated to myself: *Go back in time, Jeonga. Give up what you had for what you should have had. Go back to the time before you fell in love. Go back to before you were so in love that you didn't see that your teenage son was also falling in love with someone right under your roof. Go back to the time before Siwon and his sister came to your house.*

I imagined it, and the feeling of motion ceased. A scene became real before my eyes: A newspaper on the low table in front of me criticized Syngman Rhee. The year was 1948, and I was alone and anxious. The Japanese were gone but Korea was in turmoil. My son was thirteen years old. I sat in silence on a cushion on the smooth floor of my childhood home. I was a widow. Such deafening silence felt like a bubble all around me. It wobbled, and in the distance, I saw a rice-paper wall hanging in the air by itself and then rushing toward me while other walls materialized around me and a floor slid beneath my feet. I was thrown off balance, like the sudden jerk of a people mover in an airport when you first step on. The walls pressed in, threatening to squash me.

I crouched on the floor, covered my head. But the walls kept their short distance, making a square coffin around me. The floor was hard and cold to the touch; a chill traveled up through my feet. I gathered my knees to myself, placed one foot on top of the other to keep warm. How lonely I felt. Not worthy of love. I didn't matter to anyone. Alone. No one would miss me. No one even knew I was here.

I thought it would stay silent, but instead I heard a throbbing heart, the coursing of blood through my veins. All the noise of being inside, not outside, flesh. Even unloved, the body demanded to be known. If I'd never known desire and had never been desired, would I feel as if every centimeter of skin hungered for a tender touch? I remembered how restless I'd felt before Siwon came into my life. If he had not, I would still have found the loneliness intolerable, but now, the memory of what I'd had in life made the loss excruciating. I shook my head back and forth. I held my arms around myself. I made myself concentrate on the sacrifice I was making: Gwangmu would not father a child. Ellery would not be born. Jordan would fall in love with someone else. Generations would carry on as they had for centuries. For the good of all, the annihilation of my spirit would ensure that generations to come would flourish. *This is heroic, Jeonga,* I told myself. *Be a shell of a person, Jeonga.*

Time crawled by inside the rice-paper box in which I was trapped. I began to believe I would suffocate. Every few minutes I stretched out my hands and prodded a wall. It didn't budge. The rice paper felt cold and hard. I pushed on the opposite wall. The same obstinate, unforgiving surface. The restlessness spread to my eyes. I pressed my face against the walls to see if I could make out shapes, anything outside of this container, but I couldn't see anything. Before I knew it, I had jumped to my feet. There was no door. I couldn't go back in time and accept another path. I was not strong enough, selfless enough. My hands pounded against the rice paper of the walls through my bubble.

"Let me out. I can't do it. I can't do it alone. I don't want to be alone," I wailed. I clawed at the rice-paper walls. I kicked and screeched.

When my skin tingled, I thought it was from the cold. Baby goose bumps. But then I felt a vibration. A humming from outside. A voice was calling me. A sound I knew. Coming from below? I fell to my knees and pounded my fists on the frosted floor. The voice came again, this time from above.

"Samonim!"

Hands on the other side of the rice-paper wall. Pounding. Not my hands. Other hands from the other side of the rice-paper box. The wall shook from the impact.

"Samonim!" It was Chohui. "Samonim!" The walls fell away.

My eyes were open, but I felt another layer flip open as if I had a third eyelid. The rice-paper room I was in was gone. Instead, I was standing on a blue surface facing a dense curtain of falling water in the shape of a doorway.

Tell the secret, show people the secret came a voice from the center of my chest. The voice, which belonged to me, was steady and firm.

"Chohui, are you there?" I called.

A droning filtered through the cascading water, increasing in volume. A familiar sound attached to a memory: Seona and I as children sneaking up to a small house. It was forbidden but we went anyway, crawling up on the porch and crouching by the sliding door. My sister held her finger to her lips. An ancient ritual — that's what it was. We were not allowed to be there but Seona was curious about everything, so we followed Appa and Eomma to see a shaman.

Now I heard a similar kind of murmuring. It originated from the other side of the waterfall. Could I walk through it? Could I finally reach the living? Could I tell everyone the secrets I'd been holding? Seona's face on that day we listened in on the shaman's incantations flashed in my mind. Not only had she held her finger to her lips, urging me to be quiet, but she had nodded: *See? We can go anywhere.*

I held on to that vision and lunged through the water.

"Wait for me," I said. "I'm coming." A tiny mallet of hope hammered in my chest.

It was a startling experience. Immediately, I was incredulous. Rather than being pelted with actual water, I felt nothing. The waterfall was an illusion, a phantom. So much in this dimension was not what I expected. The incantations grew louder with each step I took. I pushed on, making out shining small globes of light ahead of me.

All at once, the torrent ceased. I was through to the other side. In front of me were round tables piled high with books and rocks, flickering flames of candles that were nearly at the end of their lives, and boxes of Kleenex. Had to be an American room. The spheres of light I had used as a guide turned out to be lamps with tasseled shades.

Across the room came the source of the droning. Two figures sat in chairs facing each other; the smaller one, whose back was turned toward me, had her hands, palms down, in the open hands of the larger person. The pair were angled toward the back of this small sitting room. The one whose expressions I could make out clearly was American. She seemed quite average even so, a plain white woman with light brown hair and the round gold-rimmed glasses that were in fashion in Korea last year. She looked forgettable except for a blouse the shade of blue that reminded me of the waterfall I'd just traveled through. I walked around with great effort, feeling like I was wading across a knee-high river with a strong current, to get a better view. The American had her hands outstretched toward...Chohui.

I blinked to be sure I could trust my eyes. Chohui. I recognized her precious bent head. Chohui's body was turned slightly away from the woman, as if she couldn't commit herself to being fully present. I felt a tenderness toward her. She was mourning me. If I still had a heart in whatever form I was in, it lifted. Dear Chohui.

I moved ever closer. What was Chohui doing here? The American woman was speaking.

"We could use tarot cards, or I could read your palm, but my way is to channel the energy of the grieving one because I find that love powers the connection." She spoke in English, but I experienced it as knowing, which caught me by surprise. I understood what she meant without hearing it as any language. I looked around to see if I was wrong — maybe someone had translated her words to me. But no one else was in the room.

Chohui sniffled. Was she crying? I attempted to touch her, but I was still too far away. What was this woman doing to her?

"Whatever way you think best," Chohui said. "My friend the chauffeur said you've helped him before. Shamans are very busy in America, just like in Korea, I guess." Again, the meaning was dropped in my mind. I didn't question it for another second. What was happening here that I had to fix? Who cared how I knew? I just knew — it was simple. A shaman? This wasn't like any shaman I'd ever imagined.

"Go to a Korean shaman, Chohui, didn't I teach you better?" I said aloud. I had to get closer to her, because at this distance, Chohui didn't seem to have heard me.

Suddenly the American woman looked right at me.

"She's here," she announced.

Chohui looked everywhere but where I was standing, which was in the middle of the room.

I followed her gaze, noting the parameters of this small windowless parlor.

"Well, this is not a good way to spend the money I left you," I said to Chohui, because, really, I could see now that this American woman was a performer, not a true medium with natural talents. She clearly needed useless props. The strange rocks on the tables, for instance. And the crystals hanging from an already low ceiling.

"How much did you pay this shaman?" I asked.

"It's the going rate," the American woman answered.

"What do you mean, rate?" Chohui asked.

"Run, Chohui, get away at once, and don't give her another cent," I shouted and again tried to move closer and intervene, but my feet wouldn't comply. They were pinned to the floor. The shaman gave me a stern look, which Chohui followed with her own eyes, but evidently she still couldn't see me because then she looked up at the ceiling and away again.

"Samonim?" Chohui said, eyes widening.

The shaman pointed to Chohui's left, precisely where I was not. Liar.

"Please, Chohui, my sisters surely know of a powerful shaman with integrity who can help us," I urged.

"She says she has sisters," the shaman said to Chohui.

Chohui's eyes welled up. "That's right, she does. But they're scared. They wouldn't come with me. Do you wish they'd come instead of me?" She pulled her hands away just then. "Do you have a tissue? I can't stop crying —"

Her voice began to fade and her form did too. My eyes blurred. I couldn't breathe. An invisible hand was around my throat and I was pushed back into the waterfall.

"The connection has to stay strong," the American woman said.

Chohui apologized and all at once, my eyes focused and I could breathe again. Chohui's hands were back in the shaman's. I'd been returned to the room but I was now on the periphery — who had moved me here? This was unacceptable. I felt anger and then I was seized with fear. I could be removed from the room without my consent.

With rapt attention, I found myself repeating, "Hold on, Chohui, hold on tight. Hold on, Chohui."

"You said on the phone that you had an urgent question?" the shaman said.

"I've been so worried," Chohui replied.

"Oh, you worried," I said. My heart melted in her direction. "I'm fine, Chohui," I shouted at her and then waved my arms and fanned the air. "Can you do something about this?" I asked the American woman, pointing to my feet and then to my chest.

"Was it your grandmother's heart that took her from this dimension?" the woman asked.

"She's not my —" Chohui and I said at the same time.

The woman blinked suspiciously. "It's such a strong, immediate connection that I just assumed," she said.

"I worked for her, that's all," Chohui answered.

"That's all?" I sank to the floor.

The shaman lifted her chin in my direction. "Give her a minute," she said to me. "Stay with us." I nodded and got back to my feet. I'd do anything to remain in this room.

"Wait — did she hear that?" Chohui said.

The shaman nodded. "She's listening. Continue," she said.

"Does she know I talked about her?" she whispered.

The shaman shrugged.

Chohui swallowed hard and then called out to the room, "I did complain about you to my friends, I'm sorry, but you weren't easy to work for, samonim. I know it was because you missed your son. We have that in common, you and me. We haven't been lucky with our families."

I wiped a torrent of tears that had surprisingly sprung up. No more clogged ducts — a miracle.

"She understands," the shaman said.

It still hurt. I thought Chohui had been grateful for the lessons I'd provided. "I made the best decisions for Chohui. She wouldn't even be able to talk to you now if I hadn't given her English lessons," I declared.

"She's glad you speak English," the shaman said.

Chohui let out a laugh. "That doesn't sound like samonim. She told everyone how she got me the best English tutor in Seoul and it certainly was helpful for me, but really she did it because she was obsessed with the United States. Plus, she cared what everyone thought. I had to be the best so she looked good."

She turned her face to the middle of the room. "Samonim, if you can hear me, I'm sorry I said that, but you know it's true. *You* wanted to learn English — that was the real reason you made me learn."

I was about to protest, defend myself, but the shaman gave me a piercing look that plunged right into my forehead, and I was silenced.

Chohui was talking to the shaman again. "Samonim meant well — I know she tried to help me. Anyway, she did not have a heart attack. You see, the night before she died, I heard her say something that's been bothering me."

"Go on," the shaman said at the exact same time I did, though she spoke in English.

"Right, so that night she was calling out in her sleep for her sister, the one who went to North Korea. She told me the whole story."

I did? I couldn't remember doing so.

Chohui continued, "Samonim was saying 'Sorry' repeatedly in her sleep, and I didn't tell her the next morning because she was always upset when she talked about her sister. They were very close, but in her sleep, she kept saying, 'I'm sorry, I'm sorry.'" Chohui's voice quavered. "I know she's been sad lately. Being in America reminds her of her son, and I just want to know if she — I'm sorry to even question it, but I have to know — did she mean to go the way she did? The bus was horrible. Because if so, I'm so sorry. I've been praying for her soul. Is she in purgatory because she killed herself?" Chohui's eyes were wide with fear.

I forgot Chohui had converted to Catholicism last year. Her friend had convinced her it was a good idea. That was probably the friend she'd met while I was at my father's grave with my sisters.

"Not a suicide," I said out loud because the shaman lifted her eyebrows in my direction.

"She wasn't supposed to be on the bus," the shaman said.

"*On* a bus? No, she was hit. Eyewitnesses said she walked in front of it like she meant to."

"She doesn't strike me as someone who would hurt herself," the shaman replied.

"Are you sure?" Chohui asked. "I should have run after her but I was on my phone — and maybe her dream was a warning, maybe I was supposed to warn her."

Well, now I was overcome with tenderness for her. Dear, dear Chohui. I'd underestimated the extent of her devotion to me.

Her eyes must have welled up just then because she dropped the shaman's hands and asked for another Kleenex, which resulted in my neck being throttled again and my vision blurring.

"Not yet — grab her hands," I called.

The shaman responded in a calm voice, "It was just a dream and now you know what happened with the bus was just an accident. Put it behind you."

Chohui placed her hands back in the shaman's. Clarity returned.

Put it behind her? Not only was this shaman getting some basic facts about how I had died wrong, she was encouraging Chohui to forget about me. I had so much more to tell her. I needed help.

"She's a suspicious old thing, isn't she?" the shaman said.

I was startled. That wasn't a compliment.

Chohui gave a feeble smile. "Samonim is like that. She's suspicious of almost everyone, but you should see her with her sisters. She trusts them and probably shouldn't. She doesn't listen to me. I mean, she didn't —" Her smile vanished and her face reddened. "I mean, they want to cremate her here instead of waiting for a proper burial in Korea. Samonim would be furious. She wanted everything done the old way. Can you tell her it's not my fault that they won't budge?"

Well, what about that! My sisters were disposing of me as fast as possible. How dare they. No wonder I was wandering in the afterlife. The betrayal. No funeral rites? Cremated here in a foreign land? My fist was pounding on my hip bone; I was stomping my feet. The floor shook with each stomp; I could feel it, but Chohui and the shaman didn't seem to notice.

"Taking a body back on a plane can be cost-prohibitive," the shaman said, nodding.

"Money? That's not the reason. They don't want to be bothered," I said. "Like I'm a piece of wood to burn up, like they can't be inconvenienced for one minute. Just wait and see what I'll do to them, I'll find a way —"

"Tell her sisters to give her proper funeral rites or she'll haunt them forever," the shaman said to Chohui in a brusque voice. She looked at me again. "Anything else?"

This shaman was ruthless, I could see. I was beginning to believe she had some actual powers after all.

"Listen here," I said to the shaman. "Tell Chohui to go to Ohio and give the letter that's in my purse to my grandniece."

The shaman repeated it verbatim as if she were in a trance.

"Good job," I said. "And tell her don't forget to arrange for the money."

"Remember the money," the shaman said.

"Don't worry, samonim," Chohui called to the room. "I have your purse. You left it in Ned's house."

She was more comforting than I'd given her credit for. And then I remembered the more important point. To the shaman, I shouted, "Tell her Jordan and Ellery need to know the truth about their family."

The shaman blinked and nodded at me several times. "Go on," she said in my direction.

Now my respect was flowing in waves toward this woman. "Forget about the wedding. She has to bring Ned and his family-tree diagrams to the hospital and tell them the truth," I said.

"You're going to meet someone. There's a wedding, and they need to be shown the family tree," the shaman said.

"Well, well. I will stay right here and use you to do my bidding," I said. "Can you let me sit in a chair, at least? I have so much to say."

"No, you won't," she snapped at me.

"I won't?" Chohui said.

"Okay, I won't sit. Now you've gone and ruined your good work," I said, laughing.

The shaman collected herself. *My goodness, her arms must be tired of holding Chohui's hands that way,* I thought. "Keep up the good work," I said to the American. "But you're wrong about Chohui's wedding."

"Forget about your wedding," she said to Chohui.

"But I'm not getting married," Chohui said.

This conversation was getting off track. "It's not about *Chohui's* wedding," I said, shaking my fist at the shaman. "She must give Ned's family tree to Ellery and Jordan in Ohio. They're the ones who want to get married. Do you understand? The family tree!"

The shaman ignored me. "I see you meeting your soul mate in two days, two weeks, two months, or two years. That's it. That's all there is. Now our time is up," she said.

Two days to two years? What kind of approximation was that? Not one worth anything.

"Are you sure?" Chohui exclaimed.

"Don't you believe in love?" the American shaman asked with a sadness in her voice I could relate to. "A young man will come along and —"

Chohui grimaced. She released the shaman's hands and I felt myself falling backward.

"Wait," I cried. But Chohui was standing up — I could see her silhouette straighten and hear her voice: "Thanks, I have to go now." An elongated sound distorted by the rumble of falling water.

"Your hour is up anyway," the shaman said. "The connection is broken. Let yourself out. I'm going to wash my hands and ready myself for my next client."

This time, there was no returning. I was shoved through the waterfall and spat out to be suspended in a putrid orange mist. I promised myself I'd never eat another persimmon for as long as I — I stopped myself. Not another persimmon ever.

The waterfall vanished. In the quiet of the other side, which was becoming increasingly thunderous, I called out, "Chohui, you must tell them the secret, that Ellery is Jordan's third cousin. Don't let them get married." There was no response. I repeated myself and tried to feel for the waterfall with my hands. Nothing. Silence. I was hanging out in this orange space, nothing under my feet, but I wasn't falling. What to make of this? No way forward, no way back. Just orange mist all around me.

"Chohui," I called and called. "Go back to the shaman or go to another one. I have so much to tell you."

But the roar of the water increased. Stupid, stupid. Why didn't I say that first? That was the most important message to get across. All I'd had to do was extract that promise from her to keep the channel open. Pay this shaman for as much time as it took. But I had forgotten the basic lesson: Start with the most important point; don't waste time.

The lost opportunity ate me up. I kicked and pulled and thrashed about. I lost a sock. And then, when I was exhausted by my tantrum, I recalled Chohui in the American shaman's room, her hands outstretched. She had reached out to me, and I had heard. Could she hear me if I reached out to her? Even without a shaman? I had to find her.

With my eyes closed, I remembered what a good swimmer I used to be. The air felt heavy. It surrounded me. A density, even a gurgling — the slightest whoosh and current of invisible water. *Where are you, Chohui?* I took a deep breath and shifted my weight to my knees and feet as if I were trying to sink to the bottom of a lake. I waved my arms to push water above my head, propel myself down. I seemed to be moving, albeit ever so slowly. But to what did I have to compare my descent? The air around me remained unchanged. But I felt movement. I tried to sink faster by bringing my knees to my chest. Was I running out of time?

I was accelerating downward. The orange air blurred around me. Even as I was being swept into a whirlpool of air, I had to hope. My body protested but I didn't care. If I suffocated, would I die again? What more could be done to me? The American shaman was wrong. The connection couldn't be broken. I wouldn't let it. I pictured Chohui in my mind's eye. Chohui tapping on the rice-paper room in which I had been trapped. Cherished Chohui. "Samonim!" Her voice reverberated in my head.

I found myself dragging my body in the direction of Chohui's voice as I remembered it. One step forward. I could move back into the world of the living. I remembered what Taeyang had told me.

"Chohui, it's an emergency," I called and took a step in the air, and my feet held firm against a carpeted floor. Another step and I walked through a wall and was inside a hotel room. A figure was lying in a bed in front of me. I approached.

"I'm here," I squawked, my voice too excited to be steady.

The figure in bed sat up abruptly, reached for a lamp, and clicked a switch and the room was bathed in a warm yellow glow.

"Go away," Chohui shouted. "Go away, evil spirit!"

"No, no, no." I held out my hands toward her.

She pulled the blanket that was across her legs straight over her head. "Samonim taught me how to ignore you years ago. You're not welcome here," she said, her voice high with fright.

I laughed out loud, and it sounded like a howl as tears of frustration cut it short. In a soothing voice, I said, "Chohui, calm down, it's me."

She threw off the blanket and scampered out of bed. This way and that, she rushed about, turning on the television and raising the volume so loud I couldn't speak over it. I tried to get closer to her but the sounds, the lights. It was dizzying. She grabbed a book off the night table and began to read. Had I told her about my strategy to read when I saw gwisin? I didn't remember but there she was using the book the way I had. It made me both irritated and mildly proud of her.

"Chohui! Stop it at once. Put that book down, I'm trying to tell you something," I ordered in what I considered a measured and kind voice. But she didn't listen; her hands blocked her ears and she mouthed the words on the page. I didn't know what to do. Her fear vibrated in waves around her and hit me in the chest. How could Chohui be afraid of me? How could I reach her so she would hear me from this side of life?

I stifled my disappointment and focused. If I could get a little closer to Chohui, she would hear me through the noise of the television, which had talking heads in multiple frames on the screen. She would hear me despite her eyes skimming the paragraphs of the novel. But every step forward seemed to push me back from the woman in the room, who was now humming. Chohui could sing? Along with the sound of the television, her humming was pushing out thoughts of me. Now I was half back in the wall. The vibrations emanating from her increased. And in the next instant, I was outside in the night air, alongside the top story of a gruesome white-gilled building. Like a dancing spine of a skeleton without a head or limbs.

CHAPTER 27

I started to plummet, so I flapped my arms. I was going to die. Crash to the pavement. And then I remembered I'd already died and breathed again. My body steadied in midair. But then the thought of Chohui's fear of me dropped me a few floors before I calmed myself once more.

I willed myself to return to the interior of the building, which was, by its sign, the Radisson Blu Aqua Hotel (my sisters had certainly spent a lot of money after I died!), only this time, maybe my sisters would allow me into their dreams. Surely they missed me as Chohui did. Despite the conflicts and misunderstandings. They were my sisters.

They were in the room next to Chohui's. I wandered in. Lumps in their beds. Who knew if they were capable of dreaming? Didn't they care about me? Didn't they wonder? Nothing emanated from their bodies. No love. No hate. Blank. They were no different than their phones charging on their bedside tables. A sadness kept me from staying any longer. I retreated.

Up into the night sky, I floated. Was this the phase of no body? Was I running out of time? How long did I drift, expecting nothing to change? Did we get to watch over the people we loved? Which part of me was sky and which part the body I remembered? Siwon had said he watched over my grandson Ned, had made Jordan have a flat tire so he would meet Ellery. How had he reached them? I wandered over the streets. Where was I? Where were they?

If I could find Ned with his books and his family-tree diagrams, could he contact Ellery? What was this space of in between and would I be able to stay? That's what made me hold on.

Swim, I told myself. I kicked my way through the air. I had to find a way to connect to the living. Maybe Ellery, like Chohui, would mourn me. If Ellery knew I was dead, she'd call for me, wouldn't she? Except why would she? To her, I was a busy old woman who'd stopped by her house; nothing meaningful in that.

I floated for an indefinite time. No waking or sleep or way to measure. No signals from Ned or Chohui or anyone who grieved for me. I pictured Chohui with the shaman again, how she'd held out her hands and allowed me into the shaman's room. *Don't forget me, Chohui,* I called out to the dark night sky around me.

What I remembered was how different Chohui had looked, how being in America suited her, being without me. She could have been any young woman about town, her hair loose around her face, her shoulders back, at ease, as if she didn't need to guard herself. With me dead, a burden lifted from her, it was true. I hoped my sisters weren't making demands of her. At the shaman's, it seemed not the case. She was free to see the shaman, after all.

How long did I drift? Days and days; the sun came up and then set. I paddled my arms to the left — they would be back in Korea by now. Could I fly there? Would Chohui's voice transport me to a shaman in Korea?

On one of those days, I paddled about in the blue sky until my fingers blurred and I had no use for them. Was it so bad to be a cloud? Clouds were part of Chohui's world. Could I drift until someone remembered me? *Focus,* I ordered myself. *Make the connection.* The shaman's room had been within reach. Chohui's dream had been within reach. I listened.

And then a voice, Chohui's voice. I heard it coming from somewhere to my left. It said, "Pretzels, please."

But nothing was there. I swam all the way to my left, then all the way back to my right, up and down, and then far below me was a minuscule object, a bird, white and glistening.

I descended fast and then faster still. Instead of crashing into feathers, I plunged into something huge, not a bird but an airplane. And then I was through the outer shell and had merged into the dark blue faux leather of a passenger seat. I swallowed to squelch the wave of vomit that threatened to be expelled. And then every part of me from my chin down seemed to go numb. The violent queasiness subsided. I had no time to wonder if this was eternal, this loss of my body.

I was all face, no arms or legs, nothing I could reach out with. All I could do was observe. I felt absurd in this state, but there was no time to dwell on it. I noticed that my mouth was the screen embedded in the back of a passenger seat. My nose and eyes felt as if they were above the screen. Pulling this way and that in small increments, I could loosen myself a little, enough to slide, but not before I saw that Mina's face was staring back at me.

"Mina," I called. "Here I am." She did miss me! My sister. She hadn't forgotten! Except she wasn't looking at me but at the screen. Her mouth was moving as she watched. Her halitosis made me gag even in this state of being merged with an airline seat. I managed to slide down and away to the edge of the armrest so I could see what she was watching. It was an American movie.

A white American woman's giant face was on the screen, her dark red lipstick glistening. Blood red had never been a good color for me. I slid back with great effort to try to catch Mina's attention. She was mouthing the words the actors were saying in the movie. The wrinkles around her eyes had become even looser and hung like a valance.

"Here, in the seat, Mina. Look up." *Sister. Big sister Mina.* I tried telepathy, but she was closed off. There were creases in the leather. Surely she could make out my eyes. But Mina's eyes were empty, as if she had no light inside. That had always been Mina to me. Not open, not present, not caring. In this blob state, I found myself scowling just from the sheer intensity of it.

"Here." I glared. "Straight ahead, look at me."

She jerked her head up and stared right at me, but she blinked without any recognition and then she closed her eyes and said to Aera, "Don't bother me, okay? I'm taking a nap. This is exhausting. Conserve your energy. Seona will die next, wherever she is in North Korea, and then it's you, Aera. You'll go, if the birth order means anything. I'll be the last."

Well, Mina made no sense. If birth order by youngest to oldest was the pattern, then I would have died first and then Seona. But I realized that my older sisters didn't know that Seona had died. They knew only that I had, and they assumed that Seona was still alive in North Korea.

Aera let out a breath and hit the screen of her television. It took much effort, but I slid with big breaths into the seat in front of my other sister. "Aera, please see me," I implored, my eyes as open as I could make them. She pushed at the screen and mumbled to herself, "Not that one, not that, oh, go back." Each push was a lurch I felt on my face.

"Damn it, Aera, I'm here." I sent as strong a message as I could, but she continued in her frustration, her short gloved fingers stabbing at the screen.

Hot breath blasted the side of my eye. A man sitting in the seat that was now my face barked at her, "Can you stop doing that?" His nose poked into the space between the seats. With the faux leather that smelled like chlorine and the lurching and his hot breath, I felt as though I might faint.

Where was Chohui? As far as I could see, which in this position wasn't far, she was nowhere to be found. I tried slithering from seat to seat and then slinking along the floor. Even when someone stepped on me, it didn't hurt; I was just blinded momentarily. It would have been comical if it weren't so pitiful. I had no time for pity, I reminded myself.

Where was she? Where was this plane headed? My speed at sliding down the aisle brought me to the end of the plane. Lavatories flanked me. If I waited, I might see her go to one. Below me in the vast compartment existed something that called to me. It was not a voice this time but a tug. As if my toe had been caught in a sudden bump in a sidewalk, if I were to be walking on a sidewalk. Another big breath and I lowered myself and merged now with the entire ceiling of the baggage compartment. I was shaped like a domed ceiling, one eye curving in one direction and the other curving in the other, and I felt immense, as if my face were now the whole width of this large plane, but I did not feel all-powerful. Simply expansive and at the mercy of whatever happened next.

Pinned to this place, I wanted to leave it before I was trapped here forever. Suitcases — those bricks with wheels and handles — were stacked in a wall, and then I saw it. This was what had called me here. A casket.

It took my breath away. I slid down the side and along the metal rivets and then I was caressing the glossy wooden surface of the coffin with my cheek. Mina and Aera had spent money on me after all. Chohui had been wrong. Or maybe Chohui had fought for me. I pictured her fighting my sisters and emerging victorious. Good thing I'd left Chohui a decent amount of money. She'd never have to work for people like them.

Inside, I could view my body. It didn't look as if it had ever been alive. An old woman's shell dressed in a powder blue suit. A skirt and jacket with a white blouse beneath it. A commonsense choice, but I looked like a flight attendant. Why did I pick such a suit to buy? The old woman was already not human. A discarded plastic mask. No part of me was in there, the separation of spirit and form complete. I felt disgust. And disbelief. They must have put a plastic mannequin in here in place of my body. Even as the knowledge was unrelenting, I didn't want to believe I could ever have had anything to do with this strange thing. As strange as the discarded skin of a snake. A sadness unfolded from my lungs and threatened to choke me.

This was not a good road of thought to travel down and so I refused to keep going. I kicked away from the top of the coffin — sharp snap of my attention, up and up. Up to the living. Away from these inert objects.

"Ginger ale, no ice," a voice said. Chohui; I knew it was her. I'd told her many times never to have cold drinks. It's not good for your health — everyone knew this.

Familiar exhaustion flooded through me even here, but I slid anyway, up to the seat in front of her. Unlike the business-class seats that my sisters occupied, the accommodations here were cheap. Itchy polyester in a tweed crosshatch of royal blue, yellow, and lime green. I entered through the pattern on the seat in front of her. Below me on the screen was the plane's flight trajectory — the cartoon image of the plane tilting toward and away from Chicago, wobbling as it steered toward the shape of California. I was too late. All was lost. Ellery was in Ohio, and Seona was either trying to heal Jordan, in which case Ellery and Jordan would get married (would Hayun break her promise to me and tell them the truth? Maybe, maybe not; I couldn't be sure), or trying to hurt him, having caused Jordan's illness to begin with, the way Siwon had caused the flat tire. I recoiled from that possibility. I refused to consider it. Instead, I concentrated on Chohui.

She was making sure my body was brought home to Korea. I gazed at Chohui's lovely face. I was sorry I had frightened her in her dream. She looked as if she'd aged ten years since I'd seen her at the American shaman's house. I watched her lower the tray table and thank the flight attendant who handed her a plastic cup with a clear liquid fizz.

"Don't drink it too fast, it's got bubbles," I said, as I often had when I was alive and in her company.

She spat out the soda and set the cup hard on the tray, which made it splash out. Her eyes were on mine. "You spilled!" I said. She squinted and stared, ignoring the mess on her tray table. "Your sleeve — watch out," I added, because she'd reached her hand out to touch my left eye and in the process, the sleeve of her shirt swept through the puddle of ginger ale. She was oblivious to it, of course. I winced and her hand snapped back before actually making contact.

Stay calm. I forced myself to be silent. Chohui had closed her eyes and was squeezing them tight.

"Go ahead, check, if you need to know it's me," I said and braced myself for her hand again, but this time when she opened her eyes, she sank down in her seat and looked everywhere but at me.

"What are you doing?" I asked.

"It's only a pattern; I'm seeing things that aren't there. I'm going to sleep," she muttered and then leaned to her right.

A woman with headphones was sitting next to Chohui, and when Chohui touched her, she jerked away as if she had been burned, bumping into the man in the window seat. I wondered what was wrong with this woman. Her reaction to Chohui annoyed me.

"Sorry, so s-sorry," Chohui stuttered.

She had no reason to apologize, but she did a few more times and then sat straight up in her seat. But she wouldn't look at me. Her head was tilted down, and her eyes were closed. In a second, she'd nod off into that cup that was still on the open tray table. I assumed her hands were in her lap beneath the table; there was nowhere else for them to go.

The man sitting in the seat ahead of her squirmed and I felt my eyes expand and then shrink back. Each movement pushed me out to the aisle, and I felt a part of me scatter. How much longer would I be allowed to stay here?

"Wake up, Chohui." I sent the command with all my strength.

CHAPTER 28

I thought I had been quite clear. I tried again. "It's me, Chohui. I know you attempted to reach me through the shaman. I was there, remember?"

"I don't care," Chohui said. "Go away."

Her fear was incomprehensible to me. This was not a dream. Why was she afraid?

"This is an emergency — I need you," I said.

"Are you all right?" a flight attendant, a man with a kind voice, asked as he walked down the aisle.

"Are there any other seats I could move to?" she asked.

Really? Was I going to have to chase her all over this ridiculously long plane? The flight attendant surveyed the rows and then shook his head.

"Sorry, but we'll be landing in San Francisco soon."

No, no, no. They were headed in the wrong direction. I had to hurry. I changed my tone. "I know you want to read a book right now and block the other world out — I showed you how to do that — but it's really me. Can you try to be open? For me?"

She nodded; even with her head tilted down, I knew I saw a nod.

"Good. Well, here's the thing: I need you to tell Ned his family tree is missing a branch."

"Family tree?" she said.

Chohui had opened her eyes and was examining the pattern of the seat-back fabric again, but I was not there; I had been tossed to her feet. The rattling of the plane's wings hitting turbulence had displaced me.

"Tell Ned that my son has family in San Francisco, that he's right about that," I called from the floor.

"Ned has a safe?" she said.

"The family secret — the secret, Chohui, do you understand?" I asked.

The woman beside her removed her headphones and sat stock-still. "Secret," she said.

I'd had no idea she could understand Korean. Chohui was as surprised as I was.

"You heard that?" Chohui said.

"Didn't you just say *family secret*?" she asked in English, although she used the Korean word for *family*.

"It wasn't me. It was the woman I used to work for. She died, but I see her," Chohui said and then launched into Korean, but the woman looked confused.

"Slow down. I know a little because my mother's Korean," she said.

"But you understood what she said," Chohui exclaimed.

"Can you two pay some attention to me?" I said. The man in the window seat had turned his head and was listening intently to Chohui and her new friend, appearing more and more apprehensive.

"What do you want?" Chohui's friend said to my face, which was now on the edge of the chair in front of Chohui, sliding up, as I'd been trying to get a better look at this mediator.

"What's samonim saying?" Chohui said.

Here I'd been worried that I wouldn't be able to make Chohui notice me, and look how easy this was. "Chohui, there's so much I have to tell you," I began but she was not listening.

"How is it possible?" Chohui asked.

"Friend of Chohui, tell her Jordan is Ellery's cousin," I said hurriedly.

"Who is Mallory?" the woman asked. She was quite attractive and looked to be close in age to Chohui.

"Ellery! Ellery is my great-granddaughter," I said.

"It's about a great-grand or something," the woman said.

Chohui wrinkled her brow.

"Call Hayun and get her to talk to Ned and tell everyone the secret," I rushed to say.

The woman in the middle seat repeated my words in Korean.

"But who is Hayun?" Chohui said.

"Tell Chohui to call the last number on my cell phone and tell Hayun to explain about the family secret," I said.

The woman did as I asked.

"Her cell phone? But she had it in her pocket when she was hit, and it was crushed by the bus. I don't have it," Chohui said.

"You could call the phone company," she suggested.

This woman was knowledgeable.

"I could do that in Korea," Chohui said.

"No, that'll take too long," I said. "Explain to my sisters that you all must go to Ohio as planned. As soon as you get off the plane in California, catch a flight to Ohio. Tell Joyce that Ellery is my great-granddaughter. Call Attorney Kim and have him wire the money to her." That was a mouthful, but everyone needed to know.

The woman asked Chohui a series of questions, their heads together. I thought they were awfully close. A few times they were interrupted by turbulence, and they laughed. So much mystery over a phone call. I squished my face into Chohui's cell phone. "Look at me," I said.

"We're landing," the woman said and she helped Chohui return her seat tray to a locked position.

"Call Ned and catch the next flight to Ohio. Tell my sisters you have to save Jordan's life!" I said to Chohui. But her eyes were closed, and she wasn't listening.

There was a low, deep rumbling, and I was flung upward. The ceiling of the plane slammed into my eyes, and Chohui and the young woman beside her fell away. I was shaken loose, and my limbs returned to me in the clouds. I wrapped my arms around myself — so cold. Fast and ferocious, a wind howled. Chohui hollered below me — a choir of screeches. I tried to keep the plane in my vision, but the clouds were stretching in towers around me. All I could do was go. I remembered, in my panic, what Taeyang had said: *Inside. Go inside.* So I relaxed my limbs and listened for the voices in the plane, and for a while there was still only the wind whooshing around me. Listen and wait. All I could do was be taken up and up. Closing my eyes, I reached out. *Chohui? Did you understand everything I said?*

It was cold as I rose higher, but then — there it was, not Chohui's voice but a sigh of relief. And then a shudder followed by the feeling of solid ground even though I was still rocketing upward. The plane was on the runway. It had landed.

Back to the plane, please, back to Chohui, I told myself. I stretched out my hands, recalled the feel of water, but I watched helplessly from the clouds as Chohui walked off. The roof of the airport was transparent, so I could see her chatting with her new friend. The trouble was, I couldn't hear what they were saying. All I could do was watch.

Every few minutes I flailed my arms to close the distance. *Call for me, Chohui,* I said. *Don't forget me, Chohui.*

My sisters Mina and Aera deplaned also. They weren't concerned about me at all. They waited for Chohui, had a conference with her standing at the gate, then left her to go another way. Chohui must be explaining my message, that I wanted them to go to Ohio. I anticipated confusion, an argument, a longer discussion. I hoped my sisters would look for me. Instead, it seemed they were all in agreement. I saw them nod. I saw Chohui relax her shoulders. Good!

Chohui watched them go and then went to one of the airport restaurants and joined her friend once more. Reduced as I was to the power of only my vision, I left the pair to follow my sisters. Where were they going without Chohui?

Mina walked with a limp to which Aera seemed oblivious. The younger of my two older sisters sped on ahead. She didn't even stop at the gate. People were lining up to board and Aera slipped right into the line without a glance at Mina. That was unkind. Maybe she assumed Chohui would help our sister. Aera boarded and eventually Mina arrived and got seated too and didn't say a word to her. What had happened? What had Chohui said to them?

The destination, according to the sign at the gate, was Incheon. My heart sank. They were flying to Korea. Chohui had let me down. All that work on the plane, and they were returning to Korea without getting the money to Joyce or giving Ellery the information she needed.

The gate closed but I didn't see Chohui board. My hopes rose, but what did this mean? Back to the restaurant I sped, and she was still there, talking to her new friend. Chohui blushed. Well, I didn't understand.

"Chohui," I called. "Chohui, what's the meaning of this?"

I settled into the vast ceiling of the airport and waited to see what she would do. She curled up and slept in a row of chairs after her new friend left to catch her plane. I watched Chohui sleep and tried to speak to her in her dreams, but she didn't let herself slip deeply enough into slumber. At every sound — people in the restaurant clinking uten-sils, the murmur of travelers passing by, the hum of the giant heating and cooling ventilation system, the announcements over the loud-speaker — she stirred, raised her head, then closed her eyes, only to snap them open again. Despite my best efforts, I was unable to get any closer than the ceiling.

It seemed to me that movement was essential to keep me from los-ing any more of myself. I flitted from one part of the ceiling to another. It was after midnight when I heard another voice call me. Was it Ellery? I stretched toward it. Did she need my help? Chohui remained in her state of half sleep so I let my grip on the airport go.

There was a tittering of voices off in the periphery now. Who was reaching out for me? The sky was a blizzard of nothingness, shards and shards of it. I had to swim toward the sounds, the feeling of sound, calling to me.

And then I was upon it, laid out on a flat black pavement. I had overshot my mark. With great and repeated effort, I gathered myself together, rolled, and pulled out every bit of me that had landed in the muck of the concrete.

I was separate now, in the bulb of the lamppost; my eye extended telescopically to a lone figure crossing the parking lot, walking as if buffeted by a wind even though there was no wind. The cars had Ohio license plates. I saw a large advertisement with the word *Meijer* with blue dots over the *i* and the *j* that made me feel like eyes were watching me. This must be Dayton, Ohio. I had to leap to another lamppost to keep up with this woman, who was walking briskly now. This wasn't Chohui or Ellery — her hair was very long, for one thing; it flew like a crushed banner behind her as she rushed about. Taller than Ellery, she wore a yellow raincoat as bright as a traffic sign.

I had to find trees and building roofs on which to cling. Vast spaces in this American city, and I had to avoid the pavement because it was too sticky to rise from. Better to stay high and leap even if I had to wrap my arms around objects as my hands faded and solidified at an unpredictable rate.

Shrubs were the best, really, for offering handholds. One bush bent particularly with my weight and I saw the woman stare before hurrying on her way. Finally, she entered a house and I used what I'd learned in the afterlife to go through the hard element of the red painted door.

I found I could cling to the leaves of plants. There was a convenient clump of them in pots by the bay window of this modest ranch house. It's why you shouldn't bring plants home from the hospital room of a sick person and why there were so many flowers at funerals and grave sites. Plants gave us a place to rest and hide.

The voices were not present here as I'd thought they'd be. I watched the woman for several days. She went, poor thing, back and forth between the hospital and her house. Sometimes she didn't even return to her house. Did I love my son that way? It shamed me to think I'd cut him off so easily. Should I have gone to his house in Chicago, America, and begged him to forgive me? He seemed happier without me. A new job and a new woman to fall in love with and then marry.

But if he was dying, I would have gone to the hospital. I know I would have. Gwangmu's death had been sudden. There had been no lingering.

Joyce — for I learned that this woman was Joyce — was devoted to her boy. Did she know he was dying because he was in love with the wrong person? That I was to blame?

I followed her as far as the entrance to the hospital, saw her through the window next to the shape of a young man in a hospital bed, but I didn't go any farther. A fear took hold of me — the hospital had a peculiar quality.

My goal was to watch out for Ellery. And of course she came, her head bowed with determination, wearing a short black trench coat and carrying a red Longchamp tote bag over her shoulder, the most stylish person in Ohio. I had to follow her despite the ominous air that surrounded the hospital, I had to protect Ellery, so I let go of the young maple tree by the sliding glass doors at the front of the building and launched in behind my great-granddaughter.

She stopped at the visitors' desk and then was in the elevator in seconds. I followed along, holding on to whatever sharp edge I could in the hallway and ceiling — these modern glass buildings didn't make it easy. I refused to lose sight of her, though, so I suffered, sliding along and ripping myself up from the horrible-smelling polished floors. I was proud of the way Ellery sailed through those halls. Clearly familiar to her. Clearly rushing to the side of her beloved. I almost cheered her on.

Ellery burst into the room and ran past Joyce, who was seated in a chair by the door. There was a strange orange fog encircling the still figure in the hospital bed. As Ellery neared, I saw an old woman move aside. She had been hovering in the air, whispering into the ear of the man in the bed. She was dressed in a white hanbok like me.

CHAPTER 29

F orgive me, Seona," I said from the doorway to the old woman
whom neither Joyce nor Ellery seemed to see. For that is who I
knew her to be; no mistake now. Old Seona, not as old as me, but older
than the woman her daughter had attempted to impersonate when I'd
first arrived in the afterlife.

"How dare you show up here?" Seona's head spun in my direction.
Her voice was a growl. In an instant, she'd positioned herself between
me and the hospital bed. The orange fog seemed to expand. Was
Seona controlling it?

I had to reach her somehow. Make her listen to me. "Joyce reminds
me of you," I said, motioning toward Seona's granddaughter, who had
stood and walked over to Ellery.

At my words, Seona glanced back at her granddaughter, her body
leaning. The shift gave me a better view. I saw that both Joyce
and Ellery were looking with tenderness at the face of the man in the
bed.

"Don't hurt your great-grandson because of me." I took a tentative step closer. The danger in the orange mist that I'd sensed must
have been coming from her.

"You have no idea what you're talking about. Stay where you are."
Her words emanated with such force from her body that she flew

upward, and I cowered. She hated me. My own sister. It was a thousand times worse than Taeyang's attack.

I'd hoped for a better reunion. How I had hoped. All these years and here she was. And she treated me like an enemy. What a fool I'd been to think she held me in special regard because we were sisters. The closest of sisters even among sisters. My vision blurred. My tear ducts worked overtime now.

All at once, out of the corner of my eye, I saw movement. Ellery turned away from Jordan and wiped her eyes. She didn't see me, she couldn't see me, but I resolved to keep trying for her sake.

I straightened my shoulders. I'd not come all this way to let Seona destroy Jordan and, with him, Ellery. "Seona, please, give me a chance to explain," I called out.

"There's nothing you can say," she said. "In your decades and decades with the living, you still didn't tell the truth about your other family."

"But that's not the real problem, is it? You're angry at me for something else. For what you wasted your life doing? How you threw your life away? Did you know how Father and Mother suffered after you eloped?"

She grimaced. I knew something had gotten through.

Ellery and Joyce left Jordan's side and seated themselves in chairs. I heard Joyce say that the doctor would be in soon with an update. Ellery, the dear girl, nodded. Joyce handed her a tissue from a pocket of her sweater. I wished I could have wiped her tears. There was too much suffering and it had to end, I told myself. Jordan couldn't die. My breath froze in my chest as I saw my sister settle into a sitting position, one leg crossed, the other knee raised, floating just above Jordan's chest. She was reaching down with her hands.

"Please don't," I called. "I have more to say — please listen. I know what you want to hear."

Seona halted. "I trusted you," she said. "We were sisters." And then she looked at me and I knew she knew. She drew back her hands and clenched them in her lap. At least they were not near Jordan's body anymore. One chance. She was giving me a chance. What I hadn't said to Taeyang, I said now to my sister.

"I failed to help your son." My voice shook, and the anguish swallowed the end of my apology. I cleared my throat and started again. "I turned him away and he slept on the street because of me. I turned him away twice, and the third time, I sent him away because I couldn't stand to look at him."

Seona covered her eyes with one hand.

I slid forward, tears in my eyes. "Sister, I'm sorry."

She lowered her hand and I saw that her eyes were wet with tears too.

"He was my son," she said. "You might as well have turned me away."

I wiped my cheeks with the back of my hand. It seemed I had never grown up. All the hurt rose to the surface. I felt like a child again. "Why did you forget about me?" I asked.

She blinked in surprise. "I never forgot."

"Then why didn't you write? Why didn't you come? You sent your husband, your son, but you didn't come. I needed you." My voice shook so much, I thought she couldn't hear me.

She took her time. She swallowed and waited until she was ready and then she said, "I was too proud to admit you were right. All of you were right. Do you remember the night I left, you said to me that I would be back?"

I had no memory of that conversation.

She sniffed and continued. "I was ashamed. Rushing off and being wrong. Then later, I had children. And Taeyang, she was older than Daeshim, she had friends in the Communist Party. There were good ideas for women in the Communist Party. I didn't imagine the border would close forever."

"Sister, I'm sorry," I repeated because the cascade of regrets was suddenly unbearable to me. I'd made choices that had hurt those I'd loved over and over again.

The air in the room was throbbing. The orange haze surrounding the bed deepened into a near red hue and rose higher, spreading to all four walls. We wept together.

"I'm sorry, forgive me," I said, taking another step closer.

At my words, my sister straightened up. "We won't speak anymore of this." Seona bent over and whispered in Jordan's ear. Her hands lowered into his torso.

I was astonished. Didn't our conversation matter? Hadn't I changed her mind?

"Then why are you still angry, Seona?" I called to her. The artificial lights in the ceiling of the hospital room flickered at my words.

"It's not me who's angry," Seona said. Her hands kept reaching down and coming out as if she were fishing for something in a small pond. Each time her hands surfaced, they were empty.

"Come away from Jordan, then," I said. "Let him live."

She motioned with her chin. "You're still making assumptions." She sighed.

Seona's words found their mark. How many times had I heard this since I'd died? Taeyang and Siwon, now Seona. Was this part of the change I needed to make in myself? The lesson I was supposed to learn? I closed my eyes, made myself relax by taking deep breaths. And then I listened.

It took me a minute, but I could hear Seona's voice. "Hang on, Jordan, stay with the living, let me help your heart along."

"You're keeping him alive?" I said, opening my eyes.

Seona blinked back tears. "His heart is getting weaker and weaker, but I can't touch it to keep it beating, I've been trying and trying." Seona let out a long wail. "I can't make contact."

I looked at the orange haze climbing the walls, nearly at the ceiling now. "There must be something we can do."

"If I could just make contact. But we're ghosts, Jeonga, we're only ghosts. All I can do is make suggestions, hope that he'll hear. All I have is my voice. You know that — you were hard to reach too. Just like him. I was watching over you, trying to keep you alive — I tried to give you time to bring Ellery's family back into our family, tried to keep all of you on the living plane as long as possible. It was not easy. Do you know how many cars I kept from hitting you by whispering in your ear? You don't look both ways when you cross the street, Jeonga." My sister raised her hands to the ceiling. "Why are we so helpless?"

"But you made him sick — how did you do that?"

"Of course I did not. How could you even think it? It was a simple bacterial infection that got out of hand, but it took him to death and the afterlife, and in that time, he found me. Because of course I was watching over him — how could I not?"

"But Siwon made Jordan's car tire go flat — how'd he do that?" I said.

"Maybe he told Jordan to swerve so he'd hit a pothole," Seona replied.

"But we do touch things. I hold on to things to move; I merged with the airplane seat," I insisted.

"Airplane seats are one thing, human bodies are another. People walk right through us."

I thought of what Siwon had said to me about touching him, knew I had been unable to feel Taeyang's movements like I'd thought I had. My husband and his girlfriend had never made contact, never touched. All I had was my voice.

"Then you've just been telling him to stay alive?" I asked.

She nodded, swiping through Jordan's body again.

"And Jordan has been to the afterlife?" I said.

She let out an exasperated breath. "The fever got quite high. He died for a minute before the doctors and nurses resuscitated him, but that minute was long in the afterlife. He confronted me. He wanted to know who you were and what I was trying to tell you about him and Ellery, so he found out she was your great-granddaughter. I couldn't hide it. He spun into such rage that he put himself in jeopardy. All he has is anger that he can't contain. It's killing him even now."

"He's doing this to himself." A stunning truth.

"I've been telling him he has to live, that if he dies now, he'll roam the afterlife and lash out at the living for generations to come," she replied. "We'll be cursed. The family will be haunted."

I sank to the floor, deep into the dark orange mist. This was not what I'd expected.

Before I could ask any more questions, there was a knock on the door frame, and Ned walked in. Walked right through me huddled on the floor. He had a small bag and an iPad in his arms. I was able to stand and slide back near the wall.

In another second, Chohui walked in, pulling her carry-on suitcase behind her. As if sensing my presence, she sidestepped me and headed for Joyce, who looked bewildered. In Chohui's hand was an envelope, which she held out to Jordan's mother. The letter! I assumed it was the letter I had had in my purse.

Ned looked over Chohui's shoulder. Seona had floated down to this crowd of new arrivals and was circling each one.

I wished I could move with as much grace as my sister. All I could manage was a sloppy step before Seona shouted at me to halt. I obeyed and was relieved to be close enough to lean toward Joyce, who unfolded the letter and read it with an eagerness that moved me. "This is from my great-aunt," she said.

"Yes, from samonim, Mrs. Jeonga Hak Cha. I'm her aide. She made every effort to come herself, but she died in Chicago on our way here. A bus hit her," Chohui explained.

At these words, Ellery swiftly put her hand to her mouth and let out a gasp. "Mrs. Cha? But I know a Mrs. Jeonga Cha. My grandmother used to work for her in Korea. Mrs. Cha can't be — I just saw her in San Francisco," she said, shock in her voice.

"It's my fault she ran out," Ned said. "I was trying to explain about —"

"You're not responsible," Chohui interrupted. "Don't think that way, Ned." Exactly what I would have said to him. I beamed at her from my position near Joyce. "Good girl, Chohui," I told her, but she didn't seem to register my presence.

"But she can't be," Ellery said again and covered her face with her hands, sobbing. Tears rose in my eyes as I saw her distress. She had cared about me after all. Joyce embraced her.

"I'm to do something else for you. Samonim wanted to wire you money," Chohui said and fished in her bag, found another envelope, and offered it to Joyce. "And this is a letter from your two other great-aunts. They want to help with your son's medical care too. They couldn't come because they had to bring their sister's body to Korea."

"Thank you," Joyce said as she unfolded the second letter. "It's very kind."

"I need your bank information," Chohui said. "Or would you talk to Attorney Kim yourself?"

Seona glared at me as she took in the amount I'd written in my letter to Joyce. "It should be ten times that," Seona said.

"That's why I was coming in person, to g-give more," I stammered. "Plus, I added Joyce and Jordan to my will."

"Took you long enough," Seona said.

"Does it matter?" I retorted.

She seemed surprised at my tone. After that, we returned to watching Ellery. She was listening to Chohui and Ned as they spoke to Joyce. On her face, a deep concentration, her brows creased, as if she was working something out.

"Wait," Ellery said at last, looking at Joyce. "Why is Mrs. Cha writing you letters? How do you know her?"

Seona moved closer to Ned, who was speaking. "I can explain. You must be Joyce. I'm your cousin Ned Cha, the grandson of Mrs. Cha. I'm sorry we never had the occasion to meet; our fathers were estranged." He turned from Joyce's shocked face to Ellery. "And you must be Ellery. Did you say your last name is Arnaud?" Ned gave himself some room to remove his iPad from its case under his arm. He tapped the screen and held it out for everyone to see.

"He's writing a book, a family history," Chohui said, leaning forward. There were exclamations all around in response.

"Here's a diagram." He pointed. "And this is the Arnaud family I've just discovered in California."

"I don't understand," Ellery said.

"I'm sorry, but it's true. I spoke to your grandmother a few days ago on the phone," Ned continued. "She was instrumental in helping me fill in the missing parts of our family tree."

"We got her number from the phone company, from Mrs. Cha's recent calls," Chohui added. "She knew that Ellery and Jordan were third cousins. I'm sure she was going to tell everyone."

Seona laughed at that. A huge guffaw. I felt the old feeling of panic combined with ancient shame, but at last it was joined with newfound relief in my heart. Everything was going to be revealed.

Ellery said, "No, that can't be right. Cousins? I can't be related to Jordan. You're wrong." She grabbed the iPad from Ned. Her hand covered her mouth. My heart went out to her.

Ned pointed over her shoulder as he spoke. "It says right there,

Hayun Jin. That's your grandmother, and then your mother — see her name right there? Jiu. And then here you are, this is you."

"Wait, no, no, that means Jordan and I are in the same family?" Ellery cried out. She thrust the iPad back at Ned. "You're wrong, I don't believe it. I don't believe it," she shouted. She searched the room, frantic, as if trying to find someone who would refute him. I wished I could have been that someone for her sake and that it could have been true. Everyone looked away except me. She rushed toward the hospital bed and collapsed in tears over Jordan's chest.

Moving swiftly was still a challenge for me, but I tried to run to her anyway. I had to explain; I had to comfort her. I pushed off the floor, determined to reach her. I covered the distance at a remarkable pace but overshot my mark and coalesced with the cardiac monitor, an electronic device on a pole with wheels so it could be moved close to a patient; the monitor gave me an unexpected vantage point.

Seona gasped. I heard her but I found myself transfixed by the view. Jordan's face was placid, almost plastic; he barely resembled the man in the photograph my great-granddaughter had shown me in San Francisco. I couldn't take my eyes off him.

Suddenly, the alarms on the machine went off. Seona flew at me, and I released my hold on the monitor. I retreated toward the door. What had I done? Seona was whirling around her great-grandson. "Don't give up. Not now, come on, stay with the living."

Nurses and doctors ran in, pushed Ellery out of the way, and asked the family to leave the room. Seona struggled to stay close, and I wasn't going to give up; we leaned in together, trying to see what was happening. "Did I do something to the machine? I didn't mean to, Seona," I said.

"Shut up and look." She pointed and I could see that the orange fog around Jordan had thickened to a deep red neither of us could penetrate.

"What's going on?" I tried to shake Seona's arm but my hands fell through the air.

"He won't listen to me," she cried. "He's furious with you. I told you to stay away from him. But you don't listen, Jeonga. You got too close."

She might as well have slapped me. I staggered back. He was angry at *me*. I'd caused him harm. I'd put his life in danger. Me. If I'd caused this pain, I had to be the one to make things right. I regained my footing. If Jordan wouldn't listen to his great-grandmother, then he'd have to deal with me.

I waved my hands over my head to get his attention. "Jordan, over here, it's me, your great-grandauntie. That's right, me. Go ahead, be angry at me. Make me suffer. I will take it. For eternity, you can hate me, but you — you must live. Please. If you don't help Ellery, who will? You can't protect her if you're where I am, in the afterlife. As ghosts, we're helpless. Believe me, we are. Look at us. You don't want to be like us. Please. Go back to her, go back to Ellery and your mother."

Seona was wailing now beside me, deep sobs rising and falling in her wisp of a self, the edges of her translucent, but I kept talking. Reminding him of what he was giving up with his stubborn fury. I told him he had a future, and living meant he could hold Ellery again. In death, you can't do it. You can't touch anyone with love. Don't hide your rage by dying, I told him. No matter what, you'll never be able to speak. Shamans can't always help you, I told him. Come back to us. Speak to us from this plane.

His rage seemed only to expand. His heart rate decreased to a dangerously slow pace. I didn't know what else to say so I stopped speaking and then it occurred to me that I was at the end. This was what death really was. When you could do nothing. Really knew you could do nothing. No words. No control over anyone or anything. I stepped back and realized I had one more apology to make.

"All right, then," I said. Rising as tall as I could, I scolded him. "You listen and you listen good. Like you, I was consumed. You may be justified in being angry. We have this one thing in common. We both let ourselves be ruled by our emotions. In your case, anger at the unfairness of the deception — you're right. In my case, fear. It led to my isolation. That's the same for you. Sure, you have all of us running to you, caring for you, begging for you to be better, but ultimately, aren't you alone in your rage? Aren't you going to make yourself further alone if you continue? You will stay in the afterlife for who knows how long. Isolation. Separating people. That's actually the worst punishment. I punished myself, and because of it, I punished others. I'm sorry. There — I said it. Did you hear me? But I do forgive myself. I did the best I could and I'm telling you, don't make the same mistake. Come back. Don't choose fury over love. Don't do what I did."

You'd think without a body, your throat wouldn't hurt from the use of your voice, you wouldn't tire from constant effort. Too many secrets. Too much unsaid until now. So much more I wanted to know. I looked at my sister whom I'd so longed to see. The answers I'd wanted. Her head was lowered, her wails now mere whimpers. Could an apology matter? I walked around the bed as close as he'd allow me to be, passing through all the doctors and nurses doing the work of trying to save him, and talked and talked even more, summoning all the energy I could, glaring at him as much as I could. And then I think I collapsed.

CHAPTER 30

The next thing I knew, I was on the cold hospital floor, and Seona was calling my name. I got to my feet. There was a steady sound of machines, the monitors showing a healthy heart rate, the peaks and dips of safety. No longer was there a red haze around Jordan and the hospital bed. The doctors and nurses stepped back, shook their heads, but their chins were lifted high and there were tentative smiles.

"My ears are ringing. Are yours ringing?" a woman said to her colleague as they backed out the door. "Why was it so loud in there?"

Seona bent down and whispered to Jordan. I couldn't hear what she said but when she straightened up, she had a tired smile on her face. At that moment, Joyce burst into the room and embraced her son. Seona took my arm and made me step back with her, giving them some space.

"He's going to make it," Seona said to me.

"What did you tell him?" I asked.

"I told him he'd made the right choice."

"Will he remember being in the afterlife?"

She shook her head. "It's already fading."

Joyce walked to the door briskly while we were talking, wiping tears from her face, and waved someone in. It was Ellery, of course, who was also wiping tears from her face with her sleeve. She seemed shy this time. She didn't hug him like his mother had. Instead, she held his hand, avoiding the large IV at his inner elbow, and caressed it. I moved closer with less effort now. Seona was right about how easy it was to walk once you trusted you could do it.

"Nearly missed our chance because Joyce wrote the letter to Mina instead of you," she said to me as we looked on. "Getting you and Chohui to America, that was a feat, but we managed it."

"But who gave Mina the idea to come with me and trick me into visiting Ned?"

"The power of suggestion," Seona replied.

"What about Aera's illness in San Francisco?" I asked.

Seona shrugged. "I told you I can't make anyone sick."

"What can we actually do here? What are our powers? If Siwon hadn't made Ellery and Jordan fall in love, none of this would have been necessary," I said. "How did he accomplish that?"

"No one can make anyone fall in love," Seona said.

At her words, my estimation of Siwon bounced back a little. "Still, he shouldn't have risked it, arranging for them to meet."

"True. He only wanted to get the truth out. Like me. We worked together. Getting Ned involved with the family tree was his idea. I didn't think you being anywhere near Jordan would help us, but you surprised me."

"I almost stayed with Siwon up there." I pointed to the ceiling. "Even if it was a sliver of him."

Seona laughed and then said in a calm voice, "He does love you. The selfish part of him wanted you for himself. I'm glad you knew a love like that even if that love came with pain."

"But love can be distracting, I didn't see what was happening to Gwangmu and Hayun because of it," I said, not ready to let myself off the hook yet.

"I know. Still, better to embrace love, knowing you'll experience both sadness and happiness, than shut yourself away from the possibility of love at all," she replied.

I agreed. We were two old women talking about what mattered. How I loved being in her company again. We flitted throughout the hospital.

One time we overheard Ellery speaking to Jordan about her job in Dayton. "You won't be able to get rid of me so easily," she said. "I won't let you get away with shortcuts in whatever medical care they say you need."

His eyelids fluttered.

"And you don't have to worry about any of it anymore — your great-grandaunt Jeonga left you enough in her will."

This part surprised me. How did she know this already? Had Attorney Kim been in touch?

"She left me some too — isn't that funny?" Ellery went on to say. "Apparently, there's a whole chart I have to show you of things we didn't know about our family."

Seona and I looked at each other.

"Oh, there's someone named Ned. He's here, an uncle of ours, you have to meet him," Ellery said to Jordan. "It's going to be okay. Do you hear me?" she continued.

His eyelids fluttered again, and I thought of how much I wanted him to open them so I could see this young man who had held so much against me. His complexion looked more organic now.

In the days that followed, Jordan regained full consciousness, and his health continued to improve. I noticed he made progress as long as I wasn't around.

Well, I made it a point not to be anywhere near him. I wandered around the hospital grounds. There were plenty of shrubs to cling to as I went along. I practiced moving between them as well, into the wide-open spaces. I practiced to trust I would make it across.

Ellery described the entire family tree to him, and to the relief of everyone, dead and living, after many conversations and tears, they decided to part ways. I didn't press Ellery with any form of a suggestion. It was her decision. I floated on a wave of calm gratitude. All would be well. I never knew there could be such satisfaction.

I turned to face the next phase of my journey.

I can tell you that, in time, Ellery met and married a friend of Ned's, someone who was also a cook. They live in San Francisco with their two children and have their own restaurant in Pacific Heights. They have a pinball machine in it. I thought it was a sweet nod to our time together on Fisherman's Wharf. Hayun is quite pleased with her role as a great-grandmother. Jordan found love with someone else. Don't worry about him. He married a doctor who had cared for him at the hospital, and they had a child just a few months ago.

His mother, Joyce, was able to resume her job at the Dayton Art Institute and enjoyed having the painting of the Golden Gate Bridge that used to hang in my apartment. Even though it has no value, she was gracious when Chohui offered it to her upon learning she worked at the institute. She has the painting in her home. Ned, of course, published his book about our family. His work received excellent reviews, enabling him to write a few more books. He spoke often with Bogum, who became quite a favorite with the younger generation in America.

Pam, Ned's sister, was the first among them to leave the living. But she had a short stint in the afterlife with my help. I knew how to get her through in record time, since I was an expert in explaining how to walk through walls. She and a few others were the reason I stayed behind a little longer.

With regard to Chohui, the American shaman was right. As predicted, Chohui fell in love with the young woman in the middle seat of the plane who helped her listen to me. Chohui works for a furniture designer in Seoul, inspired, no doubt, by my discriminating taste in interiors, which she'd been surrounded by since she came to work for me. A marriage is imminent, I hear. I found it easy to communicate with Chohui as long as her partner was around. Her partner writes books. Fantasy is what they're called. Chohui is her biggest fan.

Mina and Aera lived another year and then died within months of each other. They traveled through the afterlife together, as expected. I never saw Taeyang again. Apparently, she had fulfilled her duties to me and had gone on, at peace.

I'm able to report all this because Seona gave me lessons in floating, making it much easier for me to check on everyone.

"Don't hold your hands out — you won't hit anything, I promise," she said. And: "Put your chin down and lead with your head, the rest of you will follow."

Such a relief to steer with efficiency. Floating between and through things became easy.

"Are we like clouds, then?" I asked.

"We're what we are," she said. "Not clouds, silly Jeonga." Her words stung. I felt as though I were five years old again, admonished by my sister. Then she softened her expression toward me.

"I never get tired of looking at the moon," she said. Ahead of us, a crescent shone bright in the dark sky. I let myself take that as an apology of sorts. I knew she wouldn't give me another one. It was better to be in this world of the living looking out for those we loved than in the persimmon-colored one or the watery-air one. I shuddered at the memory of that rice-paper box. She assured me she wasn't leaving anytime soon. I didn't want to lose her again. But a separation was surely on the horizon. I knew we couldn't stay together in the afterlife forever.

I had longed for a reunion and it had come at last. Me and my sister. The best part was knowing that when I was with her, I didn't have to worry. About anything. I'd felt such responsibility after she left me that first time. Beside her, I believed that everyone would be all right. That was what I'd felt as a child and it was a relief, an immeasurable relief, to experience that again, the comfort of that knowledge.

We were drifting in place in a wide field, looking at the moon, which seemed to be watching over us. Fuller now. Seona turned to me and said, "There's more. Appa wanted to stay to see you, but his time came to go."

"That's fine, Taeyang took me to him in our house," I said, defending him to the last.

"That was just the shell of him — yes, he was able to leave that for you."

"I heard Eomma," I said. "That means she was there, part of her was there, right?"

Seona nodded. "She fought for that part. She did. You're the baby of the family; she wanted to help you. But listen, here's the thing, Jeonga."

I waited.

Seona took a deep breath, then released it. "I promised Appa I would tell you. He understood why you did what you thought he wanted. Keeping up appearances. All of it. Staying in the family house for as long as you did, protecting the family's reputation. The way he would have."

"But he was too strict with you, he caused you to leave. Would you have eloped if Appa hadn't opposed the marriage?" I said, my anger at my father flaring anew.

"He had the pressure of the Japanese local leaders to contend with. Remember, we were under their thumb. My marriage would have been the ammunition they needed to take Appa's holdings, all of it. There was one man in particular who was working to ruin our father.

We weren't free to do what we wanted. We lived as well as we did because Appa served a specific purpose for them. He tried to explain it to me. And he apologized before he left the afterlife. We worked it out."

"He regretted it as soon as you left. He was never the same. You were his favorite," I said.

"Whatever you want to believe, it's your right. But let me tell you, he was sorry you sent everyone away to protect our family's reputation. The cost to you was one he didn't want you to suffer. Gwangmu and Hayun — you know what I mean. He didn't believe it was necessary, Jeonga."

"He didn't?" I felt embarrassment roll through me, as if I'd tried to do something my older sisters could do and had failed.

"Here we speak the truth, little sister."

I bent my head and distanced myself from her and her words. She followed but gave me some space.

"I thought I was doing what Appa would have wanted me to. I protected everyone; no stone was thrown at us."

"Exactly. Appa knew that. He saw it and he was sorry."

I found myself tearing up at her words. "I just wanted him to be proud of me."

"He was proud."

"He said it?"

"Yes. And you couldn't have known. You did the best you could. He spoke to Gwangmu in the afterlife, he told me. Your son had no regrets. He said you gave him a chance to meet Hayun again when he went to study in the States."

The picture in my mind's eye of my father and my son talking about me filled me with relief mixed with an ache at the base of my throat I hadn't expected. I wished I could have been present to witness that conversation.

"I am sorry." My voice trembled.

"We're all sorry for many things," she agreed and there were tears in her eyes too.

"Thank you." Even in the afterlife, you could sense a load had lifted from your old chest and feel peace arrive in its stead. Old wounds could be healed. You had a right to leave the living without worry.

Seona and I visited everyone once more and then made our exit.

ACKNOWLEDGMENTS

Reflecting on all those who made this novel possible, I'm most grateful to Vivian Lee, gifted editor and writer, who knew exactly what this book needed. Of course, a thousandfold of thanks to Cynthia Manson, agent extraordinaire and inspiring advocate. Also I'm very much appreciative of Kimberley Lim for her invaluable suggestions. Gratitude to Little, Brown's excellent Jayne Yaffe Kemp, Tracy Roe, Lucy Kim, and Melissa Mathlin for their precision and artistry. And thank you to superb photographers Christine Petrella, Janice Chung, and Nancee Adams.

Special thanks to Alexander Chee, who encouraged me to write this book at the outset and was almost my cousin; Lisa Ko, for helping me overcome the particular obstacles of a second book; and Minsoo Kang, for expert and patient advice on Korea.

Infinite gratitude to Matthew Salesses, Joan Silber, Courtney Maum, Mary-Kim Arnold, Kirstin Chen, DeMisty D. Bellinger, Jung Yun, Juan Martinez, Michael J. Seidlinger, Chaya Bhuvaneswar, Ed Lin, Melissa Faliveno, Ed Park, Gwendolen Gross, Andrew Tonkovich, Nicole Chung, Marie Myung-Ok Lee, Jennifer Baker, Peter

Tieryas, Janice Lee, Leland Cheuk, Jae-Ha Kim, Kathy Fish, LaRose Parris, and Steve Edwards. I admire their work and am forever honored by their generosity.

Immense thanks to my cherished writer pals: Marcia Bradley, Kate Brandt, Patricia Dunn, Gloria Hatrick, Deborah Zoe Laufer, Maria Maldonado, Alexandra Soiseth, Jennifer Manocherian, Vicky Cowel, Dan Martin, Michael Biello, and Barbara Josselsohn.

For keeping me grounded and optimistic, much love and great thanks to Kim Lopp Manocherian, Vi Lee, Mary Karapontso Dwyer, Dianne Twinam, Katharine Houghton, Grace Dorman, Amy Guay, Gabe Spera, and Michael Horowitz.

Lamar Herrin, Henry Louis Gates, Jr., Diane Ackerman, Linsey Abrams, Susan Guma, Lucy Rosenthal, Suzanne Gardinier, and Joan Larkin — tremendous thanks for your guidance all those years ago.

This novel could not have been written without the support of the teaching community of which I've been a part. Thank you: Olivia Worden, Rachel Simon, Laurie McMillan, Maureen Colgan, Dana Jaye Cadman, Jessica Ready-Jackson, Paige Ackerson-Kiely, Courtney Gillette, Sweet Avigale Orefice, and the students of Sarah Lawrence College and Pace University.

I'm so grateful to those who invited me to their book clubs, bookstores, reading series, libraries, and artist communities, especially Brett Hall Jones, Lisa Alvarez, Elizabeth Bermel, Maureen McManus, Gretchen Jordan Menzies, Patrick Corcoran, Atom Atkinson, Sony Ton-Aime, Theresa Choh-Lee, HJ Lee, Tracy Fauver, Annabel Monaghan, Charlotte Ray Biancone, Karyn Gallant Zitomer, Yuliana Kim-Grant, Ji Young, and Nita Noveno, to name just a few.

In memoriam: gratitude to the inimitable Paul West and Fanchon Scheier. Thank you to Susan Clements, editor at *The Rumpus*, who published my early short pieces and always asked me if I had anything — which made me write something on the spot just for her. And I'll always treasure Brian Rogers, who wrote with me and reminded me that we could not take time for granted. The details of the afterlife for this book came to me from our conversations.

Finally, this novel is about family. In my own family, there are hauntings that offered me plenty of material from which to imagine a story. The presence of love, and the absence too. I'm grateful for my memories of my maternal grandmother, who raised me in South Korea, and for my father's memories of my paternal grandmother exiled in North Korea. I'm thankful for my mother, gone these recent years, who I missed less by imagining her in a place described in my book.

There are specific people to thank in my family, for their contributions to this book, their curiosity, their encouragement, for being — as always — my primary readers. I must begin, of course, with my husband and our two daughters. Nothing gets written to completion without their belief in me.

I'm also enormously thankful to Juyeon for details about Korea, to Sherry for being a tech genius, to Jiho for medical advice, and to Won, Johnny, Jihyuk, and all their partners for love and support. To my nieces and nephews, giant hugs and gratitude. To my cousins in South Korea, heartfelt thanks for keeping connected.

Before I end, I need to spotlight in particular my appreciation for my imo, Aunt Cathy, who introduced me to nineteenth-century English novels when I was thirteen years old and teaches line dancing in Virginia today with the ageless energy of Jeonga in my novel, and for Uncle Henry, who tells me stories about being a child on a farm in old Korea. Like my mother, who makes her way into everything I write, there's a piece of both of them in this novel for which I'll be eternally grateful.

ABOUT THE AUTHOR

Jimin Han was born in Seoul, South Korea, and grew up in Providence, Rhode Island; Dayton, Ohio; and Jamestown, New York. Her work has been supported by the New York State Council on the Arts. She is also the author of *A Small Revolution* and has written for American Public Media's *Weekend America*, *Poets & Writers*, and *Catapult*, among other media outlets. Han teaches at the Writing Institute at Sarah Lawrence College, Pace University, and community writing centers. She lives outside New York City with her husband and children.